# FATAL JUSTICE

### SALLY RIGBY

TOP
DRAWER
PRESS

Edited by Emma Mitchell of @ Creating Perfection.

Cover Design by Stuart Bache of Books Covered

# GET ANOTHER BOOK FOR FREE!

To instantly receive the free novella, **The Night Shift**, featuring Whitney when she was a Detective Sergeant, ten years ago, sign up for Sally Rigby's free author newsletter at www.sallyrigby.com

## Chapter One

Detective Chief Inspector Whitney Walker parked outside her mum's house. It was a typical 1930s terrace, with a big bay window and a stone step. She'd been born there. So had her mum, her younger brother, and her daughter, Tiffany. Three generations. And now she was heading into a meeting which could put an end to all that history.

As she stepped out of the car, a few spots of rain bounced off her jacket. It had been raining on and off since the early hours of the morning. She hurried down the path, took out her key, and opened the door. A musty smell hit her as she walked in. The house was in dire need of renovation. Since her dad died ten years ago, money had been tight. Her mum stayed at home to care for Whitney's younger brother, Rob, who'd been brain damaged following a violent attack when he was in his early teens. He was now thirty-four, but unable to live on his own. Even though Whitney helped her mum out financially, there was nothing left over for general maintenance. The paint was peeling from the windows, and the cream wallpaper had turned yellow. She'd offered to do some painting on her days off, but her mum had refused, saying she didn't want to change anything because it reminded her of Whitney's dad.

'It's only me,' she called.

There were sounds coming from the lounge, and inside she found her mum sitting on the sofa next to Rob.

'Hi, Mum.'

'What are you doing here?' Her mum frowned.

'I said I'd be here for when the social worker arrived.' The forgetfulness was getting much worse. If she spoke to her mum about things from the past, there was no problem, but anything recent and it was hit and miss whether she remembered. Whitney looked at her watch. Hopefully the meeting wouldn't take too long. Even though it was quiet at work, and she'd been able to get away, she didn't want to be gone for too long. 'Shall I put the kettle on? I could do with a coffee.'

She'd been running late that morning and had only managed to finish half a mug. Caffeine was her addiction, and if she didn't get a hit every couple of hours, she became grumpy.

'If you like, love,' her mum said. 'Do you know where everything is?'

'Of course I do. What are you up to, Rob?' she said to her brother, who was running his favourite toy car up and down the arm of the sofa.

'I want a biscuit, but Mum said no.'

He was still wearing his pyjamas, which looked like they hadn't been washed for ages. She should've noticed sooner.

'You can have one when the social worker arrives.'

'Okay, Whitney.' He didn't look at her, just continued playing.

'Why don't you go upstairs and get dressed?' she suggested.

'Mum said I didn't have to.' He stuck out his bottom lip.

'Are you sure? We're having a visitor; don't you want to look nice for her?' she cajoled.

'No,' he said in the voice which meant it was pointless her trying to persuade him.

'It was just a suggestion,' she said, giving a shrug.

She glanced around the room. It obviously hadn't been cleaned for a long time, and when she walked over to the fireplace and ran her finger along the top, she could've written her name in the dust. It wrenched at her gut when she thought back to how house-proud her mum used to be. There was never anything out of place. And the house sparkled.

Whitney should have done something about it, but she'd been so busy recently. She would have to make more of an effort.

She was about to go into the kitchen when the doorbell rang.

'I'll get it,' she said, heading out of the room.

She closed the lounge door behind her, as she wanted to speak to the social worker without her mum or Rob hearing.

The social worker stood on the path holding a big green-and-white spotted umbrella over her head, as it had started raining properly. She looked to be around fifty, older than many Whitney had met in Lenchester. That pleased her. She'd be more understanding with her mum than some of the younger ones.

'Come in. You can leave your umbrella in the porch. It was only spitting a while ago, and now look at it.' She held open the door.

'Yes. Luckily, I had my brolly in the car. I take it you're Whitney? I'm Jean Hedges.' She held out her hand and Whitney shook it.

'Good to finally meet you. I'd like a word in private before we go in to see Mum.'

'Of course.'

'I'm worried she isn't coping. When I ask her, she says everything's fine, but when I look around the place, I can see it isn't. I don't know what the options are.'

She did know. She just didn't want to have to face them.

'I'll be honest. It's not looking good. It would be hard enough for her to be here on her own, but with Rob to look after, I suspect it's soon going to become impossible.'

'Could you arrange for some help? A cleaner and someone to take care of Rob. Perhaps they could help with the cooking, too.'

'Funding aside, I'm not sure it's an option,' Jean said. 'When I popped in last week during the afternoon, your mum was still in her nightwear watching the TV, and Rob was in the kitchen unattended, making himself some beans on toast. There was a tea-towel draped over the hob. If I hadn't arrived, there could have been a fire.'

'Why didn't anyone tell me? You have my contact details.' She didn't even attempt to hide the annoyance in her voice.

'Because nothing *actually* happened. But you can see the problem. It's getting to the stage when there needs to be someone here full-time overseeing them both.'

But who? They couldn't afford a live-in carer. And with a mortgage to pay and a daughter at university, it was impossible for Whitney to give up her job and care for them. Not only that, she couldn't throw away her career. It was her life.

'She's only sixty-five. Too young to be like this. It's got worse so quickly. Six weeks ago, the house was fairly clean, and she seemed less confused. But now...' Tears welled in her eyes and she blinked them away. 'And there's Rob to consider.'

'There are some lovely homes for your mum to move into, and some excellent live-in facilities for people with Rob's difficulties,' Jean said.

'Lock him up, you mean? I couldn't do that. He's used to his own bedroom, and having the freedom to go into the garden and play. Or hang out watching the TV. He doesn't go out on his own, but he goes to a special group at a local day centre twice a week where he's got several friends.'

'He hasn't been for four weeks.'

'Why not? It's not like he can't get there. He gets picked up and dropped back off. Did they stop coming for him?'

'From what I understand, your mum told the driver not to come any more.'

This was crazy. How come she didn't know?

'I don't want him going into a secure home which restricts what he does and takes away his freedom.'

'There are some great places around. It's called assisted living. Residents look after themselves, but there's a carer on call twenty-four hours a day. I can look into it for Rob and see what's available. He'd be with people like himself and will make friends. It's not something you have to decide now; we can talk it through with them both and arrange a visit.'

Would he make friends? Could he cope without their mum being there? What if he moved in and hated it? There would be nothing she could do. He'd be left all alone. So many thoughts were swirling around her head.

'I don't know. I need to think about it.'

'I'll call you next week and we can talk some more. Let's go and have a chat with your mum and see how things are going.'

They went into the lounge. Her mum and brother hadn't moved.

'Hello, Mrs Walker,' Jean said.

'What are you doing here?' her mum asked.

'I've come to see you, as I do every Thursday.'

'Okay. Whitney, why are you here?' A confused expression crossed her face.

'I've been here a while, Mum. I went to let Jean in.'

'Are you staying for dinner?' her mum asked.

'I've only just had breakfast, and it's too early for dinner. I'm here to meet with Jean.'

Whitney tensed. She couldn't bear to see her mum like this; it was soul destroying. She used to be so active, so much fun. But now. Even when she could remember things, she'd sit there looking a bit vague. Jean was right. Something had to be done. 'Who wants a cup of tea or coffee?' she asked, remembering she hadn't yet put the kettle on.

'Tea, please,' the social worker replied. 'Milk, no sugar.'

'I'd rather have sherry,' her mum said.

'It's only ten in the morning. Don't you think it's a bit early to start drinking?' Whitney gave a little laugh. She didn't even know her mum liked sherry, or whether there was any in the house.

'But I want some now.'

Jean sat down on the sofa next to her. 'Mrs Walker, I've been talking to Whitney about the possibility of you moving into somewhere more comfortable where you can be looked after, and you won't have to worry about being on your own.'

Whitney glared at Jean. They hadn't decided to mention it now, so why was she? It was Whitney's decision when to say something, not hers. Only a few minutes ago, the woman had said there was no rush.

She didn't like being put on the spot.

'I'm not on my own, I'm with Rob. I don't want to go anywhere.' Her mum's fists clenched by her side, and she appeared agitated. 'You can't make me go if I don't want to.'

'No one's going to make you do anything, Mum. It's just something we've been considering. It's hard for you having to look after Rob.'

'I can look after myself,' Rob said. 'I can cook now, can't I, Mum?'

Whitney looked helplessly at Jean. It was going from bad to worse.

'Yes, Rob. You're a very good boy, and we can manage together,' her mother said.

It was like her mum had suddenly gone back to normal. The confused look had gone, and she seemed to understand the situation.

'Don't worry, Mum. It'll be fine. Like I said, it's something we're considering at the moment. We won't do anything without your consent. We want to make sure you and Rob are okay, because I can't always be here. My job can be chaotic, and I don't want to be worrying that you two are struggling.'

'There's no need for you to worry,' her mum said.

'Why don't w—' She was interrupted by her phone ringing. It was work. 'I have to get this.' She left the room and pulled the door shut behind her. 'Walker.'

'Sorry to disturb you, guv,' Matt Price, her detective sergeant, said.

'What's the problem?'

'A mutilated body has been found on some waste ground beside the old racecourse. It's a nasty one.'

What the fuck? Lenchester was turning into murder central. It was only a few months since they'd solved the Campus Murders case, and here was another one.

'Okay, meet me there in twenty minutes.'

## Chapter Two

Whitney pulled on her blue wellington boots and headed down the overgrown path towards the location of the body. In the distance, beside the cordon, Matt was talking to one of the uniformed officers. She wrapped her coat tightly around her to stop the wind from whistling through. Thankfully, the rain had stopped, but it was still cold and exceptionally muddy.

'Hey, Matt,' she said when she got within speaking distance. 'Have you seen the body?'

He walked over to her. 'Not yet. I was waiting for you. I've been talking to PC Reeves, the first officer attending. He's secured the scene and is waiting for the crime scenes team to arrive. Dr Dexter's already here.'

'Okay, let's go.'

They walked past a line of wild brambles towards the tent which had been erected around the body to stop it being seen by the public. Not that there was anyone around at the moment, the weather was so bad. Stepping plates were in place to ensure they didn't trample on the vast amount of litter and broken bottles, all of which were potential evidence. On reaching the tent, she put her head around the opening where Claire Dexter, the pathologist, was taking photographs.

'Morning, Claire. What have we got?'

Whitney walked in and tensed at the sight of the naked body in front of her. The victim was missing his penis and testicles.

'Holy crap,' she said. 'What the fuck happened to him?'

Matt, who'd been standing behind her, darted out of the tent, and she could hear him throwing up on the grass.

'Sounds like his breakfast,' Claire said, chuckling.

However gruesome the situation, Claire could always be relied on to see the funny side. She had to be like that, or how else could she do her job and remain sane?

'What can you tell me about cause of death?' she asked.

'Wait until I've got him on the table and done the cutting. Then you can have my report. I will say, it's interesting the way his clothes have been folded so neatly and left beside him.'

Whitney glanced to the side of the body. Claire was right. She looked back at the victim and noticed he was still wearing socks.

'Why were they left on?'

'I have no idea until I remove them back at the lab and see if there's anything underneath.'

'Do you think he was mutilated here or moved?'

'Whitney. For God's sake, you know how I work. I'm not prepared to make any assumptions. You'll have to wait.'

Whitney shut her mouth. Claire was their best pathologist, but also the most uncompromising, and often on a short fuse. Should she call Cavendish? The forensic psychologist had worked with her on the last murder case, and she was sure George would want a look at this crime scene. It wasn't every day a mutilated corpse came along. Especially one like this.

'Sorry.'

'All I can tell you is I can't see any obvious cause of death, not counting the mutilation which, in itself, wouldn't have killed him.'

'Where are the missing body parts?' she asked, risking another question.

'I haven't found them yet,' Claire said.

'Could they be in his socks?'

'It's a possibility, though looking at them from the outside, not likely. Now, if you don't mind, I've got a lot to do before we can move the body, so please leave me alone.'

Claire turned and began taking more photos. Whitney didn't take offence at her manner; the pathologist was the same with everyone.

Before leaving, she decided to take another look at the victim's face. There was something familiar about him, but she couldn't quite place it. Having lived in Lenchester her entire life, she often came in contact with people she knew or had known when she was younger.

'Do we have any identification?' she asked.

'Well, not on his person, obviously,' Claire said, giving a wry grin. 'Let me photograph the clothes, and you can move them to see if there's anything there.'

After Claire had taken several photos, Whitney pulled on her disposable gloves, took out an evidence bag, and picked up each item of clothing to examine before dropping it in. But there was nothing. All the pockets were empty. There was no phone and no wallet. Nothing to identify him.

'Of course not. That would've been too easy,' Whitney

muttered to herself, letting out a sigh. 'But he's definitely familiar.' She stared at him a while longer, noticing a faint jagged silver line running along his forehead. Then it hit her. 'It's Russell Atkins. I recognise the scar. It came from a brutal tackle in a football match. I was there when it happened. The whole school turned out because winning meant we'd be top of the league table and win the championship. He went to North Lenchester Academy, my school. He was a few years ahead of me, but I remember him because he was Head Boy. And very popular. Half the girls in my class had a crush on him. What the hell happened?'

'That's what I'm here to find out,' Claire said, arching an eyebrow.

'I definitely need to speak to George. We're going to need her help with this one.' She pulled her phone out of her pocket.

'If she's got time,' Claire said.

'Why wouldn't she?'

'The last time I spoke to her, she was preparing her application for the associate professor role in her department. Said she had a lot of work to do for the interview and presentation. You know George. She's preparation personified and certainly won't be leaving it to the last minute.'

Whitney frowned. George hadn't mentioned the interview when they'd spoken a week or so ago. Actually, it was more like a month. Then again, it wasn't like they were best friends, so why would she? Especially if she thought Whitney wouldn't understand because she wasn't academic. Claire, on the other hand, was both clever and academic, so she'd know all about it.

'I didn't know you kept in touch.'

'I did a lecture for her last week, and she told me after.'

'Well, I'm still going to call her. If she's too busy, I'm sure she'll tell me.'

She pulled out her phone from her pocket.

'Hello, Whitney.' George answered after a couple of rings.

'Hey. How are you?' she asked.

'You've caught me at a bad time. I've just come out of an informal interview for a new post.'

'What post?'

Would George still be able to help on her cases if she got the job? They'd only worked together on one, and even though it started off badly, in the end it had made all the difference. Thanks to George, Whitney's daughter Tiffany was rescued from a pair of psychotic twins who'd have murdered her if they'd had the chance. Whitney would forever be in George's debt for that.

'Associate Professor in my department. I shouldn't be saying this, but several people in influential positions have intimated I'm the favourite for it. The official selection process is extremely stringent and begins next week.'

'That doesn't surprise me. You're so good at your job. What does the interview process involve?'

Interviews in the police force were difficult enough. Whitney could only imagine how hard George's interview would be. The thought of it made her insides curl.

'Today it's the familiarisation programme, which includes informal interviews and a lunch where the applicants meet and chat with members of the department. It isn't formally assessed, but people will definitely pass on their opinions. It will be interesting to see the competition. No one else from our university is applying. The shortlist consists of four outside applicants and me. Next week I have to give a presentation on my research to the Selection Panel, plus anyone who's interested. Most will come from my department, though it's open to anyone in the university. Formal interviews by the Selection Panel take place the day after the presentations.'

'Good luck. It sounds stressful.'

'I'm well prepared,' George said. 'Did you call for anything in particular?'

'I thought you might be interested in a case we've just got.'

'I'm sorry. As much as I'd love to be with you, it's not possible. I can't miss the lunch. But it doesn't mean you can't phone me if you have any questions.'

'Don't worry, I totally understand,' she said.

'Thanks. Before I go, why don't you give me a quick rundown?'

Whitney smiled to herself. George couldn't resist; she was that sort of person.

'It's certainly a doozy. I'm at the crime scene, and in front of me is a naked man. Well, naked apart from his socks. He's also minus his penis and balls. I'm with Claire at the moment. It's pretty gross. But work comes first, and I won't keep you any longer.'

She knew her words would tempt George. But would she come? Was it wrong she was trying to lure her? Probably, but George was her own person. She never did anything she didn't want to.

There was silence for a few seconds.

'I didn't expect that. How can I not come and take a look? Give me directions and I'll be there as soon as I can.'

'What about the lunch?' Whitney asked.

She didn't want to put her off, but equally she didn't want the responsibility of getting her in trouble.

'It's not for a little while. I'll make sure I'm back in time. This is one scene I don't want to miss.'

## Chapter Three

George pulled on her coat, picked up her bag, and headed out of the office, sneaking down the corridor to the side door of the old Victorian building where her room was situated. It was madness to be nipping out when she had the lunch to attend, but she had a fascination with murders involving mutilation and was interested in the psyche of the perpetrators. Over the years, there had been several famous cases involving mutilated bodies. Not just chopped into bits to transport or dispose of, which was a whole different scenario, but mutilation which had some significance.

Fortunately, because of the awful weather, she'd decided to bring her car into work, and she battled with the wind to keep her umbrella from blowing inside out as she hurried to the university car park. What happened to the lovely spring weather of a few days ago?

It took around twenty minutes to reach the address Whitney had given her as it was on the other side of the city. As she approached the waste ground, there were several police cars parked and the usual yellow cordon tape around the crime scene area with officers strategically placed around it. She found a free space up the road and, after parking, she walked briskly to the scene, until reaching one of the uniformed officers.

'Sorry, you can't go any further,' the officer said, holding his hand up to stop her.

'I'm here to see DCI Walker. She's expecting me. I'm Dr Cavendish.'

'Dr Cavendish to see DCI Walker,' he said into his radio.

'Send her down,' a crackly voice said.

'You can go now. It's straight down there,' he said, pointing at the stepping plates which led into the waste ground. 'But sign the security log first.' He held out a clipboard, and she signed herself in.

She headed where he'd indicated, but before reaching there accidentally walked right through a muddy puddle which was at least four inches deep. She glanced at her shoes, which she'd worn especially for the informal interview and lunch. Damn. Now she'd need to change them before she could go back.

They were black patent leather with a small heel. Being five foot ten, she only ever wore small heels, as she didn't like to tower too much over everyone. Not that she didn't enjoy being tall. She did. It gave her a certain amount of respect and authority, which is why she'd chosen them for today.

She debated going back to the car to see if her wellies were in the boot but decided against it as she couldn't remember the last time she'd worn them and it would just waste time.

As she drew closer to the tent, she saw Matt and Whitney in deep conversation. Whitney smiled and waved. It would be good to catch-up with the officer again, even under these circumstances. There might have been friction between them when they initially got to know each other, but they'd moved past that. Whitney was a refreshing change from the people George worked with. The detective always said it as she saw it. If she didn't like something, she'd tell you – she was open and honest about her feelings. Something George struggled with on a daily basis.

There was also a connection between the two of them since their last case involving Whitney's daughter. When she saw Whitney and Tiffany together, she had a twinge of regret she'd chosen her career over having a family. But it was her choice and most times she was happy with it. She'd done very well, and when she made associate professor, it was going to be even better.

'Look at the state of your shoes. Don't you have any wellies?' Whitney asked as she approached.

'By the time I realised, the damage had been done. I don't have much time, so tell me what you know about the victim.'

'Come and see for yourself. Matt, you can stay out here.'

'Thanks, guv. I couldn't bear looking at it again.'

'That bad?' George asked, noticing how grey his complexion was.

'I haven't seen anything like this before,' Whitney said.

'Really? Surely you must have seen mutilated bodies?'

'We live in Lenchester, not in London. I've seen missing limbs on occasion, but not missing genitals. It looks… Well, let's not talk about it out here. Let's go in.'

She followed Whitney into the tent and saw Claire in the opposite corner, putting her camera into its case.

'Morning, Claire,' George said.

'Another gawker.' Claire shook her head.

'Not exactly. I wanted to see the body in situ.' She walked further into the tent and up to the body.

The naked male victim appeared to be in his forties, had dark hair streaked with grey, and was well toned, with no flab. Her eyes focussed on the hole where his genitals should have been. Dried blood was splattered around the open wound. A wave of nausea washed over her, but she swallowed hard, determined not to let it take hold. Before becoming a forensic psychologist, she'd intended on being a surgeon like her father, but found herself unable to even look at blood. She'd spent many hours in the hypnotherapist's chair and had mostly got over it, but wounds like this still affected her. A hand resting on her arm made her start.

'Are you okay?' Whitney asked.

'Yes, I'm fine. You know my history with blood.'

'I'm sorry, I didn't think it would affect you like this. I thought you'd be interested from a psychological perspective.'

'I am. And I'm not going to let anything get in the way. I'll be fine.' She breathed deeply a couple of times and forced herself to look at the body. This time it was easier.

'What's that all about?' she said, pointing to the socks.

'You mean you don't have some theory already circulating around your head?' Whitney quipped.

'Maybe the killer doesn't like feet,' she suggested.

'What happened to his missing bits?' Whitney mused.

'Saved in a jar? Thrown in the bin? He was forced to swallow them?'

'You're kidding, right?' Whitney screwed up her face.

'It's been known.'

'They're not in his mouth, throat, hands, or anus, if that helps,' Claire said. 'Now, if you two have finished, I need to arrange for the body to be moved.'

'Just give us a couple of minutes, so George has time to fully inspect it,' Whitney said.

George noted the fact the victim didn't seem to be positioned in any way, and how he was left in full view and not hidden.

'How long has he been here, do you think?' she asked Claire.

'Let me do my tests back at the lab and I'll let you know. Off the record, I'd say at least ten hours. The dry patch underneath implies he must've been placed here before the rain started,' Claire said.

She exchanged a quick glance with Whitney. It wasn't often the pathologist was willing to share anything until she'd confirmed it back at the morgue.

'Come on, let's leave Claire to get on,' she said to Whitney.

'We'll wait to hear from you, Claire. Hopefully you'll have something for us later today,' Whitney said.

'You never know your luck, if people leave me alone and I can get on with my work.' Claire dismissed them with a flick of her hand.

They walked out of the tent and inspected the surrounding area where the scenes of crime team had started working. 'Look over there,' George said. 'Tyre marks. Do you think they're from the car belonging to the person who dumped the body?'

'It's going to be the devil's own job trying to get any evidence in this weather. Do you have enough time to come to the station with me so we can discuss this further, or do you have to get back for your lunch?'

George checked her watch. It started in thirty minutes and not only were her shoes caked in mud, there were splatters up her tights and over her skirt. She couldn't go in that state, which meant going home and getting changed.

But there wasn't time. It would be better to miss it completely than to show up late and have all eyes on her. She did have some jeans, a jumper, and a pair of trainers in the car, which would be fine for wearing in the incident room.

Was she making a mistake? She didn't like letting people down, but equally it was only part of the familiarisation programme, and she knew everyone apart from the other candidates, who she wouldn't see again. She'd phone the departmental administrator and explain she'd been called away on an emergency. That should suffice.

'I'm not going dressed like this,' she said, pointing at her clothes. 'I'll come back with you to the station.'

'That's not like you,' Whitney said.

'You need me, they don't. It's not like it's the formal interview. I'm sure it won't matter.'

Ducking out of the lunch wasn't something she'd have considered doing in the past. But since working with Whitney, she'd changed. She wouldn't allow herself to be governed by the rules in quite the same way as she used to. That didn't mean she'd given up rules altogether. She liked them. Especially the security they gave her. But now she'd break them if she believed it would produce a positive outcome.

'Well, if you say so, then I'm happy about it. We need your input. But don't blame me if it comes back to bite you on the bum,' Whitney said.

'It won't. Next week is the important time, when I have the presentation and the formal interview. You have me at your disposal for a few days, at least. Come on, let's leave so I can change out of these clothes.'

## Chapter Four

George and Whitney each grabbed a coffee from the machine on the first floor of the station.

'How's Tiffany?'

'She's getting there. She's stopped jumping every time there's a loud noise, and she went to the pub with her friends at the weekend. The first time she'd been out at night since it happened. The counsellor you suggested made all the difference. When I'd suggested she went to one, she flat out refused. I don't know how you managed to change her mind.'

George had met Tiffany for coffee several times in one of the university cafés. The young girl had opened up about the nightmares she'd been having but made George promise not to tell her mum because she didn't want her worrying. She'd agreed, providing Tiffany went to see the counsellor she recommended.

'It helps to speak to someone outside of family. I'm very fond of her.'

'And those feelings are reciprocated. It's always

"George, this… George, that…" A lesser woman would be feeling jealous.' Whitney laughed.

'You have nothing to worry about. You're an incredible mother. It's because of you Tiffany's been able to face her demons.'

'Now you're making me blush,' Whitney said.

'I mean it.'

'Let's get to work before this turns into an emotion-fest and makes us both uncomfortable.'

They made their way to the large incident room, which held desks for around twenty people. Grouped in pairs, each desk had a computer screen on it. The board was situated on the far side of the room, close to the door leading to Whitney's office.

As usual, the room was buzzing with chatter. They headed towards the back, by the board.

'Listen up, everyone,' Whitney said. 'I'm sure you've heard we've found a body.'

'You mean a partial body.' Frank, the oldest member of her team, gave a loud belly laugh.

'Okay, let's get all the jokes over with, and then we can start,' Whitney said.

George loved being with the team. The atmosphere was friendly, with no real competitiveness. So different from the university, where you really had to watch your back, as everyone was trying to outdo each other. She wondered briefly if anyone at work had noticed her missing, as the lunch was about to start. There was nothing she could do about it now. She'd phoned and explained her absence was unavoidable and she'd be there as soon she could.

'Well, one thing's for sure, he won't be feeling a right dick,' Doug said.

Everyone laughed. After a few more equally bad jokes,

Whitney raised her hands, indicating for everyone to be quiet.

'Fun time over. We have some investigating to do. We haven't had this confirmed, but I believe him to be Russell Atkins. He went to my school.'

She wrote his name in the centre of the board, followed by a question mark. 'Ellie, do a PNC check, see if he's in the database reported as missing, or if he's in our records for any other reason. Also, see if there's anything on social media. If you don't come up with anything, check the DVLA database. I don't want to have to wait for DNA or dental records. The family needs to be informed as soon as possible. If I'm right about it being Russell, we need his address, where he works, family, friends, and anything else you can find.'

'Yes, guv,' Ellie replied.

'Before I assign actions, I'll hand over to Dr Cavendish for her insights so far.'

George smiled at everyone, remembering what it had been like the first time she'd spoken to the team. They were shocked Whitney had invited her in. At the time, they'd been sceptical about how much help she could give. Now they seemed to accept her.

'It's good to see you all again, albeit under less than ideal circumstances. My initial thoughts are this murder is personal. Killers don't normally cut off genitals without having a very good reason, usually directly linked to the victim. With that in mind, it would be fair to assume the killer knew the victim in some way. They could have been a family member, spouse, friend, or colleague.'

'Excellent,' Whitney said as she went to the board and wrote *victim known to killer*.

'At the moment, it's impossible to develop a more detailed profile until we have forensic information from Dr

Dexter. However, we already know certain facts. It's likely to have been a crime of passion, which knife crimes typically are. Also, having viewed the incision, the killer had certainly handled a knife before. Then there's the fact the socks were left on the body and the remaining clothes were neatly folded at the scene. Why? What's the killer telling us? Finally, we mustn't forget the physical requirement of moving the body. As I've already mentioned, we'll know more once the pathologist has got back to us.'

She nodded at Whitney, to indicate she'd finished. Had she given them enough? Probably not, but at the moment she had nothing else to discuss and not much to contribute to the investigation.

A frisson of excitement coursed through her. This case was interesting. Until she'd met Whitney, George's work had mainly been on the academic, theoretical side. Getting a taste of what it was like in the real world proved to be extremely stimulating. She didn't want to leave the university. She loved her work, the students, and her research. But actually seeing how she could make a difference was extremely satisfying.

'SOCO are at the scene. It's a mud bath out there, so I'd be very surprised if they get much from it. We need to focus on investigating people who knew the victim. What do you make of the location, George?' Whitney asked.

'Where the body was left is interesting because although it wasn't placed in a highly populated area for everyone to see, it wasn't buried either. Also, it was left in such a way as to indicate the killer was sending a message. We need to find out what.'

'But the body was found quite quickly,' Whitney said.

'Who found it?' Matt asked.

'A jogger on his early-morning run.'

'In this weather?' Frank said.

'Not everyone's a fair-weather exerciser,' Matt said.

'Some people don't exercise at all,' Doug added. 'Do they, Frank?'

'What's this? *Get at Frank* day?'

'You can take it,' Doug said, grinning at him.

Frank sat back in his chair and banged his hands on his stomach. 'This is all bought and paid for,' he said, laughing.

George joined in. She enjoyed the banter that went on between this close-knit group of detectives. She'd got to know Ellie, Frank, and Matt well during the last case. Doug and Sue she knew a little but hoped to get better acquainted with as they worked together.

'Enough hilarity, if you please,' Whitney said, drawing it to a close. 'George, do you have anything else to add?'

'Nothing, other than to agree with you. The investigation should focus on people known to the victim.'

'Thanks,' Whitney said. 'We have—'

The door opening interrupted her, and Detective Superintendent Tom Jamieson, Whitney's immediate boss, walked in.

Whitney's face changed from smiling and relaxed to tense and on alert. Although following the arrest of the campus murderers he'd been a little easier on her, George knew Whitney believed it to be only a matter of time before he returned to how he was before. They clashed at every turn. As Whitney was so fond of pointing out, he'd come in through the Fast Track scheme, and for her that meant he was totally inexperienced in the parts of policing which mattered most.

'Don't let me interrupt,' Jamieson said. 'I've heard a body's been found. What have you done about it, so far?'

'We have a white male in his early forties, found on the

waste ground next to the racecourse on the edge of the city,' Whitney said.

'And we've ascertained it's murder already?' Jamieson asked.

'We're awaiting the post mortem results from Dr Dexter, but we're assuming so, as the body had been mutilated.'

'In what way?' Jameson asked.

'He's missing his genitals,' Whitney said.

Jameson grimaced. 'Has he been identified?'

'I thought I recognised the victim. We're checking records to confirm. If I'm correct, we'll inform the family.'

'Unfortunately, I can't come with you as I'm due in a strategic planning meeting shortly,' Jameson said.

Whitney's lips turned up in a slight smile.

'Not a problem, sir. I'll take Dr Cavendish with me. Under the circumstances, it might be useful to have her assistance when visiting the family, as it's such an abhorrent crime.'

'Good idea. Report to me later on how we're doing. In the meantime, I want it solved PDQ. Dr Cavendish, are we to expect more murders, or is this a one-off?'

'Too early to say. This type of murder is extremely personal, but as we have no idea of the motive, we can't close ourselves off to the possibility there could be more,' George said.

'True. Right, I'll see you later.' He directed his words at Whitney.

Everyone was quiet until he walked out of the incident room, and once the doors shut, the noise started.

'You lucked out there, guv. Thank goodness for the strategy meeting, otherwise you'd have had to spend time with him,' Frank said.

'That's the Super you're talking about,' Whitney

admonished, but with a grin on her face so they all knew she didn't mean it as a reprimand.

'Guv, I've got the information you need,' Ellie said.

'Great.'

'The licence was renewed last year, so the photo is current,' Ellie said.

George followed Whitney over to Ellie's desk. On the screen was Russell Atkins' driving licence, showing his photo.

'I was right. The victim is definitely him,' Whitney said.

'You want me with you when you speak to the family?' George asked.

'I would, but I know you're busy. I only said it to pacify the DSI. Unless you're able to come with?'

Should she? She didn't have any classes or tutorials, though she'd actually planned on running through her presentation to make sure all the PowerPoint slides were accurate. She could do it in the evening. She had plenty of time. When you lived on your own, you could do exactly what you wanted. She'd lived with someone for a few months last year, and it turned out to be disastrous in so many ways. Now she didn't have that issue, there was nothing stopping her. She'd come up with an excuse if anybody from work questioned where she was.

'Yes, I can,' she said.

'Good. Ellie, if you could quickly get me contact details. Frank, I want you to access all the CCTV footage around the area and look for anything suspicious. Sue, you'll need to help him. Matt, as soon as Ellie has some background information, I want you to head to his work-place and find out if anyone has a grudge against him. Doug, I want you to check to see if any sexual offenders have been released into the area recently. We have to cover all possibilities. I'm hoping by the time George and I have been to see the family, we might have something to work with from Dr Dexter. In the meantime, everyone, keep in touch. Let's hope this is an isolated incident, because we don't want any more mutilated men turning up on our patch.'

## Chapter Five

'We'll take my car,' Whitney said once they had Atkins'
contact details. His next of kin was listed as Diana Atkins,
his wife. 'I'm glad it's you and not Jamieson coming with
me. Just because he's being reasonable, I still don't trust
him. He's out for himself and his own promotion. If I get
in the way or do something to damage it, he'll soon
change. In the meantime, I'm going to enjoy the peace and
quiet he's giving me.'

'Good idea. Make the most of it,' George said.

She glanced at George in her well worn jeans and
jumper. Her short blonde hair was a little messy, probably
from pulling the sweater over her head. It made her look
much younger than her thirty-four years. She'd never seen
George dressed like it before. The couple of times they'd
been out in the evening, she'd worn something smart.
Whitney was quite envious of the doctor's sophisticated
air.

'If the village Russell Atkins lives in is anything to go
by, he's obviously done very well for himself. According to

Ellie, he's a strategy consultant for an international consulting firm.'

Maidenwell village was ten miles out of the city, and she didn't visit often as it was relatively crime-free. It was typically upper-middle class and full of the *county-set* who sent their children to private school and kept horses at the local stable.

'I don't know it,' George said.

'I'm sure you'll feel at home because they're all your type.' She cast a quick glance at George, hoping she'd taken her comment the way she'd intended.

'My type? Talk about déjà vu. Didn't you mention my *type* when we first met?'

'Yes, but now I'm saying it affectionately. Unlike before, when I was being mean. For which I apologise.' She grinned at her.

'Apology accepted. I thought the victim went to your school?' George asked.

'He did, but he must have made plenty of money along the way to afford one of the houses in Maidenwell. I bet even the smallest one is five times the size of mine. Anyway, tell me about this job you're going for. It surprised me when Claire told me, because you hadn't said anything.'

Whitney hadn't intended mentioning it to George because she didn't want to make her feel uncomfortable. It was George's decision if she didn't want to tell her. But if this new job was going to impact their working relationship, surely she had a right to ask?

'I'm sorry. I didn't think you'd be interested. I know your view on academia and how it doesn't mix with the real world.'

Previously, it would have been a correct assumption to make, though Whitney had come to the conclusion some of the stuff George came out with made sense. Not that she'd admit it to anyone.

'That's got nothing to do with it. You're my friend, and of course I want to know if something exciting, like a new job, is happening.'

'I'd hardly call it exciting.' George shrugged.

'Any new job is exciting, or is this you being your usual calm, logical, and unemotional self?'

'I'm being realistic. Associate Professor is the next step and a solid achievement for someone my age. It will look very good on my CV. Obviously, there's an increase in salary, though not a huge amount. For me, it's more an acknowledgement of how proficient I am at my work. I'm not excited as such, but I do expect to be offered the position, as I'm already working at the university, thought of highly, and everyone has indicated the job's mine for the taking.'

Years ago, Whitney's promotion to Inspector had been stymied by a particularly nasty DCI, so she knew firsthand how things didn't always turn out as expected. She wasn't sure whether to say anything, as she didn't want to upset her friend. Then again, knowing George, she wouldn't take it the wrong way.

'I don't want to put a damper on it, but don't take what they said as gospel. I know from experience how quickly things can change.'

'I won't,' George said. 'Anyway, that's all there is to tell. As I said earlier, today was the familiarisation and next week it's the presentation and interview.'

'What are you presenting on?' She glanced at George, who looked a little uncomfortable and kept her eyes focussed on the windscreen.

'Working with the police, and helping with the investigation of the Campus Murders and the arrest of Henry and Harriet Spencer.'

Whitney tensed. 'Is that why you didn't tell me? Because of Tiffany?'

'Not exactly. I'm not mentioning anyone by name. Nobody knows Tiffany was the twins' fifth victim, and I won't disclose it either. With hindsight, I didn't tell you because it was such an awful time, I didn't think you'd want to relive it.'

Whitney let out her breath. 'It's okay, I understand. But next time I'd rather you didn't keep it from me.'

They drove out of the station car park and headed onto the main dual carriageway towards Maidenwell. After twenty-five minutes, they drove into the village and down a long country avenue lined with huge oak trees. Every hundred yards or so were large wrought-iron gates leading to houses which couldn't be seen from the road.

'We're looking for number forty-four, which should be coming up on the left,' Whitney said.

She stopped by the gate, leaned out of the window, and pressed the button on the intercom.

'Hello,' a woman's voice came through the speaker.

'DCI Whitney Walker and Dr Cavendish to see Mrs Atkins.'

'Is she expecting you?'

'No, she isn't. We're here on a police matter.'

After a few seconds, there was a buzz, and the black gate slid open. She drove up the long drive, which was lined with small, very well pruned, circular bushes. It looked like something from a stately home.

'How the fuck can Russell Atkins go from North Lenchester Academy to this?' Her eyes were on stalks as she absorbed the grandeur of the house in front of them. It was a large, two storey, red brick Georgian building, with an imposing dark green door in the middle and four windows either side. It was enormous.

'It's certainly arresting,' George said.

'I suppose you lived in something similar growing up,' Whitney said.

'I admit my family home is large, but don't hold it against me.'

She wasn't surprised, but curious why George now lived in a small Victorian terrace. Although it was immaculately decorated and filled with expensive antique furniture.

'No, I definitely won't. Let's go and see Diana Atkins and break the news.'

They got out of the car and headed towards the stone steps leading up to the front door. Whitney lifted a large brass knocker and tapped several times. Within a few seconds, the door opened.

'Mrs Diana Atkins?' she asked.

'I'm the housekeeper. I'll find Mrs Atkins for you.' She held open the door for them to step inside.

George and Whitney exchanged glances as the woman walked off.

'A housekeeper,' Whitney said. 'It's all right for some.'

'I'm not saying anything,' George said.

She glanced around the large open hall, admiring the wood panelling which lined the lower part of the walls and the high ceilings with ornate ceiling roses and coving. On the walls were large oil paintings of country scenes, and although they weren't to her taste, she nonetheless recognised as being good-quality art.

'Mrs Atkins is in the drawing room, if you'd like to come with me,' the housekeeper said on her return.

They followed her down the hall to one of the doors on the right. The woman knocked and opened the door for them to enter. The room was large and square, with antique furniture and long flock curtains with a huge pelmet. Floor to ceiling shelves full of books lined one of the walls. There were three large sofas and a single chair facing the large open fireplace, beside which logs were stacked with great precision.

Diana Atkins was sitting in the chair holding a newspaper, an Irish terrier at her feet. The woman got up as they walked into the room, folding the paper and placing it on the table next to her. She was striking, in her early forties, much taller than Whitney, and immaculately dressed in a calf-length, straight, navy skirt, a soft pink blouse, and navy court shoes. A string of pearls hung around her neck. Her glossy, straight, shoulder length dark hair was tucked behind her ears.

'Good morning, Mrs Atkins. I'm DCI Whitney Walker and this is Dr George Cavendish. We're from Lenchester CID. We'd like to talk to you about your husband.'

'My husband isn't here at the moment. He's away on business. I'm expecting him back on Saturday morning,' she said, smiling.

'Please sit down. We have some news for you.'

The smile froze on her face, and she did as she was asked. Whitney and George sat on the sofa closest to her. 'What is it?'

'I'm sorry to have to tell you, this morning we found a body on the waste ground near the old racecourse, and we believe it to be your husband,' Whitney said.

Colour drained from the woman's face, and her lips pressed together. 'My husband? No. That can't be. He's away in London working. Are you sure?' Her hands were clenched tightly together in her lap.

Whitney drew in a breath. She'd never get used to this.

'We need you to formally identify him, but we are certain it's Russell.'

She stared at the woman. How would she react? In her experience, it ranged from hysterical crying, to disbelief, to absolute shock and an inability to speak. Or acting like they'd just been told something totally inconsequential and were trying to remain in control. Judging by Diana Atkins' rigid face, it was the latter. Probably a case of stiff upper lip, which posh people seemed to value.

'How did he die?' the woman uttered, her voice hardly above a whisper.

'We're treating the death as suspicious, which means the coroner has ordered a post mortem. At the moment, Russell is with our forensic pathologist. Once we have her report, we'll know more, and of course we'll keep you informed,' Whitney said, avoiding answering her question outright.

'You mean he was murdered?' The woman drew in a loud breath, and she leaned back in the chair.

'I'm sorry, we can't tell you anything else at the moment. Not until we're sure.'

'You say he was found near the old racecourse, but what would he be doing there?' She shook her head.

'That's what we're trying to find out. Is there anyone we can call to be with you? Family? Friends?' Whitney asked gently.

'Thank you, but there's no one close by. I'd rather be on my own.'

'If you're sure.'

'I am. When do you need me to come and identify him?'

'We can do it later today. First of all, we'd like to ask you some questions, if you're up to it.'

'Yes, of course. If you could wait a moment.' She rang

the brass bell on the table beside her chair. Within seconds, the housekeeper appeared.

'Isobel, please bring me a glass of water and a pot of tea for three. Would you both like tea?' she asked.

'Coffee for me, please,' Whitney said.

'I'll have tea,' George said.

'Make that a glass of water, tea for two, and a coffee. You were saying,' she said to Whitney once Isobel had left the room.

'I know this is a huge shock, but in order for us to find out what happened to your husband, we need as much information from you as possible.'

'I understand,' she said softly. 'Whatever I can do to help.'

'Do you come from around here?' Whitney asked.

'No. I come from Northamptonshire. A small village called Chapel Brampton.'

'How did you meet Russell?'

'We met at the Pytchley Hunt one Christmas Eve fifteen years ago. He was there with a friend.'

'He liked hunting?'

'He loved anything to do with horses. We keep our own horses here in the stable. Why does it matter?' she asked, frowning.

'We're trying to get a picture of what he was like. Tell me, did he work away from home often?'

'Yes, in his line of work he has to travel an awful lot.'

'He must have been doing very well to afford a place like this,' Whitney said, gesturing with her hand around the room.

'Actually, it was my family's money which enabled us to buy this house. When my parents died, we used my inheritance. To be honest, I wanted to live in Chapel Brampton, but Russell was very attached to Lenchester, and so I agreed to move here.'

That was how he did it. How did he feel being a kept man? Well, not so much a kept man but the fact his wife had so much money they could afford to live here and move in posh social circles.

'Do you work?' Whitney asked.

'Part-time for an art gallery. We commission young artists and help them set up exhibitions.'

'Fascinating work, I imagine,' George said.

'Yes, it is. Art is my passion. At Oxford I studied History of Art and English Literature.'

'Do you have any children?' she asked.

'No, we don't.' A shadow crossed her face. 'We tried for a long time, but it wasn't to be. I wanted to look into IVF, but Russell didn't. He said if we didn't succeed it would depress him too much. We both threw ourselves into work instead.'

Whitney felt sorry for the woman. She didn't know what she'd do if she hadn't had Tiffany. She made her life worthwhile.

'Does your husband have a home office?' she asked.

'Yes. I can show you.'

'Thank you.'

She led them out of the drawing room and down the long corridor until they came to the last door, which she opened. In contrast to what they'd seen of the rest of the house, this room was furnished with modern furniture. A large, light wooden desk was under the window, with two easy chairs next to it, and two large paintings of hunting scenes hung on the far wall. A leather sofa ran alongside one of the other walls, and another was lined with books. Whitney strolled over to the bookcase and had a look. It was an eclectic mix, with the emphasis on sporting and economic books, although there was also some neatly stacked fiction in there.

'Didn't Russell use his laptop for work?' Whitney asked, noticing one on his desk. There was a photograph next to it of him and Diana standing next to their horses.

'He uses a tablet supplied by the firm.'

'Did he work much from home?'

'Yes. He was in here a lot.'

Whitney glanced again at how immaculate everything was. 'He certainly kept it clean and tidy.'

'We have a housekeeper. It's her job to keep everything spotless.'

That was where she was going wrong. She needed a housekeeper. If only she could afford one.

'What about his car? Did he take it with him when he went away?'

'He has a driver when he goes to London. His office will tell you the name. His car is in the garage.'

'Do you mind if we look through the desk to see if there's anything which might help the investigation?' she asked.

'Not at all. Whatever will help your hunt for Russell's… Russell's…' Her voice broke.

Whitney rested her hand on the woman's arm and led her to one of the chairs beside the desk. 'Why don't you sit down for a moment, Diana? You've had a huge shock.'

'Thank you.'

She sat in silence while Whitney and George continued looking around the office.

'We'd like to take Russell's laptop back to the station for our digital forensic unit to examine.'

'Take whatever you like,' Diana said, sounding back to normal.

'When was the last time you spoke to him?'

'He phoned two days ago to say his business was taking longer than anticipated and he would be back on Saturday.'

'You don't speak to him every day?' Whitney asked.

'We try to, but it seldom happens as we're both so busy.'

'It's routine in suspicious deaths like Russell's to ask the family their whereabouts during the time in question so they can be excluded from our enquiries. Please could you account for your movements over the last forty-eight hours?' Whitney asked.

'Wednesday I was at an art exhibition in Lenchester's Museum Gallery for a couple of hours in the morning. Yesterday afternoon I went to Rugby to visit a gallery in the High Street. They're featuring a young artist who we're interested in acquiring. The rest of the time I was at home.'

'Can you give me the name of the gallery in Rugby and the person you saw there?'

Diana took out her phone from her pocket and looked through her contacts. 'The gallery is called Monique, and it's at 57 High Street. I went to visit Monique Jefferson herself. She can vouch for me.'

Whitney wrote down the details.

'Can anyone corroborate your movements during this time?' Whitney asked.

'The staff at the Museum Gallery know me, and Isobel is here every day from nine until four. I take the dog out for his evening walk around six-thirty, and I do remember on Thursday stopping to speak to Mike next door as he was bringing in his wheelie bin.'

'Thank you for your help. That's all we need for now. We should be finished in the office soon.'

'I'll leave you to it, as I have things to be getting on

with. A funeral to arrange.' She stood up, appearing much calmer than before.

'We're not sure yet when the body will be released.'

'I understand, but I'll still have other arrangements to put in place. If you'll excuse me, Isobel will show you out.'

'I'll be in touch later to arrange for you to formally identify Russell. Someone will pick you up.' Whitney pulled out a card from her pocket. 'Here's my card, if you need to speak to me.'

Mrs Atkins took the card and left the room, closing the door behind her.

'What did you make of her?' Whitney asked George.

'She's handling the news very well,' George said.

'She probably didn't want to break down in front of us. Some people are like that. Especially...'

'Don't say *my sort*,' George said, glaring at her.

'I wasn't going to,' she said, not wanting to admit that was exactly what was about to come out of her mouth.

Whitney pulled on her disposable gloves and passed a pair over to George. She opened each of the drawers in his desk. Everything was ridiculously tidy and well laid out. She picked up the computer, ready for them to take.

'Found anything interesting?' she asked George, who was scanning the bookcase.

'Not in terms of the books, but definitely in the way they're all classified. Everything is in alphabetical order. With all those books, what a mission it would have been to set up.'

'The whole house is the same. Nothing out of place, even the drawers in Russell's desk. I like things tidy, but this is tidy in its extreme. This can't be the work of Isobel. There's something else at play here.'

'Definitely. She's only acting under instruction. Are they both like that, or is it just Diana?' George said.

'What makes you think it's her and not him?' Whitney asked.

'If it was him, it would be mainly his office. But as you said, it seems to be the whole house. Or what we've seen of the house. Did you see the way she folded her newspaper when we walked into the room? Everything was just so. I'd like to look at their bedroom. I wonder if they share or if they have their own?'

'Do all posh people have their own bedrooms? I thought it was only the Royal Family.' Whitney's mum and dad had shared a bedroom until the day he died. It seemed weird couples wouldn't sleep in the same room.

'I can't speak for everyone,' George said.

'Do your parents have their own bedrooms?'

'Yes, they do. But that's because of the hours they both keep, and they don't wish to disturb each other.'

'And nothing to do with them being posh,' Whitney quipped.

'I'm not discussing this further, because I know your views,' George said, shaking her head. Her eyes were twinkling, so Whitney knew she wasn't upset.

'Let's get back to the station and maybe we can start putting together some sort of profile. Hopefully Claire will have something for us, too.'

## Chapter Six

They arrived back at the station early-afternoon, and as they entered the incident room, Whitney's phone rang.

'Walker.' She paused. 'I can be there in half an hour. I'll bring George.' She ended the call and continued to the desk beside the board.

George bristled. Whitney had a tendency to make decisions which included her, without consulting first. Though she supposed it was understandable, as this was Whitney's investigation. But being a typical eldest child meant George struggled when others wanted to take charge of her life.

'Listen up, everyone. We've just got back from interviewing the victim's wife and have dropped his laptop off at forensics. George and I are going to see Dr Dexter to find out what she's got for us. In the meantime, how are we getting on with the research? Ellie?'

'I've been looking into his background. Matt's visiting his workplace to interview the staff.'

'I want you to track down when and where he last used his credit card. His wife mentioned he uses a company to drive him when he goes to London. Contact Matt and ask him to check it out for us and find out exactly what appointments he had in London. We don't have his phone yet; see if you can ping where it was last used. Frank, how's the CCTV search going?'

'Unfortunately, there aren't many cameras when you get that far out of the city.'

'Why don't you track the cars coming and going. If the murderer was just dumping the body, you might see a car heading in that direction and maybe fifteen minutes later heading back. There must be something. The body didn't get there by itself.'

'Yes, guv.'

She admired the way Whitney handled Frank. Despite the number of years he'd been on the force, he often needed hand-holding.

'Doug, do a background check on Diana Atkins and her alibi. I'll text you the details.'

'Okay,' Doug said.

'Once we've been to Dr Dexter, we'll start putting together a profile.'

Whitney turned to George. 'Are you okay to come with me to see Claire, or do you have to get back?'

Strictly speaking, she should go to work, but the temptation was too great. 'I'm coming. I'd like to hear Claire's findings.'

They left the station and made their way to the mortuary. It was newly built and adjacent to the hospital. As soon as they entered, they were hit by the cold, antiseptic smell so typical of places like that. They walked to the end of the corridor and pushed open the doors into the lab. To the right, in the small office area, Claire was sitting at her desk, peering through a pair of large, black-rimmed glasses at a computer screen. As usual, she was dressed in brightly coloured patterned trousers with an equally bright un-matching patterned shirt. She glanced up.

'Good afternoon, ladies. We meet again.'

'Afternoon, Claire,' they both responded.

'I've done my preliminary post-mortem and sent bloods to toxicology, but I wanted to let you know what I'd found,' she said, a mysterious tone to her voice.

'Can we see the body?' George asked.

'Come with me.'

Claire pulled on her white lab coat, which was hanging on a hook on the wall, and they all went to one of the stainless-steel tables where a body was stretched out, covered by a sheet. Claire lifted it off, revealing the victim. There was a Y-shaped incision on his chest where she'd done her work. George leaned in and took a good look, in particular where the dismemberment had taken place.

'Fascinating. What do you think of the way the mutila-tion was carried out?' she asked.

'It appears the perpetrator had some experience of cutting flesh. That could be from animals or humans. If you look around the wound, there are no hesitation marks,' Claire said.

'So, this might not be their first victim?' Whitney said.

'It's one explanation. And obviously something for you to investigate. But equally, it could be the perpetrator has a surgical background. Or maybe worked as a butcher. There are lots of occupations where the ability to use a knife is important. That's your area of expertise, not mine. What I can tell you is the incisions were made by a right-handed person, most likely using a fillet knife, which has a flexible and robust blade, enabling it to easily cut under the skin.'

'Anything else for us?' Whitney asked.

'Yes. There were ligature marks on his wrists and

ankles from where he'd been tied up with rope and struggled. There was also some soil under his fingernails which was a different colour from the soil where he was found. I've sent it for analysis, along with fibres from his hair and body, which I suspect are from a carpet. Cause of death was suffocation. He was moved to the scene post mortem, which we can tell from lividity and rigor. Time of death somewhere between six and ten on Thursday evening.'

'Was he drugged?' Whitney asked.

'We won't know until we get the report from toxicology. However, I did find a puncture wound in his leg which could be the result of being injected with a needle.'

'Is that it?' Whitney asked. 'You could have told me all this on the phone.'

Claire turned to them with a smirk on her face. She was clearly enjoying this.

'Of course that's not it. I'm just getting to the good stuff. I checked the contents of his stomach and guess what was in there?'

'His genitals?' George asked.

Claire nodded. 'And it gets even better.'

'Better? What could get better than that?' Whitney asked, giving a shudder.

'They'd been cooked first,' Claire said. 'Fried in oil, I suspect.'

George rubbed her brow. Not only did they have someone cutting off the genitals of their victim, but they also cooked the parts and fed them to him. It took the crime to a whole new level. What did it mean?

'Do you know whether he was force-fed?' Whitney asked.

'Difficult to tell,' Claire said. 'There was no sign of food around the outside of his mouth, or up his nose, or around his ears, as you would expect to see from someone turning their head to avoid being fed. But the *meal* was cut into small pieces so the perpetrator could have placed them into the victim's mouth and forced him to swallow. Maybe threatening to kill him if he didn't.'

'So, he was likely sedated, then taken somewhere, tied up, mutilated, fed his own body parts, and finally suffocated. The suffocation appears an anti-climax,' George said.

'Yes, I see what you mean,' Whitney said. 'It's like the murderer was building up to something and suddenly killed him. Why would they do that?'

'As much as I find this intriguing, I've really got to get on. So, if you two can finish ruminating somewhere else, I'll write my report, and as soon as I hear back from toxicology, I'll let you know.' Claire waved them off in her usual dismissive manner.

'Before we go. What about the socks?' Whitney asked.

'I removed them and there was nothing out of the ordinary. I don't know the meaning behind leaving them on. Unless it was a message. Though I'd have thought the mutilation was enough. Now will you go?'

'Been good seeing you. We'll catch-up soon.' Whitney grinned in Claire's direction.

'Bye,' George said.

They left the doctor and headed out of the lab.

'She's so funny. It's a good job we know her and don't take her attitude to heart. Still, she's the best forensic pathologist in the country. We're lucky to have her,' Whitney said.

'Agreed. She's thorough. She's fast. She's insightful, and she always goes the extra mile. What else could we ask for?' George said. 'Where to now? The office?'

'Are you sure you don't want to go back to work?' Whitney asked.

'What is it with you? I've already said I'm fine. I've missed the lunch and sent my apologies. I'll come back to the station with you, and I may go back to the university later. But please stop asking. I can make up my own mind.'

Whitney held her hands up in mock surrender. 'Okay. Okay. I'm only concerned you don't get into trouble. Excuse me for caring.'

She could kick herself for not realising.

'Sorry. I'm not used to people looking out for me.'

'Well, get used to it. I owe you big time, and I'm always going to be here for you.' Whitney gave George a hug.

'Sometimes I wonder if it was better when we were at odds with one another. All this hugging stuff doesn't sit right with me.' She shifted awkwardly on the spot.

'I'll inject some emotion into you. You wait and see. In the meantime, let's get back to the station and start solving this murder.'

## Chapter Seven

Whitney scanned the incident room once they arrived back, having grabbed some sandwiches on the way, as they hadn't had time to eat lunch. Matt had returned. Ellie was sitting at her computer. Frank and Sue were also looking at a computer screen, presumably at the CCTV, and Doug was standing by the board. The rest of the team would be out doing house-to-house enquiries, not that there were many houses in the area surrounding the waste ground. She thought the world of her team. Especially those currently in the room, who were her most trusted members. They'd stood by her when Jamieson wanted her removed from working the last big case. And thanks to them, and George of course, they'd solved the case, and she'd redeemed herself.

Not to mention they'd saved Tiffany's life.

'Stop what you're doing. I want to tell you what we found out from Dr Dexter.' She waited until she had their attention. 'After removing the genitals, the murderer cooked and fed them to the victim.' Whitney paused, waiting for the fact to sink in. She was greeted with a chorus of groans and vomit sounding noises.

'You've got to be kidding me. What sick fuck would do that?' Frank said. 'It has to be the grossest thing I've ever heard.'

'George is going to give us a rundown on what she thinks of the perpetrator, so far.'

Had she put George on the spot? She should have asked if she had any more insights beforehand. George didn't look perturbed, though, as she stepped forward and leaned against the desk.

'Now we know about the victim swallowing his own body parts, it confirms my view it's personal. I'd say the victim definitely knew the murderer. We're awaiting confirmation as to whether the victim was sedated, but it seems likely. The murderer would need to be strong enough to move the body. However, the obvious sexual component would indicate the perpetrator is likely to be a woman. In terms of the investigation, it's definitely worth looking into his private life to see whether he had affairs. Had he scorned someone? Was anyone stalking him? I'm not totally discounting the murderer being male. It could be the work of a jealous husband.'

'So basically, it could be anybody,' Frank said.

'Profiling isn't an exact science. We use the information to help steer the investigation,' George said.

'What about his wife?' Ellie asked.

'I checked, and she was at the museum on Wednesday and art gallery Thursday afternoon, as she claimed,' Doug said. 'The neighbour also confirmed seeing her on Thursday evening around six-thirty when she was walking the dog. He saw her return about an hour later. Do we have a time of death?'

'Between six and ten pm on Thursday,' Whitney said.

'Which puts her in the clear,' Doug said.

'Possibly. She's still a person of interest, until we know for sure.'

Whitney wasn't convinced Diana had anything to do with her husband's death, but she wasn't prepared to dismiss her involvement just yet.

'Do you think this is a one-off?' Matt asked.

'It's hard to be certain. The only way we'll know is if we find another body. At the moment, I suspect it might be a single incident,' George said.

'Thanks, George. Matt, what did you turn up at his workplace?'

'I got the name of the company he used to drive him to London and to his appointments. I'm going out to interview the driver later when he gets in from his current run. I also spoke to Atkins' personal assistant regarding his schedule, and he didn't have any meetings yesterday or today as he'd taken two days of annual leave. So, he only used the driver on Wednesday.'

'Go back to his office and find out what he was like socially. Was he having an affair, or had affairs? Anything non-work related you can dig up. Also, ask them to check if his phone is there. We need to find it. Ellie, do we know when he last used it?'

'It pinged the tower by the Imperial Hotel near Leicester. I'm going to call them to see if they have any record of him staying there.'

'If he did go to Leicester, how did he get there? Check his credit card and see if he went by train.'

'I'll do that first and then contact the hotel,' Ellie said.

'Okay, let's plot the sequence of events. The victim goes to London for appointments. He takes two days of leave, yesterday and today, which his wife doesn't know about. He goes to a hotel sixty miles away from home, which implies he was going to meet someone. I'm guessing the hotel will be somewhere small and of out the way, where he's not going to be spotted. We'll know soon enough and—'

The phone on her desk rang.

'Walker.'

'It's Mac. We've found an app on the laptop you brought in which you'll be interested in.' Whitney listened before asking him to forward the information.

She finished the call and smiled at everyone. 'It looks like we're getting somewhere. It seems our victim used SnapMate. It's a site where teens hang out, and he's been chatting with young girls. He goes by the name Billy.'

'Grooming them?' George asked.

'We'll need to look at the content of the messages, but it's certainly pointing that way.' Whitney shook her head. People who preyed on young children made her sick to her stomach.

'If we're right, it places a different emphasis on who we're looking for. It could be a girl he was grooming and maybe met. It could be the parents of the girl he was grooming who found out. It seems likely, considering the nature of the crime, that his activities had something to do with it,' George said.

'Okay, everyone, get on with the tasks you have. I'm going back to see the wife, but not without a search warrant. I'll get onto it straight away. Priority now is finding his phone.'

'Once his laptop is returned to us, we can check if the two devices are linked,' Ellie said.

'How will that help?' she asked.

'If we can't find his phone and they are linked, we should be able to access all his apps and anything on there without it.'

Whitney shook her head. She wasn't that old, but this techie stuff was definitely passing her by.

Once the search warrant came through, Whitney and a forensics team went back to the Atkins' house. Diana answered the buzzer, as it was after four and Isobel had gone home. They drove up the long drive and parked. She already had the door open waiting for them.

'I didn't expect to see you back here. I thought you were going to phone and let me know about identifying Russell,' she said as Whitney walked up the steps.

'New information has come to light, and we have a warrant to search the house.'

'What information?' Diana frowned.

'While the team are here, we'll go to make the formal identification, and then we can go to the station and discuss everything,' Whitney said, deliberately ignoring the question, as she hadn't yet decided how much they would divulge to her.

'Do they have to search the whole house? Will they make a mess?' Diana asked.

'They'll be very careful and will ensure to tidy up behind them. Obviously, it's not going to be as spotless as it is at the moment.'

Diana leaned against the wall, resting her chin in her hand. Her eyes were glassy with tears. It was the first time she'd displayed any real emotion. 'Do you want us to leave now?' she asked.

'Yes.'

'Can I bring my own car?'

'Are you sure you're up to it?' Whitney asked gently.

'I'll be fine. I need to stop at the supermarket on the way back.'

It was like the earlier display of emotion had been returned to its box, and she was back to being brave. Whitney would have to check with George whether it was the way the *county-set* usually behaved.

She felt sorry for the woman, because once her husband's predilections were known, she doubted anyone would be on her side. It was tough.

They left the house and headed in convoy to the morgue. On the way, Whitney phoned Claire to let her know they were coming and told the pathologist Diana didn't know the circumstances surrounding the death. When they walked into the lab, Claire was sitting at her desk.

'Hello, Claire. This is Mrs Atkins,' Whitney said.

'We can do this one of two ways,' Claire said. 'I can show you photographs, or you can view the actual body.'

Diana Atkins looked first at Whitney and then Claire. She sucked in a loud breath. 'I want to see his body.'

The pathologist nodded, and they followed her into a room off the main lab area. Whitney and Diana stood behind a glass partition through which they could see the body on a table, covered with a sheet. Claire went back into the lab and over to the body.

'I'm sorry we have to put you through this. But we need a formal identification,' Whitney said as she nodded at Claire to get on with the process.

The pathologist lifted back the sheet covering the body, only revealing his head, which looked normal. Diana gasped and wobbled on her feet. Whitney took hold of her arm.

'Is this your husband, Russell Atkins?' she asked.

'Yes, it is.' The woman's voice cracked.

Claire covered the face with the sheet and came back to the side room.

Whitney turned to Diana, who stood upright, her face drained of colour. 'Would you like a glass of water?'

'No, thank you. I'm fine. It was just a shock to see him lying there so still and lifeless.'

'I understand. But at least it's over with now.' She turned to Claire. 'Thank you for your time. We'll be going now.'

After leaving the morgue, they drove straight to the station, and once back there Whitney took Diana into one of the interview rooms.

'I'll arrange for some coffee,' she said, leaving the woman alone.

Whitney wanted George with her and hoped she hadn't already left. She was in luck, as when she entered the incident room, she found George sitting at the desk beside Ellie's.

'I expected you to have left and gone to work,' she said.

'I caught up on my emails here and decided to stay in case you needed me.'

'Great. I've got Diana Atkins downstairs. She's identified the body. Now I want to inform her about the exact nature of his death.'

'Are you going to tell her about SnapMate?'

'Yes, as I'd like you to scrutinise her reactions.' Telling her everything could be viewed as a risky move, but it would be out soon enough in the media.

Carrying a tray with three coffees, Whitney and George went back into the interview room.

'I've brought Dr Cavendish with me,' she said, handing out the drinks.

The woman nodded in George's direction.

'You haven't told me how Russell died. I couldn't tell when I identified him,' Diana said.

'He was suffocated, after his body was mutilated.'

Diana's eyes widened. 'Mutilated? How?'

She sucked in a breath, bracing herself for delivering the news.

'There's no easy way to say this. When we found Russell's body, he'd had his genitals removed.'

Shock etched itself across the woman's face, and she remained silent for a while.

'Why? Who would do something like that?' she finally asked.

'We believe the murderer was sending a message.'

'What sort of message?'

'After examining Russell's laptop, our digital forensics team discovered he'd been active on SnapMate, a site for teens. We believe it's related to that.'

Diana's face paled. 'A site for teens,' she repeated. 'What does that mean, exactly?'

Whitney exchanged glances with George, nodding for her to explain.

'Men go onto these sites in order to meet young children. They'll pretend to be a teenage boy or girl and make friends with them. Once they've gained their trust and friendship, they may suggest exchanging photos of an intimate nature. Something they wouldn't want others to see. This is what we call grooming. Often during the grooming process, the child is persuaded not to trust, or to be wary of, their friends and family. The aim is to isolate them and make them totally dependent on their new "friend". After a while, they may arrange to meet in person. Only then will the child find out they haven't developed a relationship with someone their age. It's not unusual for the older person to use the photographs as blackmail to coerce the child into having sex.'

'And you believe that's what Russell was doing?' Diana Atkins asked, her voice shaky.

'We're unsure how far his involvement went,' George said. 'This is what we're looking to find out. It's still the early stages of the investigation.'

'It would really help if you can let us know anything about his behaviour which you believe might be relevant,' Whitney added.

'Yes, of course.' The woman's hands were resting on the table, but there was no mistaking the tremor. 'I need to think about it. Do you need me for anything else?'

'Not at the moment. Will you be okay to drive, or would you like one of my officers to drive you back in your car?' she asked.

'I'll be fine, thank you.' Diana gave a weak smile.

'If you need anything, let me know. I'll keep you informed of the investigation.'

'Will it be on the news?' the woman asked.

'We haven't yet announced it to the press, but once we do, then yes. It will be.'

'Will you tell them everything? About him being… being…'

'Initially we'll only report the circumstances surrounding the death in broad terms, but it may come out in the future,' Whitney said, fully aware what she meant.

'To be expected.' She shook her head. 'If it's okay, I'm going to head home.'

'Of course. And remember, you can contact me anytime, if you want to.'

Whitney escorted her to the back of the station and out into the car park. The woman's life had been totally destroyed. It just went to show, having plenty of money meant shit. Diana Atkins' world had been changed forever. She'd always be known as the paedophile's wife, and no money could change that. Would she move away from Lenchester and back to where she came from? Whitney would, if it was her.

'Thank you. I appreciate your help.' Diana held out her hand and Whitney shook it.

## Chapter Eight

'Matt, you're with me. We're off to Leicester to the hotel where Russell Atkins checked in on Thursday,' Whitney said when she walked into the station on Saturday morning. 'He left his phone there.'

'Guv, before you go, I've got a lead on one of the girls he'd been talking to on SnapMate. Her name's Rebecca Church, and she lives in a village near Market Harborough. She's fifteen,' Ellie said.

'Text me her details. After we've been to the hotel, we'll go to her house to interview her. We'll need to get permission from her parents first. Contact them and let them know we'll be there later. Hopefully they'll be around, as it's Saturday. Good work, Ellie.'

Ellie blushed a little and smiled. Whitney was lucky to have her on the team. Her research skills were phenomenal. If anyone was going to find something, and find it quickly, Ellie would be the one.

They drove the sixty miles to Leicester in just under an hour. Coming off the motorway, they headed into a village called Orton, where the hotel was situated. It was a typical country hotel. Stone building, with ivy growing up the walls, set in beautiful grounds. It was very peaceful.

They walked into the hotel and approached the reception desk.

'DCI Walker and DS Price to see the manager,' Whitney said to the receptionist, an older woman wearing a navy jacket with the name of the hotel embroidered on it.

'I'll get her for you.'

The reception area had wood panelling on the walls, low beams, and an open fireplace which had seats and coffee tables facing it. She could imagine staying there on holiday. It seemed very relaxing.

'DCI Walker?'

Whitney turned at the sound of her name, and a young woman approached.

'You must be the manager,' Whitney said.

'Yes, I'm Eloise Graham. I understand you're here about one of our guests.'

'Do you have somewhere more private we can go?'

'We can talk in my office. Follow me.'

They walked around the back of reception into a small office which had a desk facing the window and three easy chairs placed around a small dark-wood coffee table. They all sat down.

'We're interested in Mr Russell Atkins, who was booked in to stay with you for Thursday and Friday night.'

'Yes, I know Mr Atkins.'

'What can you tell us about him?'

'He's stayed with us several times in the past, though not for a few months. This time he was booked in to stay for two nights, but we don't think he actually slept here on either of them.'

'What makes you say that?' Whitney asked.

'His bed hadn't been touched. When he didn't check out at ten and didn't answer the internal phone, we opened his room and went in. We found his phone and a small travel bag in his room. But no key. He must still have it.'

'Did you try to contact him?'

'We couldn't, because the only number we had was his mobile. I was hoping he'd get in touch.'

'Unfortunately, he won't be. We found Mr Atkins' body yesterday morning in Lenchester.'

The manager's jaw dropped. 'He's dead?'

Whitney nodded. 'We'd like to look at the room and will take his phone and belongings. Was anyone with him when he checked in?'

'He always checked in alone, and this time was no exception. On occasion, he did bring someone back later in the evening, but they'd gone before reception opened in the morning.'

'And that's acceptable to the hotel, is it?' Whitney asked.

'The room rate is for two people, so if he wants to bring someone back, it's nothing to do with us,' the manager said.

'We'd like to speak to any of your staff who might have seen him with an evening guest.'

'You need our night porter. Once reception closes at nine, he's the only one on duty. He'll be here from seven this evening. Mr Atkins' phone and suitcase are in our lost property area. We packed his toiletries bag and clothes and put them in the case. He didn't have much. I'll take you to his room now. You can collect his belongings from me once you've finished.'

'Thank you.'

They followed her up the wide wooden stairs until they

reached the first floor. They turned left and walked along the corridor, stopping at room six.

'The room's already been cleaned because we're expecting another guest this evening.'

'Did you change the bed linen, even though it appeared he hadn't slept on it?'

'We change everything, just in case. Some people can make up a bed so it looks unused.'

'Do you still have the linen?' Whitney asked.

'Yes, but we can't identify which it is. Once it's removed, the cleaners put it in bags for the laundry service to collect.' Eloise glanced at her watch. 'In fact, I believe it's already gone. They come every other day, and today's the day. I'll leave you to it, as I've got a ton of paperwork to do.'

Eloise turned and headed towards the stairs as Whitney and Matt walked into the room. It was fairly basic, with a double bed in the middle, two easy chairs beside the window, a wardrobe, and a door leading into the bathroom. Next to the kettle and two mugs were sachets of coffee and tea. Whitney looked into the bathroom cabinet and the cupboard under the sink. It was all empty. But very clean. She headed back into the bedroom and over to the window. The view was spectacular, overlooking the countryside. In the distance was a stately home.

'Let's go. There's nothing here for us.'

'Hang on a minute.' Matt dropped down onto his knees and peered under the bed. 'There's something here.' He reached and pulled out a pink hair tie.

He placed it into the evidence bag Whitney was holding.

'We'll test it, but it could have been there for a while.'

After leaving the room, they went back to reception and asked for Eloise. She came out holding Russell's phone and suitcase. Whitney dropped the phone into an evidence bag and took the suitcase. Once they were back in the car, they drove towards the village where Rebecca Church lived. When they were only a couple of miles away, Whitney called Ellie.

'Did you manage to speak to her parents? We're close to the house now.'

'I spoke to her mum and she's expecting you. I didn't say what it was about, just that you thought Rebecca might be able to help with some of our enquiries. She pushed me on it, but I pretended not to know anything.'

'Excellent. We'll see you later. We shouldn't be more than a couple of hours.'

The house, a 1960s semi-detached, was on the outskirts of Orlington village. They walked up the long path to the front door and knocked.

A woman dressed in a uniform belonging to one of the local supermarkets answered.

'Mrs Church?' Whitney asked.

'Yes.'

'I'm DCI Walker and this is DS Price from Lenchester CID.' Whitney held out her warrant card. 'I understand one of my officers spoke to you earlier about talking to Rebecca. Is she home?'

'She's just got up. What's this all about?' she asked.

'We're hoping she can help with our enquiries regarding an incident that happened in Lenchester.'

'Rebecca's never been to Lenchester, so I don't see how she can help.'

'May we come in? We'll explain everything to you and Rebecca.'

'As long as it doesn't take too long. I work at Four Square in Market Harborough and my shift starts in an hour.' Mrs Church ushered them into the house and through to the small lounge, which had a burnt-orange sofa and two easy chairs all facing the television. In one of the chairs was a young girl dressed in jeans and a pink sweatshirt with a unicorn motif on it.

'Rebecca?' Whitney asked as the girl looked up.

'Yes.'

'Would you like a cup of tea?' Mrs Church asked.

'Do you have any coffee?' Whitney said.

'Yes. For two?'

'Yes, please,' Matt said.

'Do you mind if we talk to Rebecca while you're in the kitchen?' Whitney asked.

'I'm not sure. Has she done anything wrong?'

'At the moment, all we want is some information to help us with our enquiries.'

'I suppose you can start. I won't be long, anyway,' Mrs Church said.

Whitney was surprised she was happy to leave Rebecca with them. She wouldn't have, if it was Tiffany. Then again, Rebecca might not want her mum to know what she'd been up to online, so it could be a good thing.

'Is that okay with you, Rebecca?' Whitney asked.

'Yes, I suppose so,' she said, looking at Whitney from under her eyelashes.

Whitney sat on the sofa, and Matt sat next to her.

'I'd like to ask you about SnapMate.'

'I don't know anything about it,' the young girl replied.

'We know you've been on there,' Whitney said gently, conscious of how carefully she had to tread.

Rebecca's jaw clenched, and she flushed a deep shade of red. 'How do you know?' Her voice was barely above a whisper.

'It's to do with a case we're working on. Have you been in contact with a boy called Billy?'

'Y-yes,' the girl said, averting her gaze.

'Have you known him long?'

'A few months.'

'Do you chat with him a lot?'

'Every day.'

'Have you ever met him?'

'We were meant to meet yesterday, but he didn't turn up.' Tears formed in her eyes and she blinked them away.

'And before yesterday?' Whitney asked gently. The poor girl was going to get such a shock when she found out. Judging by the tears, she was extremely fond of him.

'No. He doesn't come from here, and he took a day off from college to meet me.'

'Have you seen photos of him?'

'Yes, I've got one on my phone.'

'May I see?'

Rebecca took out her phone and pulled up a photo, handing it to Whitney to take a look.

A good-looking boy of about eighteen. Exactly what Whitney had expected.

'How well do you know each other?' she asked.

'Really well. He's like my best friend.'

'Already?'

'He understands me. We can talk about anything. He's helped me deal with what's going on in my life. Things haven't been easy at home.' She glanced anxiously at the door.

'Can you tell me more?' Whitney cajoled.

'Mum's got problems at work, and they're making her do extra hours. She can't refuse or she might lose her job. We need the money because my dad stopped sending any child support.'

'What else did you talk about?'

'School, because it's been hard there, too. My friends have been really mean and leaving me out of everything.'

She needed to broach the subject of whether they shared intimate photos of themselves, but she didn't want the girl to clam up.

'I'm sorry to ask, but it is important for me to know. Did Billy ask for any photos of you where you were showing parts of your body?'

The young girl bit down on her bottom lip and nodded. 'Yes. He said it was just for a laugh. Please don't tell my mum. Why do you want to know?'

'We believe Billy isn't who you think he is.'

'Of course he is,' Rebecca said adamantly. The door opened, and Mrs Church walked in holding two mugs of coffee.

'What have I missed?' she said.

'I was discussing with Rebecca someone she might have known online.'

'These kids are online all the time. I can't get her away from her phone. Mind you, I'm as bad.' Mrs Church laughed.

'We have reason to believe one of the boys Rebecca knows was actually a forty-one-year-old man posing as a teenager in order to attract young girls.'

The colour drained from Rebecca's face, and she slammed her hand over her mouth.

'What? The filthy bastard,' Mrs Church growled.

'These men groom the young girls they speak to and eventually arrange to meet them with a view to having sex with them.' There was no way to sugar coat it. The woman had to know.

'Rebecca? D-did you meet this man?' Mrs Church's voice wobbled.

'No, Mum, I didn't.'

'But you know him?' Mrs Church said.

Tears returned to Rebecca's eyes, and she brushed them away with her back of her hand. 'Yes,' she said, sniffing.

'These men prey on young girls like you. There was no way you could've known,' Whitney said to reassure her.

'But I still don't understand why you're here,' Mrs Church said.

'The man who called himself Billy online has been murdered. We found his body yesterday in Lenchester. On his laptop we found evidence of him using SnapMate and talking to young girls. It's an app teens use to meet people. We traced Rebecca as being one of the girls he'd spoken to.'

Mrs Church glared at Rebecca. 'What the hell were you doing on this app? You know I don't want you hanging out with boys. You've got your exams and schoolwork to think about.'

'It was just a bit of fun, Mum. I didn't actually meet up with anyone.'

'And this dead man? Did he ask to meet you?'

Rebecca looked away. 'I arranged to meet him yesterday after school in a café, but he didn't turn up. I waited for half an hour and then came home.' She started crying, and Mrs Church went over and sat on the arm of the chair, pulling her daughter close.

'Well, thank goodness he didn't. Is there anything else my daughter can help you with?'

'We'd like to see the photos you sent each other. Email them to me. Here are my details.' Whitney pulled a card from her pocket and handed it to Rebecca.

'Photos?' Mrs Church said.

'They weren't of him. He must have got them online. They were just a hot guy,' Rebecca said.

'Let me see,' her mum said.

'I'll show you later.'

'Rebecca, if you can think of anything that might help us get to know this man better, please let us know. Can you tell me what you were doing on Thursday between six and ten in the evening?'

'Why? Is she a suspect?' Mrs Church said.

'This is routine. We're asking everyone who knew the victim their whereabouts at the time of the murder so we can eliminate them from our enquiries.'

'Because there's no way my Rebecca could murder anyone,' Mrs Church said.

'I was at home doing my homework.'

'Can anyone vouch for you?' Whitney asked.

Rebecca shook her head and looked at her mother.

'I was at work, so she was on her own,' Mrs Church said.

'Do you use a laptop for your homework?' Whitney asked, remembering something George had once mentioned.

'Yes.'

'Can you let me see your work? It will have a time and date for when you saved it.'

Rebecca went over to the dining table and opened up the laptop. After a few moments, she showed her home-work to Whitney, so the date could be checked. Luckily, she hadn't done anything since and saved over it, because it clearly showed Rebecca had worked on it during the time in question.

'Thank you very much, Rebecca. We'll be going now. We may need to get in touch with you again. Actually, before I go, please could you send me the photos. Then we know it's done.'

'Okay,' she said, looking at Whitney's card and keying the number into her phone.

Once the photos came through, Whitney and Matt left the house and went back to the car.

'Poor kid,' Whitney said. 'And that bastard Atkins. Who'd have thought he'd have turned out to be such a monster? He was so nice at school. It was as George explained. He got her to trust him and persuaded her to exchange photos. I'm assuming the reason he didn't turn up to meet her was because he was already dead. So, all we have is: sometime after he arrived at the hotel on Thursday, he went out to meet someone and didn't come back. Could it be someone he knew? Were they tailing him? Or had he arranged to meet another girl from SnapMate and it went wrong? We need to get back to the office. Just because the victim was an arsewipe doesn't mean we shouldn't do our job and find his killer.'

## Chapter Nine

They returned to the incident room, and Whitney immediately took the victim's mobile to Ellie.

'His phone's turned up. See what you can find.'

'Will do,' the young detective said.

Ellie had been trained to use the self-service kiosk to extract mobile phone data. It was a huge advantage in this type of investigation, as they could look at the phone straight away rather than having to wait for the digital forensic unit to get to it. Mac had pulled out all the stops to get Atkins' laptop looked at immediately, and their case took priority over his other work. It didn't always happen.

'Frank, I want you to check Rebecca Church's mum's alibi. She works at Four Square in Market Harborough.'

'Yes, guv.'

Whitney's next stop was the desk in front of the board, and she placed the victim's small suitcase on it. Inside she found two pairs of underpants, two pairs of socks, a clean shirt, and a toiletries bag containing a toothbrush, toothpaste, floss, condoms, and an electric razor. In other words, nothing out of the ordinary, apart from the condoms,

seeing as the man was married and unable to have children. After re-packing the case, she put it in an evidence
bag for one of the team to take down to the evidence store.

George had asked to be kept up to date on what was
going on, so she took out her phone and gave her a call.

'Hi,' she said once the phone had been answered.
'We've just got back from speaking to Rebecca Church.'

'How did it go?'

'She'd arranged to meet Russell Atkins yesterday, but
he didn't turn up. Obviously, as he was dead. You were
right about the photos. It seems they did swap intimate
ones. I've got them on my phone but haven't opened them
yet. Hang on a minute while I take a look.' She flicked
through what Rebecca had sent. 'For fuck's sake,' she
muttered when she came to the naked images.

'What?' George asked.

'The photos. Why do these young kids do it? Don't
they realise what they're getting themselves into? They
really should be educated more about the Internet's nasty
side.'

'It's not easy. Very often parents aren't aware of it,
either. How did Rebecca take it when you told her about
Atkins?'

'Shocked, obviously. She thought she'd been chatting
with an eighteen-year-old boy, not a forty-one-year-old
man. They were good friends. He'd certainly done a good
job with the grooming. We've now found his phone, and
Ellie's going through it. It should give us something to work
with. Do you know when you'll be able to come in?'

'I'm not sure, because I've got so much to do. There
are parts of my presentation I want to change, which
means amending many of my PowerPoint slides.'

'I know you've already told me, but when's the presentation?' She felt guilty for having to ask, but there was so much going on it had totally slipped her mind.

'Monday.'

'I'm sure you'll nail it. And is the final interview on Tuesday?' She'd remembered it was the day following.

'Yes. They're taking the candidates alphabetically, which makes me second. My appointment time's eleven.'

'When do you find out whether you've got the job?'

'They'll get everyone who viewed the presentations together and discuss their thoughts. The Selection Panel will also need to meet and discuss each candidate. I expect I'll know by the middle of next week.'

'Bloody hell. Talk about recruitment by committee.'

'That's education for you.' George laughed.

'Do we still call you Doctor Cavendish?' Whitney asked.

'I'll be known as Associate Professor Cavendish,' she said.

'We'll call you the Prof then,' Whitney joked.

'I haven't got the job yet. But yes, you can call me that if you wish.'

Whitney smiled to herself. This was a new side to George. When they'd first met, no way would she have agreed to it.

'I do wish.'

'Have you found out whether he'd been grooming any other girls? I'd be very surprised if it was only Rebecca,' George said.

'The app is downloaded onto his laptop, and we know he's been chatting with others. I'm waiting to see what Ellie turns up on his phone. He's probably got the app on there, too. We'll be able to see if he had private texts or calls with these girls away from SnapMate.' She glanced up and saw

Ellie heading in her direction. 'I better go. If I don't speak to you before, good luck. Let me know how it goes.'

'Thanks,' George said.

Whitney ended the call and put the phone back into her pocket. She walked towards Ellie.

'What have you got?' she asked.

'Plenty. Some time ago he'd been texting a girl called Amy Bond. He met her on SnapMate, and there's a string of private messages on there, too. I'm finding her details now. There's also another girl called Cleo he'd been chatting to on the site, but I'm coming up against a brick wall with her. She appears untraceable. I'll get the digital forensic unit to see if they can help.'

'Let me have Amy Bond's details as soon as you have them.'

'Are you going to interview her?'

'Yes. But at the moment, I want to run through where we are. Listen up, everyone,' she called out as she headed back to the board. 'I want to go through everything we have so far. The victim, Russell Atkins, is a forty-one-year-old consultant. He lives in an upmarket area, thanks to his wife's money. The place is like a show home. Everything's immaculate, with nothing out of place. His wife, Diana, appeared shocked when we told her about his grooming activities.'

'Is she a suspect?' Frank asked.

'Forensics were at the house yesterday. I asked them to check everything, in particular to look for a syringe or any other potential weapon. They didn't find anything. But just because the house was clean and she seemed shocked by what he'd done, doesn't automatically eliminate her.'

'She'd have to be one sick wife to do that to him,' Frank said.

'She wouldn't be the first. Remember Mrs Bobbitt and what she did to her philandering husband,' Doug said.

'True,' Frank said.

'Good point. I'll run it past George,' Whitney said. 'We have at least two, possibly three, girls we know he's been grooming on SnapMate. Matt and I visited one of the girls, Rebecca Church. Fortunately, when she went to meet Atkins, who she thought was a young boy called Billy, he wasn't there. They'd traded intimate photos, which I'm sure he would have used to persuade her to go back to his hotel room. We have a second girl who we'll interview tomorrow. At the moment, we can't trace the third girl. How's the rest of the research coming on? Background check on Atkins? His work and social life?'

'I'm going back to his workplace on Monday. I'll interview the staff again, paying particular attention to any relationships,' Matt said.

'There was a monthly payment on his credit card for a gym membership at Flexible Fitness,' Ellie said. 'When I contacted them, they said he was a regular attendee. Usually visited three times a week, but not on any specific days because of his work. Apart from Saturday, early afternoon, when he was usually there. He'd spend an hour going around various pieces of equipment. They liked him, said he was sociable, and there hadn't been any instances of him pestering their female clients.'

'That sounds more like the Russell Atkins I remember from school. He puts on a good front. It'll be interesting to have more detailed information of what he's like at work from his colleagues. What else have we got?'

'The house-to-house hasn't turned up anything, so far. There aren't many residences close to the waste ground,' Doug said.

'What about the CCTV?' Whitney asked.

'Nothing out of the ordinary, so far,' Frank said.

'What do you call out of the ordinary?' Whitney asked.

'Well, there were no cars headed in that direction from the city centre which came back within half an hour.'

'What about in the other direction? Where do the CCTV cameras start if they were coming in from the A14?'

'That's my next job.'

'Good. I'm going to see Jamieson to give him an update on where we are at the moment. Carry on with what you're doing. I want you all here tomorrow morning at seven-thirty.'

Whitney headed to Jamieson's office. It was unusual for him to be in on a Saturday. The door was ajar, and he was sitting at his desk. She gave a gentle knock before walking in.

'I wanted to let you know where we are with the Atkins murder. We're investigating possible leads at the moment and believe it's connected with him grooming young girls on SnapMate, a site for teens. We've found evidence on his phone and laptop. I've interviewed one of the girls.'

'Is she a suspect?' Jamieson asked.

'No, she has an alibi.'

'What about her parents?'

'She lives with her mother, who was at work at the time of death. Her alibi's being checked. We've also managed to track down another teenager who he'd been chatting with, and we'll be speaking to her tomorrow. There's a third girl we're trying to find, too.'

'The wife?' Jamieson asked.

'Forensics were at the house yesterday and didn't turn up anything. What you do need to know is after their removal, the penis and testicles were cooked, and the victim ate them.'

'You've got to be kidding me. That's disgusting.' His face turned grey.

'It certainly wasn't a pretty sight to look at,' Whitney said.

'Thanks for letting me know. Keep me up to date on everything. We've arranged a press conference this afternoon at four-thirty. I want you with me.'

Now she knew why he'd come in. He wouldn't miss the chance of being in the public eye.

Whitney brushed her hair and smeared on some lip gloss before making her way to Jamieson's office so they could go together to the press conference.

'Sir,' she said as she walked into his office.

He'd changed into his best uniform, which seemed to be fitting a little better these days. Had he been on a diet? She wasn't going to ask him. They didn't have that type of relationship. It was very much a *put up with one another* type.

He didn't like how she'd say it as she saw it and wouldn't kowtow to him. And she didn't like… well, she didn't need to go over all that again.

'Anything else turned up since earlier?' he asked.

'Nothing. All we can report is his name, the fact we're treating the death as suspicious, and he was left naked. I believe we should withhold information about the exact nature of the mutilation. We certainly don't want to incite any copycat killers. We can say he died from suffocation, which is true.'

Jamieson nodded in agreement. 'Okay, let's go.'

They walked to the conference room and met Melissa, the PR officer, outside. She ushered them in and they sat behind a table. Reporters were at the front of the room and cameras at the back.

'Thank you for coming today,' Melissa said. 'I'd like to hand you over to Detective Superintendent Jamieson.'

He leaned forward slightly. 'We're here to report the death of Mr Russell Atkins, which we are treating as suspicious. He was found on the waste ground near the old racecourse yesterday. We would ask any member of the public to come forward if they saw anything unusual in and around the area over the last two days. We're particularly interested to know if there were any cars parked there for a short period of time. Any questions?'

'What was the cause of death?' a reporter asked.

'We're awaiting confirmation from the pathologist; however, it's believed Mr Atkins was suffocated.'

'Was there anything out of the ordinary at the crime scene?' a female reporter in the front row asked.

Why had she asked that? Had someone leaked information?

'Mr Atkins was found naked, and his body had been mutilated.'

Whitney glared at Jamieson. What happened to their agreement not to mention it?

'Mutilated in what way?' the reporter continued.

'I'm not able to disclose details at the moment. I repeat, if any member of the public has any information, please contact our office. All calls are dealt with in strict confidence. Thank you very much for attending.'

Jamieson got up and Whitney followed him into the corridor. As they were walking, she turned to him.

'I thought we were withholding the mutilation.'

'I changed my mind. We've still kept confidential the exact nature of it, plus the folded clothes and the socks, so that should suffice. Knowing the body was mutilated will make people more interested in the case and convince them to contact us with any information.'

'And possibly incite a copycat.' Whitney was unable to hide her frustration.

'But we'll know because of what we've omitted.'

'That's not the point. We're putting ideas in people's heads.'

'I made my decision,' he said.

'Your call,' she muttered, annoyed he'd made it without paying any attention to what was going on with the rest of the investigation.

He turned to her. 'Yes, it is my call.'

They got to the stairs, and she left him, seething all the way to the incident room. Once more, he'd managed to wind her up. But she'd have to put it on the back burner and get on with the case. Jamieson wasn't going anywhere until he managed to wrangle a promotion.

## Chapter Ten

'Guv, I've got something,' Frank said when Whitney walked into the incident room the following morning.

What the hell was Frank doing in before her? It had to be a first. Especially on a Sunday.

She hurried over to his desk. 'What?'

'I spotted a car on the Leicester Road at six in the evening on Thursday, and the same car returning four hours later. I managed to see the number plate, and the car belongs to Tina Church, Rebecca's mum.'

Whitney's heart pumped in her chest. This could be the lead they were looking for. Tina Church had said she'd been at work on Thursday night.

'I thought you checked her alibi yesterday,' she said, locking eyes with him.

Frank averted his gaze. 'Sorry, guv. It slipped my mind. I was so busy on the CCTV.'

'Well, do it now. Pronto. I'll get Ellie to arrange for her to come down to the station.'

She resisted the urge to haul him over the coals, as his attitude to work had improved over the last few months.

Ever since Tiffany's abduction. The episode had shaken him. He'd known her daughter since she was a young girl.

She headed to Ellie's desk. 'Could you phone Tina Church and ask her to come into the station today at eleven?'

'Will do.'

'Also, the other girl who Atkins was grooming. Amy Bond. Where does she live?' Whitney continued.

'Lenchester,' Ellie said.

'Lenchester? Why on earth would he be shitting on his own doorstep?'

'Perhaps he didn't realise that's where she came from,' Ellie said.

'Get in touch with her parents and see if they can bring her in tomorrow after school for an interview. Don't say it's related to the death of Russell Atkins. Say we're speaking to a lot of young women who might have known someone via an online site. If they ask anything else, plead ignorance and say you're phoning on my behalf.'

'I'll do it now,' Ellie said.

She went back to her office and pulled the door shut. She keyed George's number into her phone. It went straight to voicemail.

'Hey, it's Whitney. Sorry to bother you, and good luck for your presentation tomorrow. One of the other girls Atkins was grooming, Amy Bond, is coming in tomorrow afternoon around four-ish. It would be good if you could be here to observe the interview. But no pressure.' Whitney laughed. 'More importantly, Tina Church's car was seen on CCTV heading in on the Leicester Road and returning four hours later. Tina is Rebecca's mum. We're arranging for her to come in this afternoon at two. Anyway, good luck. I know you're going to kill it.'

Whitney headed back into the incident room. She stopped at Frank's desk.

'Did you contact Four Square about Tina Church?'

'Yes, guv. They said she wasn't working on Thursday. It was her day off.'

'Nice one. Start doing a background check on her.'

She walked over to Ellie. 'Did you speak to Tina Church?'

'Yes. She wanted to know why we had to speak to her and not Rebecca.'

'What did you tell her?'

'I said there were things about the case we felt she needed to know, but they weren't appropriate for Rebecca. She accepted my answer and will be here at eleven.'

'Good response. Well done.' The young officer shrugged, but Whitney could tell she appreciated the praise.

Before going back to her office, she went to the station cafeteria and grabbed a coffee and roll, as she'd missed breakfast. She took advantage of her spare hour to complete some paperwork and was glad when, at five minutes past eleven, she received a call to say Tina Church had arrived. She went downstairs to the station's reception area.

'Mrs Church. Thank you for coming in,' she said as she approached the woman.

'Call me Tina.'

They walked to one of the interview rooms and went inside.

'Can I get you a drink? Tea, coffee, or something cold?'

'Coffee would be good. Milk, no sugar.'

'Leave it with me. I'll be back in a moment.'

Whitney headed to the incident room, hoping to find Matt there. He was. She walked over to his desk.

'I'm with Tina Church. Could you bring us two coffees, both milk, no sugar, and also stay for the interview? Bring the file with you.'

'Yes, guv,' Matt replied.

Before returning to the interview room, Whitney popped into the adjacent office so she could look through the one-way mirror at Tina Church. She was staring into a compact mirror, adjusting her hair and putting on some lipstick. She was an attractive woman, with dark hair cut into a short bob. A bit too heavily made-up for Whitney's liking. She was medium height and build. Would she be able to lift his body and place it at the dump site? She could've dragged him. The ground was so wet and muddy any tracks would have disappeared.

She went back into the interview room. 'Coffee will be here shortly,' she said, smiling.

'What do you want to talk to me about? I had to lie to Rebecca and say I was meeting a friend, so she didn't realise I was coming here,' Tina said.

The door opened and Matt came in holding a tray with three mugs of coffee, which he placed on the table. Whitney handed them out.

'Are you familiar with the Imperial Hotel, near Leicester?'

'I'm not sure. Why?' The woman glanced at each of them, frowning.

'Russell Atkins, the man who'd been chatting with Rebecca online, was booked in there for two nights. Only after he checked in, he disappeared and was found dead on Friday morning. He died sometime between six and ten on Thursday evening, as I mentioned to you when we were at your house. When asked what you were doing at this time, you stated you were at work.'

The woman avoided eye contact with Whitney. 'Yes,' she muttered.

'We've checked with the supermarket, and Thursday was your evening off. Where were you, and why did you lie to us?' Whitney asked.

'I didn't think it mattered.'

'Why on earth would you think that?' Whitney stared at the woman.

'I didn't want Rebecca to know where I'd been.'

'Then you should have contacted me later and explained, instead of us finding out on our own. It doesn't look good.'

'I don't see why. It's not like I even knew the man.'

'We don't know that.' She gave a frustrated sigh. 'I repeat. Where were you on Thursday evening, when you were supposed to be at work?'

'I'd rather not say.' Tina stuck out her chin, going from embarrassed to belligerent in a matter of seconds.

'It's not an option,' she said.

The woman was hiding something, and Whitney was quite prepared to sit it out until she found out what.

'It had nothing to do with the murder, so I'm not prepared to say.' Tina folded her arms tightly across her chest.

'Your car was seen on the Leicester Road heading towards Lenchester at six on Thursday. Why?'

Tina Church paled. 'I went to meet a friend.' Her voice was barely above a whisper, and she slumped in the seat.

'Where did you meet this *friend*?' Whitney leaned in and locked eyes with her. She hadn't expected the woman to cave so easily.

'Look. I had nothing to do with the murder. Nothing. When you told me about Rebecca, I was totally stunned.

But I can't tell you who I was with. If it got out, there'd be hell to pay, and I'd lose my job.'

'Mrs Church, I don't care what you get up to in your spare time, but you won't be leaving the station until you tell me who you were with, and where you went on Thursday evening. It's not up for negotiation.'

Whitney leaned back in her chair and stared at the woman who remained silent, looking down in her lap. She sensed Matt was about to say something and nudged his foot with hers to stop him. She'd been in enough situations like this to know when there's an ultimatum, whoever speaks first, loses. Their silence was putting pressure on Tina Church to talk.

'If I tell you and I get sacked, then it's on you,' Tina finally said.

'I can live with that.'

'Thursday evening I was out with Jerry Porter, the manager of the supermarket. We've been seeing each other. No one knows, because he's married. We met at The Crown in Mulberry village and had a meal. We left there at eight.'

'And what did you do until ten, which is the time your car was seen driving back towards your home?'

'What do you think?' The woman blushed.

'Where did you go?'

'We were in his car. We parked in a country lane where there was no traffic.'

'What, he couldn't afford a room?' The words were out of her mouth before she could stop them.

'It was a spur of the moment thing,' Tina said.

'We'll need to contact him and the pub to confirm your story,' she said.

'Why?'

'We'll be discreet. Providing it all fits with what you've

told us, it won't go any further,' Whitney said gently, suddenly feeling sorry for the woman. It can't have been easy admitting what she'd been up to.

'Thank you. May I go now?'

'Once we've checked your alibi. Please write down the details.' She handed the woman a sheet of paper.

Whitney and Matt left the interview and headed back to the incident room. Doug was sitting at his desk. 'Tina Church is here. I want you to check her alibi for Thursday evening. Here are the details.'

'Yes, guv.'

'I'll be in my office. Let me know when you've contacted them.'

After ten minutes, Doug poked his head around her door. 'Everything checks out.'

'Another lead falls by the wayside,' she said, shaking her head.

She left her office and went to see Tina Church.

'About time,' the woman said as she walked into the interview room.

'Thank you for waiting. We've verified your alibi and you're now free to go.'

Whitney waited while Tina Church picked up her handbag from where she'd placed it on the floor next to her, and then showed her out of the station.

They were still no closer to solving the case than before. Damn.

## Chapter Eleven

George walked into the incident room and was hit by a cacophony of sound. Groups in conversation. Shouting from one side of the office to the other. So different from the university where there was rarely more than two people per office, and it was quiet while they were working. George enjoyed the excitement of coming here. She liked the camaraderie, and the atmosphere was thrilling. But she couldn't do it all the time; the noise would drive her crazy. She liked to be on her own, as she needed her space. Here, they were very much on top of each other. It suited Whitney, especially as she was very often the one making the most noise.

Whitney was talking with Matt over by the board, which currently displayed a picture of the victim, and three girls which George assumed were Rebecca Church, Amy Bond, and one other. She headed over to them.

'Hey,' Whitney exclaimed when George was close to her. 'How was the presentation?'

'As good as can be expected.'

'You mean you rocked it?' Whitney smiled like she meant it, and her eyes twinkled.

'It went well.'

'I'm glad you could make it. I thought you might have to prepare for the interview tomorrow.'

'I needed a change of scenery. Tell me what's happened since you left the message.'

'We talked to Tina Church about being in the area, and she admitted to an illicit meeting with the manager of the supermarket she works at.'

'And was that confirmed?'

'Yes. Which means we have no suspect.'

'Have you checked into Diana Atkins?'

'Yes, and her alibi's sound. She was home alone some of the time, but she'd be pushing it to get to Leicester and back in such a short space of time. Plus, there's no record of her car on the CCTV.'

'Fair enough.'

'I must admit, it did cross my mind she could be responsible. Even though she was shocked and clearly disturbed, there was still an element of calm about her. Then again, she is like you in many respects.'

What the hell did she mean by that? George couldn't see any similarity between her and Diana Atkins.

'Care to elaborate?' George said in a cool voice.

'You know what I mean. She's posh, and into horses.'

'So, she's the same as me because she's posh and likes horses. Seriously, Whitney, I thought you knew better. I'd hardly say those attributes meant we were alike. Does she smoke, like I do? Does she like fast cars? I don't suppose you asked her that.'

'Sorry. It's just she has that British stiff upper lip thing going on. Like you. And I didn't know if it was the reason for her reaction to everything. Because she was taught to keep her emotions in check.'

'You could be right,' George relented. She actually did know what Whitney meant, but she didn't want to be put into the same box. 'And what about the girl coming in to be interviewed?'

'She's fourteen and should be here soon. I'd like you to watch from outside and give me advice on the questioning. I'll wear an earpiece. I don't think it's a good idea for us all to be in there. For a start, it's intimidating, and she's only here helping us with our enquiries. Plus, I want to know what's going on in terms of her facial expressions and her word choice, et cetera.'

'Not to mention it would be pointless me being in there, as you're the one doing all the talking.'

'I don't know what you mean.' Whitney grinned.

George looked at the photos of the three girls. 'What about her?' she asked, pointing to the photo of a young girl with shoulder-length dark curly hair. 'Cleo.' She read the name printed below the photograph.

'We can't trace her. There were some conversations on the app, but no mention of any meetings. We checked the other messaging app on his phone, but no trace of a conversation there. He could've deleted it though.'

The phone on the desk rang, and Whitney picked it up. 'Walker.' She paused. 'Show them into the interview room, and we'll be there shortly.' She replaced the phone. 'Matt, you and I will interview Amy Bond, and George will be outside.'

After stopping at Whitney's office to pick up an earpiece and mic, they made their way there.

George stood behind the one-way mirror. Amy was petite and had straight blonde hair which hung just below her shoulders. She looked younger than fourteen. Her face was make-up free. Her mother, in contrast, was highly made-up, and wore a flowery dress with a navy cardigan over the top. Amy was fidgeting in her chair, looking uncomfortable, and when Whitney and Matt walked in, she blushed a deep shade of red. Whitney sat opposite the girl, and Matt sat opposite her mother.

'Thank you for coming in to see us,' Whitney said.

'What's this all about?' Mrs Bond asked.

'We need to ask Amy some questions about an online app she uses.'

'Okay,' Mrs Bond said.

'Amy, we understand you've been on SnapMate. Is that correct?'

The young girl looked at her mother and bit her bottom lip. 'Yes,' she said quietly.

'Amy?' her mother said, frowning. 'What's SnapMate?'

'It's somewhere to meet other kids. Everyone goes on there, Mum. It's not only me. It's a bit of fun.'

George shook her head. These youngsters all thought it was a *bit of fun*. They seemed totally oblivious to the danger they were putting themselves in. Something had to be done to change it.

'And on the site did you meet a boy named Billy?' Whitney asked.

'Yes.'

'Did you talk to him often?' Whitney leaned in slightly.

'Yes, we're good friends,' Amy said.

'Did he ask to meet you?'

She nodded. 'We wanted to meet, but he's away at college. We're going to see each other in the holidays.'

'College?' Mrs Bond said. 'You're fourteen years old. You can't see someone who's at college.'

'He's eighteen, Mum. Not much older than me,' Amy said.

'Well, I think it's too old for you. And when—'

'Mrs Bond, may we continue?' Whitney interrupted.

Amy's mother turned to face her daughter. 'We'll discuss this when we get home. Yes, you may continue.'

'Tread carefully, Whitney. Especially when talking about any photographs,' George said.

'I'd like to be a bit more specific about how friendly you were with Billy. How often did you message each other?' Whitney asked.

'Every day. Although I haven't heard from him since Thursday.' She lowered her head. 'Is he okay?' she asked, looking out from under her eyelashes.

'How long have you known him?' Whitney asked.

'Eight weeks.'

'You must have got to know each other quite well in that time?'

'Yes.'

'What sort of things did you talk about?'

'He tells me things to do with college, and I tell him things about school.'

'Did you tell him any secrets? Anything you haven't told other people?' Whitney probed.

Amy rocked in her seat. 'I told him when one of the girls in my class was bullying me.'

'You didn't mention this to me,' Mrs Bond said.

'Because you'd go into school, like you did last time, and make things worse. Billy understood.'

'Typical grooming behaviour,' George muttered.

'Did you exchange photos?' Whitney asked.

'Her body language suggests she's uncomfortable with your question. Possibly because of the nature of the photos. Don't be surprised if she doesn't admit to it with her mother present,' George said.

'Y-yes.'

'Are they on your phone?' Whitney asked.

Amy nodded.

'May I see?'

Amy looked at her mum and went bright red again. 'I… I…'

'Show the photos to DCI Walker,' Mrs Bond said.

Amy pulled out her phone from her pocket and showed a photo to Whitney.

George could see it was one of a young man leaning against a tree.

'Is this the only one?' Whitney asked. 'Did he ask you to send any intimate photos of yourself?'

'No.' Amy shook her head.

'She's not telling the truth. But don't push it,' George said.

'Amy, what were you doing between six and ten last Thursday evening?' Whitney asked.

'I was at school until six for choir rehearsal, and then I caught the bus home with my friend Holly, who lives two doors down from us. I don't go out anywhere during the week because Mum doesn't let me.'

'What's this all about?' Mrs Bond asked.

'The person Amy's been in contact with is actually a forty-one-year-old man who preys on young girls on these sorts of sites.'

'And have you arrested this disgusting pervert?' Mrs Bond asked.

'Unfortunately not. He's dead.'

## Chapter Twelve

_When you first heard about Russell Atkins' death, you no doubt wondered what sick person could have done it. Nobody in their right frame of mind would remove a man's genitals and force him to eat them._

_And then you heard about him and his disgusting predilections for young girls and how he groomed them to satisfy his perverted needs._

_You became conflicted. Of course you did. That disgusting, piece of shit of a man, stole the rest of those young girls' lives._

_And I should know._

_Not because he'd done it to me. But it's been done to me in the past._

_It's with me every single day._

_Why didn't I realise what he was doing?_

_Why did I let him get away with it?_

_Because I was only ten when it started, and he threatened to ruin my parents' lives forever if I didn't comply. For three years. Three long years, I dreaded every time my parents gave a party and people came to the house. I tried to go out if I knew he'd be there._

_But he'd find me. Wherever I was, he'd find me._

_He was so good at what he did. Convincing me to acquiesce to his_ disgusting needs. I knew no one would believe me, even if I did tell. Which, of course, I didn't, because my parents would've hated me for what I'd done. Or so I believed. And the worst thing was, he acted like what we were doing was normal. I believed him. Why wouldn't I? I had no other experience.

I hated it. It hurt and made me cry. I even tried to find out, in a roundabout way, if my other friends had to do what I did. But it was hard to actually ask them without letting on what had happened to me. And I'd been sworn to secrecy. He told me he'd know the moment I mentioned our little secret to anyone. I believed him.

Then one day he had a stroke and ended up in a wheelchair. My parents were devastated.

I laughed and laughed and laughed. I was free.

Except I wasn't free, because the memories overwhelmed me. Never loosening their grip.

So, back to Mr Russell Atkins. Why did I mutilate him?

Because he thought with his dick, so what better punishment? And yes, he was alive when I did it.

You should've seen his face when the knife came out. I would've taken a photo, but I didn't need to. His expression is etched on my mind.

What else do you want to know? The socks? The folded clothes beside his body? Why I left the body where I did?

Let's take them one at a time.

The socks are directly related to me. I hate feet. Can't bear to look at them. Why? Of course there's a reason. It's not just because they're ugly. Remember what I told you earlier, about the man who destroyed my life? He had a fetish for feet. He'd make me suck his big toe. He got off on it.

I can't talk about it anymore.

What about the folded clothes? Nothing of interest there. It was a case of, what else could I do with them? I didn't want them. They were evidence, and I didn't want to risk anything being traced back to *me. So I did what normal people would. Folded the clothes and placed them beside him.*

*Next. Location. Really, it's not of any consequence, although I suspect someone will think it is and look for a clue about me. They can look, but they won't find anything useful.*

*Now we've gone through all that, I'm guessing your question is, why Russell Atkins? I made it my business to find out about him. The same as I made it my business to find out about other men grooming young girls for sex.*

*My aim in life is to eradicate scum like that from the face of the earth.*

*Russell Atkins might be my first, but I can assure you he won't be my last.*

*Between you and me, I'm expecting the second body to be found shortly. I hadn't planned on it happening so soon, but when the opportunity presented itself, I took it, because I might not have had another chance.*

*Don't pretend to be shocked and disgusted by my behaviour.*

*I know you respect and admire me for taking a stand against these monsters.*

*If everyone did the same, we'd have a much better world in which to live.*

## Chapter Thirteen

Whitney glanced up as George came into the incident room.

'What are you doing here? I thought you had your interview?'

'I've already had it. It finished a few minutes after twelve, so I thought I'd come to see what was happening. I've got nothing on until a meeting at three this afternoon.'

'And?'

'What?'

'How did it go?'

'As well as can be expected.'

'What does that mean?' Whitney shook her head. 'Never mind. Extracting information from you can be like getting blood out of a stone, sometimes.'

'There's nothing to say. I won't know anything until a decision's been made. How's the investigation going?'

'Not well. We've alibied everyone. The house-to-house hasn't brought up anything, and there have been very few leads coming through on the phone lines. The porter at the hotel didn't have anything useful to add, and the hair tie we found had nothing incriminating on it. At the moment, we're backtracking on all the CCTV. Checking who's been released from prison recently, whether there's anyone with a history of murders like this. It's a tricky one.'

'What about his workplace? Any joy from there?'

'No. From what we've gathered, he was popular. There were no stories of him getting together with any members of staff. He was an ideal employee. Except we know he wasn't.'

'If it was young girls he wanted, I'm not surprised he left the women at work alone. He's not stupid. He put up a good front. But you'll find something,' George said.

'Guv,' Matt called from across the office. 'There's been another murder. Same MO.' He grimaced.

'Crap. That's all we need. Where?' Nausea coursed through her body in anticipation of the sight awaiting them.

'The old disused railway station at the back of Cross Street.'

'Let's go. Are you coming, George?' she asked.

She frowned. 'I can't. The meeting. Stay in touch.'

Whitney and Matt took one of the pool cars and drove to the site where the body had been found. They parked up at the same time as Claire Dexter.

She confirmed with the attending officer that all the correct procedures were in place, then they all signed the log and walked together towards the body. Matt hung back a bit.

'What's the matter, Matt? Are you nervous about what you're going to see?' Claire joked.

'Leave the poor guy alone,' Whitney said. 'After the last one, you know he has a fragile stomach.'

They continued along the old track until they came to the body. Her breath caught in the back of her throat. A slightly overweight man in his thirties, with receding mid-brown hair, was laid out on the ground. Naked, minus his genitals, and wearing socks. There was hardly any blood. It was the Russell Atkins scene all over again.

Claire pulled on her overalls and gloves, took out her camera, and started work.

Whitney walked back to Matt, who was several yards away. 'No need for you to go any further. Let's search the area to see if there's anything. Have the crime scenes team been called?'

'Yes, they're on the way.' He gave her a grateful nod.

'Look over there. Some tyre tracks on the grass.' Whitney pointed a few yards in front of them. 'How can a car get down here?' She scanned their surroundings.

'It's possible to drive beside the railway track. There's an entrance further along,' Matt said.

'Let's take a look.'

They walked along the track. It was wide enough for a car, but mostly gravel, so there weren't any tyre tracks to suggest a car had been that way. After about half a mile, they came to the gap. There was plenty of room for a car to come off the road and drive towards the place where the body had been left. There was also a patch of grass with tracks.

'Right, we need to cordon off all the way up to this entrance. Get it done straight away. Make sure forensics come here to check out these tracks. Now we need to iden-tify the body.'

They headed back to the attending officer. Matt stayed with him, and she walked over to speak to Claire.

'Same as last time?' she asked.

'It looks like it,' Claire said.

'Anything on the body to identify him?'

'I've photographed the clothes if you want to go through them.'

Whitney pulled on some disposable gloves and went around the body to the pile of clothes. In the pocket of his trousers she found a set of keys, a phone, and a wallet, which was empty apart from a ten-pound note and a driving licence in the name of Kelvin M Keane.

'Interesting the killer left identification with the body, unlike with Russell Atkins. What do you make of that?' she asked.

'Not my area of expertise. Speak to George if you want some sort of analysis,' Claire replied tersely.

Whitney smiled to herself. One day she'd learn to get it right with Claire. Though where was the fun in that? In the meantime, she'd leave the pathologist to get on with what she did best.

'Good idea. I'll speak to you soon.'

Whitney returned to Matt and the attending officer. After ensuring everything was in hand, she left with her sergeant for the station.

When they arrived back, she handed the phone and licence to Ellie. 'Go onto the DVLA site and find his address, then start going through his phone.'

While waiting for Ellie, Whitney called George. It went to voicemail, so she left a message.

'It looks like the same MO. The only difference I could see was the killer left the victim's wallet, keys, and phone in his trouser pockets. Hopefully you can call in tomorrow and we'll go through everything together.' She put her phone down.

'Guv, I've got the victim's address: 228 Whitworth Street, Lenchester.'

'Thanks. I want you to go through his texts and flag

anything suspicious. Doug,' she called to the detective sitting at the next desk to Ellie. 'Find out what you can about him. Marital status. Where he works. I'll go to his house. Matt, you can come with. We have his keys so we can go inside if there's no answer at the door.'

Whitney and Matt drove to Whitworth Street, which was in an older part of the city. They parked outside the small, terraced house where Keane lived, and walked up the path. Whitney rang the bell several times, but there was no answer. She was about to try the Yale key on his set of keys when she heard a sound behind them.

'What are you doing?' A tall but stooping, slim, grey-haired woman in her late sixties came up the path, glowering at them.

'I'm DCI Walker.' Whitney pulled out her warrant card and showed it. 'Do you live here?'

'Yes.'

'And your name is?'

'Beryl Murphy.'

If she was connected to the victim, she didn't want to have a conversation outside. 'May we come in? We'd like to talk to you about Kelvin Keane.'

'What's the little shit done now?'

'I'd rather we spoke inside,' Whitney said.

The woman pulled out a set of keys from her coat pocket and opened the door. They followed her inside. The house smelt musty.

'This way,' Murphy said.

They followed her into a small lounge. The furniture looked like it came from the seventies. A brown Draylon three-piece suite, centred on the television. There were no photos or pictures on the walls. On the shelf over the electric fire, looking out of place compared with the rest of the room, was a small, antique, gold carriage clock.

Whitney and Matt sat on the sofa and Beryl on one of the chairs.

'Is Kelvin your son?'

'Stepson. His father died fifteen years ago. Leaving me nothing, apart from this house and his son to look after.'

Whitney drew in a breath. Usually she mentally prepared herself before delivering news of this nature, but she hadn't had the time. 'I'm sorry to have to tell you, we found Kelvin's body earlier today.'

'Dead?' Her green eyes widened as she stared at Whitney.

'Yes.'

'What happened?'

'We're treating his death as suspicious. We found him by the disused rail track in Cross Street. His body had been mutilated.'

'Like the other man? Russell Atkins. It was on the telly.'

Should she mention the grooming? It would move things along much quicker if she did.

'Yes. We suspect the deaths might be linked to online grooming of young girls.'

'Not again.' The woman shook her head and slumped in the chair.

'He's done something like this before?' As far as she knew, there was no record of this, or Ellie would've highlighted it.

'Not Kelvin. His father. He was a window cleaner until he got badly beaten up by one of his customers for putting his hand up the skirt of the man's twelve-year-old daughter. He couldn't work after that.'

'Was your husband charged for what he'd done?'

'Thankfully, no. It was bad enough me knowing what he'd done, without the neighbours finding out.'

'Please could we take a look at Kelvin's room?'

'Upstairs, first room on the left.'

Whitney and Matt left the lounge and headed upstairs. They went into Kelvin's bedroom. Like the rest of the place, it was dingy. His laptop was open on a small white table under the window. She pulled on some disposable gloves and opened the top drawer of his bedside cabinet. Inside she found creased photos of young, naked girls. 'Dirty bastard,' she muttered under her breath.

She dropped them into evidence bags.

After taking everything they thought would be useful, they went back to the lounge where Beryl was sitting, staring into space.

'We've taken some items from his room for our forensic team to analyse. Our scenes of crimes unit will need to go over the house. I'll arrange for them to come by soon.'

The woman shrugged. 'Do I have to be here?'

'To let them in. After that you can leave. We'll also need you to formally identify Kelvin's body. I'll send a car to pick you up while SOCO are here, if you like?'

'Yes, I'd like to do it then.'

'I'm sorry for your loss.'

'Don't be. I'm not.'

Whitney stared at her. Did she mean it? It certainly appeared so. She might change her mind once it properly hit her.

The clock above the fire chimed. 'Lovely clock,' she said.

'A present from a previous employer.'

'That was very kind of them.'

'I suppose so.'

'One more question. You were married to Kelvin's father, yet you go by Murphy?'

'I went back to my maiden name after he died. Didn't

want people to associate me with him.' She sneered. 'Have we finished?'

'Yes. We'll see ourselves out. I'll be in touch and let you know when my officer will pick you up.'

They went back to the car. 'No love lost there,' Matt said as Whitney pulled out into the road.

'It doesn't seem like it. But it could just be her way. Finding out her stepson was the same as his father would be hard to take.'

'Unless she already knew he was like that. She didn't seem surprised. Look at those photos he kept in his drawer. They were hardly well hidden. She could've found them as easily as we did,' Matt said.

'True.'

When they got back to the station, Whitney dropped off the laptop with the digital forensic unit. Once they were in the incident room, she copied the photos and sent the originals off to forensics. She pinned the photos on the board, underneath the second victim.

'Doug, what have you found out about Keane?' Whitney asked as she went over to his desk. The detective was staring at his computer screen.

'He's single. Aged thirty-five. Works as a campus security officer at the university. He's been there for three years. No criminal record. Nothing else to tell you.'

'Go to the university and speak to the head of security. See if there's anything else you can find out about him.'

'Ellie, what's on his phone?'

'He rarely texted anyone, and when he did, it was mainly for work. But he does have the SnapMate app on there.'

'Can you get into it?'

'No problem,' Ellie said as she pressed several keys. 'He left himself logged in.'

Whitney peered over her shoulder at the opened app.

'Can you download and identify all the young girls he's had conversations with?'

'Yes. Leave it with me.'

'We're looking for any red flags. Assuming he was lured to meeting someone, we'd expect to see details of it somewhere. Have you looked at his emails yet?'

'There are very few in his inbox, and nothing remotely incriminating. He doesn't have any other chat apps on his phone, so I expect all his conversations took place on SnapMate.'

Whitney paced the room. What was she missing? Both victims used the app. Both victims were mutilated. Both victims… She stopped dead in her tracks.

'Why Lenchester?' she asked, not to anyone in particular. 'Both victims come from Lenchester? Doesn't that strike you as odd?'

'What do you mean, guv?' Ellie asked.

'This is an international site. So teens could be chatting with anyone from any area. So how come our killer managed to find two men from Lenchester?'

Ellie smiled. 'You haven't connected with anyone online, I take it.'

Whitney frowned. 'No. Why?'

'Because you can put in the preferred location of people you want to get to know. It's no good trying to find someone to meet up with if they live two hundred miles away.'

Whitney rolled her eyes. How come she hadn't known? It was obvious after Ellie had pointed it out. Would she ever go online to find someone? She doubted it. She didn't have time for dating or getting to know someone as a friend. She had enough on her plate with worrying about her mum and Rob and looking after Tiffany. Not to mention work. These days, she barely had time to sleep. No. It definitely wasn't for her.

'So, it would be easy to pick off men from Lenchester. Which means either the killer comes from around here or has some link with the place.'

She went over to the board and wrote "Lenchester".

While she was staring at the board, her phone rang. She pulled it out of her pocket.

'Walker.'

'Hi, it's Becky, from Radio Lenchester.'

'Hey. How are you?'

Whitney and Becky Ellis went back a long way. Over ten years, in fact, when Becky first joined the radio station as a researcher and helped Whitney out on a baby abduction case. Well, she didn't actually help, and talking with Becky had got Whitney into trouble and sent her in the wrong direction on the case she was working on. But they'd crossed paths several times since, and they'd helped each other out when they could.

'Very well, thanks. I've been promoted to head of the newsroom.'

'Congratulations, I'm really pleased for you. How can I help? I take it you're not phoning just to tell me about your promotion.'

'No. An anonymous letter has been sent to me, here at work. You'll want to see it. It's allegedly from the murderer of Russell Atkins. Only they mention another victim. Has there been a second victim we don't know about?'

They'd hardly had time to process the death and already it was out in the public domain. Talk about not making her job easy. She rolled her eyes towards the ceiling.

'I can't say anything at the moment.' She winced at the pathetic fob off she was giving to the woman.

'You mean there has?' Becky said.

'Leave the letter where it is. Don't handle it any more. I'm coming to see you.' She deliberately evaded the question. Well, for now.

## Chapter Fourteen

Becky met Whitney in the reception area of the radio station, and they took the stairs to the first floor. The building was modern, and the walls were full of posters of presenters, old and new. This was the first time Whitney had been in there, as in the past she'd met Becky outside, in a café. She often listened to Radio Lenchester and especially liked the afternoon presenter, who made her laugh.

'Where are the studios?' she asked.

'Behind reception. I'll show you on the way out, if you like?'

'Thanks. I've never been in one before.'

'They're nothing fancy. A desk with a mic and a computer screen. The letter's in my office.' They turned left at the top of the stairs into a large room. 'This is where the sales team sit.' She gestured to a block of six desks, all empty apart from one, where a man was talking on the phone.

'It's very quiet in here,' Whitney said.

'They're mostly out visiting clients, selling advertising.'

They walked into another open plan office, which was

as noisy as the sales office was quiet. There were TV screens on both walls and several people sitting at computers. 'This is the newsroom. Where it all happens. I'm over there.'

Whitney followed Becky over to a small room and closed the door behind them.

'The letter?' Whitney asked.

'On my desk.'

She pulled on some disposable gloves. 'Who opened it?'

'I did, as it was addressed to the head of news.'

'We'll need to take your fingerprints so we can eliminate them. The envelope will have gone through the postal system so will have many prints on it, but there's a good chance the letter will only have yours and the person who sent it.'

'Unless they wore gloves,' Becky said.

'Yes. Which is likely. Then again, sometimes people slip up. Even a fragment of a print can be enough to give us an identification.'

Whitney read it aloud:

*Dear Head of News,*

*I'm writing to you because I want everyone to know justice is being served. I will not tolerate men who prey on young girls for sex.*

*My mission in life is to ensure all young girls grow up to be happy women without having desperate memories dragging them down and ruining their lives.*

*We have our priorities all wrong in this country. We care more about crimes against property than we do about crimes against the person. We hear time and time again about rape victims not reporting their attacks because of the ordeal they are put through by the police.*

*Men like Russell Atkins get away with what they do to young girls because their victims are afraid to say anything. Well, they don't need to say anything, because I will make sure they don't do it again. The wheel is come full circle: I am here.*

*Atkins was my first. There has also been a second.*

*Beware all men in Lenchester who believe it's okay to prey on young girls.*

*I'm coming for you.*

Whitney pulled out an evidence bag and placed the letter and envelope into it.

'It looks like we have a serial killer,' Becky said.

'Strictly speaking, no. To be classed as a serial killer we require three bodies, not murdered at the same time.'

'But if this letter is correct, you have two so far, and the murderer indicates there will be more.'

'True. Have you copied this letter?'

'I took a photograph of it on my phone.' Becky averted her gaze.

'I know it's tempting, but I don't want you to publicise it.'

'Why not?'

'Because we'd be playing into the murderer's hands. We don't want the public to take their side. She…'

'You think it's a she?'

Whitney could've kicked herself. She hadn't meant to tell her. She'd grown to trust Becky over the years, but this letter made such a good news story, it would put their ratings through the roof, especially as they'd be the first to carry it. It would certainly attract national interest, which wasn't something Whitney wanted.

'We don't know yet. We've been putting together a profile, and it certainly points that way. But if we want the public's help in catching them, releasing this letter won't assist us, as they'd have zero sympathy for the victims.'

'What about if we sit on it for a few days and then reassess?'

Whitney couldn't prevent her from releasing it, so it was probably the best she could hope for.

'Okay. But please don't do anything without first speaking to me. I don't want the investigation jeopardised.'

'It's a deal,' Becky said, smiling. 'Now, how about we go to the studios? You can watch a programme being broadcast.'

She was sure spending an extra ten minutes there wouldn't make any difference, so she agreed and followed Becky downstairs and through the double door behind reception to where the studios were. There were three doors, each with a light above it, two of which showed red.

'The red lights mean someone is in there. Either broadcasting live or recording a programme or news items.'

Whitney's phone rang. She glanced at the screen. It was her mum. 'Sorry, I need to get this. Hello, Mum. I'm a bit busy at the moment. Is it urgent?'

'I can't find my handbag,' the panicked voice replied.

'Why do you need it? Are you going out?'

'I want to go to the shops. I think it's been stolen.'

Whitney sighed. She couldn't leave her mum on her own, trying to find the bag which was bound to be somewhere she wouldn't think of, like the fridge. The other week, her mum was convinced her keys had been stolen, and Whitney found them in the biscuit barrel. It was only by chance she'd even checked there.

'Give me twenty minutes. I'm sure you've just put it somewhere. We'll find it. Don't worry.'

'Okay. When will you be here?'

'In twenty minutes. I've got to go. See you soon.'

'Problem?' Becky asked.

'My mum's not doing so well. Early onset dementia. It seems to be getting worse.' She bit down on her bottom lip, determined to stop the tears which threatened to spill.

'I totally understand. My nan lived with us from when I

was young. She got Alzheimer's. It was so upsetting to watch her when she became really bad.'

'It's not easy. It looks like I'll have to give visiting the studios a miss.'

'Next time you're here, we'll take a look.'

'Thanks.'

Whitney left the station and drove to her mum's house.

What was she going to do?

The social worker's words came flooding back to her. It seemed the decision was being made for her. If her mum couldn't look after herself, then no way could she look after Rob. Tears spilled down her cheeks. How the hell was she going to explain to them both they could no longer live there? It would be worse for Rob because he needed to feel safe. He hated any change or upheaval.

She expected her mum would soon get used to living in a care facility. She'd probably enjoy being with other people. Plus, if the dementia got worse, it wouldn't matter where she was because it wouldn't mean anything.

She gave a loud sniff and brushed away the tears with the back of her hand. One step at a time. It was how she'd always done things. How she'd raised a daughter on her own. She'd survived that and would survive this, too. She'd find the missing handbag and then get back to work.

It took less time than she'd anticipated to reach her mum's because the traffic wasn't as heavy as usual. She parked on the road and hurried up the path and knocked.

Her mum used to have a rule about not letting yourself in, even though she had a key. Whitney was never sure why. Was her mum going to be engaged in some activity she didn't want her to see? It had been the rule for years. But nowadays, Whitney was flexible over when she stuck to it.

There was no answer, so she knocked again, then let

herself in, rationalising she was in a hurry and there was no guarantee her mum had heard.

'Mum, it's me,' she called out as she closed the front door behind her.

She grimaced at the dust on the hall table and promised herself she'd come around and do some cleaning soon. Perhaps Tiffany would help. The place was in dire need of a going over. Although it had only been a few days since she was last there, somehow it seemed even dirtier than before.

'Hello, Whitney,' her brother Rob said as she walked into the lounge. As usual, he was sitting on the sofa. He was playing computer games.

'Hello, little brother.' She ruffled his hair.

'I'm bigger than you,' he retorted.

Which wasn't hard, seeing as she was smaller than most people she knew. Apart from her mum.

'You're right. Where's Mum?'

'She's looking for her handbag. I didn't take it. Promise.' His face fell.

'I know you didn't. I'll help her find it.'

Whitney left the lounge and headed for the kitchen. Her mum was in there, standing with her hands on her hips, staring at the cupboard.

'Hi, Mum.'

'Why are you here? Don't you have work?'

'You phoned and said you couldn't find your bag, so I've come to help.'

'My bag. That's it. I knew I was looking for something, but I couldn't remember.'

'When did you last have it?'

'When I went to the supermarket at the weekend.'

'Have you checked your shopping bags? It could be with them. Where are they kept?'

Her mum frowned. 'On the hooks in the hall where the coats are.'

'Let's go and look.'

'You won't find it,' her mum said adamantly.

'How do you know?'

'Because I didn't put it there.'

'I'll go and check, in case, and if I can't find it, we'll take a look somewhere else.'

'Okay. If you insist. But it won't be there. I know it won't.' Her mum pulled out a kitchen chair and sat down, her arms folded.

Whitney returned to the hall and looked inside the shopping bags hanging on the hooks. As she'd suspected, inside the third was the missing black handbag. She'd have recognised it anywhere. Her mum had used it every day for the last twenty years, ever since her dad had bought it for her one Christmas.

'I've found it,' she called as she went back into the kitchen.

'Thank goodness. I really thought it had been stolen.'

'Who would steal it? You don't have any visitors, apart from me and Tiffany.'

'The social worker could've taken it. You can't trust anyone these days.' She took the bag from Whitney and clutched it tightly to herself.

'I'm sure she wouldn't have. Anyway, you've got it now. Which shops are you going to? Would you like me to give you a lift before I go back to work?'

'I'm not going anywhere. Would you like a cup of tea?'

'Sorry. I can't stop. I'll be here at the weekend, and we can have a good chat.' She kissed her mum goodbye and left, fighting back the tears which seemed to be on constant alert.

She forced her mind back to the case. The letter would

hopefully contain evidence they could work with, so the sooner it was with forensics the better. She despised the victims for their abhorrent behaviour, but couldn't let it interfere with her job.

There was a vigilante on their hands, who had to be stopped.

## Chapter Fifteen

'Fascinating,' George said as she stood reading a photo-copy of the murderer's letter. 'Absolutely fascinating.' Wednesday wasn't a busy day for her, so going out in the morning for a couple of hours to see how the investigation was progressing, wasn't a problem.

'Who do you think you are, Sherlock Holmes?' Whitney quipped.

George stiffened as she glanced up at Whitney, who was laughing, and then reluctantly joined in. She thought she understood Whitney's humour, but sometimes, especially when she was concentrating, it bypassed her.

'This letter tells us so much about the murderer.'

'Care to share it with us all?' Whitney asked.

'That's what I'm here for.' George grinned, pleased with herself for being able to join in with the banter.

They headed over to the board, and Whitney pinned up the letter.

'Listen up,' Whitney called out in her usual manner. 'The local radio station has received a letter from the murderer. George has some valuable insights into the person who wrote it. Stop what you're doing and pay attention.' Silence fell over the room. 'Over to you,' she said to George.

'The note is short, but it gives us plenty to think about. First of all, the murderer sent it to the radio station. Why?' George looked around, waiting for an answer. It was like she was lecturing. She hoped Whitney wouldn't pull her up on it. It always worked better when people could work things out for themselves.

'Publicity?' Matt said.

'Good. Why do they want publicity?'

'Because they're making a statement and want people to sit up and take notice,' Matt said.

'Exactly,' George said. 'This is a statement. It's also highly political. The person who wrote it criticised our laws for favouring property over people. They mention victims of certain crimes often don't report what has happened. This is personal.'

'You think the murderer has herself been a victim of grooming?' Whitney asked.

'It seems likely some sexual crime happened in the past. Or she knew someone who was the victim of one.'

'Are we definitely looking for a woman?' Whitney asked.

'In part, the letter reads like it comes from a female. The use of emotive language, like *I want everyone to know justice is being served*, indicates a feminine voice. But at the end, *I'm coming for you*, is more masculine and aggressive in tone.'

'Are you suggesting there might be two murderers?'

'It's a possibility, and one we shouldn't ignore,' George said. 'More than one person could have contributed to the writing of the letter and to the crime.'

'Could it be the work of a vigilante *group* rather than a single person?' Matt asked.

'It's possible.'

'Once we get the results from forensics and Claire's findings, we should have more to go on,' Whitney said. 'Is there anything else on the note you wanted to comment on?'

'Only that Lenchester is highlighted. *Men in Lenchester should beware*. This indicates a connection with the city.'

'It could simply be that they live here and it's easier for them to murder close to home.'

'That's entirely possible. Many crimes are committed in a familiar location. It makes disposing of the body easier. In this case, the bodies were situated in out-of-the-way locations only a local would know. But equally, they were not left in such a way they wouldn't be found. Knowledge of Lenchester would certainly help in this.'

'So aside from the vigilante group angle, where else are you suggesting we focus our investigation?' Whitney asked.

George glanced at Whitney. Not so long ago, no way would she have included her like this. When they first started working together, George had been kept at arm's length and only included when Whitney deemed it necessary. Now she was part of the team. An important part. It felt good.

'As you said, we need forensics to help. I also think we need to look more at the social media sites both men were on,' she said.

'That's a given,' Whitney said.

'Also of interest is the Shakespeare quote,' she said.

'What quote?'

'"The wheel is come full circle: I am here" is a quote from *King Lear*. I believe it was Edmund who said it.'

'How do you know?' Whitney narrowed her eyes. She

often did that when she was confronted with things of an academic nature. 'Are you an expert on all Shakespeare's plays, too?'

'I just know.' George shrugged. 'Probably from school.'

'But what does using it mean?'

'The murderer is well read, and a bit of a smart-arse,' George joked.

'Guv, Dr Dexter's on the phone,' Ellie called out.

'Transfer it to my office. Come with me,' she said to George.

They went to the office. Whitney answered and flicked a button.

'Hello, Claire. I've got George with me; you're on speaker,' she said.

'I'd better be careful what I say then,' Claire said.

'Hello, Claire,' George said.

'No classes today? You're becoming a part-timer.'

George tensed. Was Claire intimating she wasn't doing her job properly? That was absurd. Okay, her attention had been diverted, but the work she was doing here with Whitney was enhancing her work at the university. It was invaluable. As for being a part-timer, George worked every night at home, as well as going in early for work. So, if she decided to take time off here and there to help with the enquiry, then as long as her university work wasn't suffering, it didn't matter. And she resented the inference it did.

'There have been no complaints. I do my job well. I always have.'

'You know I was joking, don't you?' Claire said.

George glanced at Whitney, who was arching an eyebrow in her direction. Why did she have such a problem with social cues? 'Of course, I realised,' she lied. 'I was joking back.'

Whitney snorted and stifled it with a cough. 'What do you have for us, Claire?'

'I've had the toxicology report back on the first victim. He'd been given a sedative. Also, he'd had some alcohol, the equivalent of one glass of wine.'

'Anything to report on the second victim?' Whitney asked.

'Similar to the first, in many respects. The mutilation. The feeding of the cooked parts. Ligature marks. I'm waiting on toxicology for the rest.'

George marvelled at the way Claire could reel off these facts. Facts that would disgust most people. Yet to Claire it was a run-of-the-mill occurrence. Then again, if she got upset at everything, she'd be unable to do her job properly.

'Had he been sedated?' George asked.

'I've already told you; I'm waiting to hear back from tox,' Claire snapped.

'Was he restrained by the wrists and ankles like the first victim?' Whitney asked.

'What is it with you two? Aren't you listening to me? I've already said there were ligature marks. These were on his wrists and ankles and similar in nature to the ones used in the first victim.'

'Cause and time of death?' Whitney asked.

'Suffocation, like the first victim. Time of death between ten p.m. Monday and two a.m. Tuesday.'

'Thanks, Claire. When are you likely to get the tox results?' Whitney asked.

'When they arrive.'

Although they couldn't actually see Claire, George sensed she was rolling her eyes towards the ceiling.

'Other trace evidence?' George asked.

'No finger prints on the body and nothing under the finger nails. But there were traces of carpet fibres on the torso and head, like before. It's a wool carpet with a twist, expensive. But at the moment we can't identify the make. We're working on it.'

'Let's hope you come up with something,' Whitney said. 'Anything else?'

'That's it for now. I'm busy, so I've got to go.'

Claire ended the call before they even had time to say goodbye.

George laughed. 'Claire is certainly one of a kind,' she said.

'I'm surrounded by them,' Whitney quipped.

'If you've finished casting aspersions in my direction…'

'Which is exactly what I mean. Only you would say "casting aspersions".' She made quote marks with her fingers.

'At least now we've got more to work with. Have you heard back from forensics regarding the tyre tracks?' George asked, choosing to ignore Whitney's comments.

'Not yet.'

They walked back into the incident room. Ellie was standing by the board, the phone in her hand.

'Okay, I'll let the DCI know,' she said as she replaced the phone.

'Who's that?' Whitney asked.

'Mac, from the digital forensic unit. I asked him for help, as I contacted the owners of SnapMate, who are a tech company in the States, and they refused to give us details of their users in Lenchester. I thought techie to techie might do the trick, but he had no joy either.'

'What do we know about them?' Whitney asked.

'SnapMate was started by a young guy about ten years ago. Damian Smart. They say on the site they have security measures in place to stop predators. They also state in their terms of service that members shouldn't give out any of their personal information. Hundreds of thousands of kids are members across the world. They all have the app on their phones.'

'If they don't give out personal information, how's that going to work, if the aim is to find *friends*?' Whitney asked.

'Because once they make friends, these kids will give out their personal information. Which is why these sites have become stomping grounds for paedophiles,' Ellie said.

'Can I see the site on screen?' Whitney asked.

Ellie pulled it up, and they stared over her shoulder reading it.

'Shit,' Whitney said. 'These kids don't hold back talking about themselves. Armed with that information it would be so easy for the likes of Atkins and Keane to pretend to be one of them.'

'I agree,' George said. 'They have age restrictions of thirteen to nineteen. But how the hell can they police it?'

The lack of control over the Internet frustrated her greatly. She didn't blame the parents. These days, kids were often more computer savvy than those who were meant to be supervising them. And even though plenty of parents monitored their children's phones, if an app was free it could be download without permission. Something had to be done about it.

'It's a playground for paedophiles,' Ellie said.

'We need to check the girls Keane was chatting with and see if there's any link with the ones on Atkins' phone. Ellie, can you do that?' Whitney asked.

'From what I can see, Keane only chatted with one girl. Her name is Bea. He arranged to meet her Monday lunchtime,' Ellie said.

'Can we track her down?' Whitney asked.

'I've been trying to.'

'Doug, did you speak to the head of security at the university?'

'He wasn't there. His assistant said he'll be back later.' He checked his watch. 'Actually, I'll leave now. He should be there by the time I arrive.' He took his jacket from the back of his chair and slipped it on before heading out of the door.

'We need to focus on vigilante groups. They could be carrying out these murders,' George said.

'Ellie, research any you can find in the area, and also other groups that could have links with people here. Ones specifically targeting paedophiles living locally. Anything you can dig up,' Whitney said.

'I know there's the Hunter Group in Birmingham. I came across them last year. They might have connections in Lenchester,' Ellie said.

George followed Whitney as she walked over to the board and wrote *vigilante* on it.

'What sort of people join vigilante groups?' Whitney asked.

'Those who are unhappy with the way the police deal with sex offenders. Or with the prison sentences they're given. When paedophiles are released from jail and put into the community, it often incites a lot of anger. Very often vigilantes will be survivors of abuse themselves,' George said.

'But the problem is they can get it wrong. There have been several cases where innocent people have been beaten up and chased out of the city due to mistaken identity,' Whitney said.

'Indeed. But if you speak to members of these groups, although they may be sorry for the mistaken identity, it doesn't stop them from believing what they do is right. They feel vindicated by the fact they're protecting the public from evil. In their minds, their behaviour is totally justified,' she said.

The mind of a vigilante she found as fascinating as that of a killer.

'We need to know more about how these groups operate,' Whitney said.

'Last year an alleged paedophile was out on bail and he hung himself after a meeting with a member of a vigilante group,' George said, recalling a case she'd recently read.

Frank had come over during their conversation. 'Well, if you ask me, they deserve what they have coming to them. I have no sympathy,' he said.

'We can't let our personal opinions get in the way of doing our job,' Whitney reminded him.

'I'm just saying what most people in this room think. The two victims deserved everything they got. If it was one of my daughters they'd been grooming for sex, then they wouldn't be living. I can assure you.'

'We've already alibied the parents of the girls we know about. We need to find out if there are more girls we don't yet know about. Frank, look into other social media sites where teens hang out and let's see if our victims went on any of them. It's possible they would use the same aliases they used on SnapMate.'

'Okay, guv, I'm onto it.' Frank headed back to his desk.

Ellie came over. 'Guv, there's a group operating in this area calling themselves Justice Hunters. I've seen some articles written about them. They were started up last year by Len White, after he moved up from London. I've got his contact details here. He works at Hamilton's, the online electrical wholesale place.'

'Thanks, Ellie. Find out more about this group. Names of members, if you can, and do background checks on all of them. George, you and I need to pay this man a visit.'

George paused.

Should she stay with Whitney or go back to work? She did have a mountain of marking to do, and she didn't want to get behind. Claire's words earlier, even though she said they were spoken in jest, had got to her. She was an academic, not a police officer, and she needed to be seen in that light. Especially when she got the promotion, and all eyes would be on her and her research output. Having said that, one of her research projects would be on the police force and their use of forensic psychologists. It could have a far-reaching impact on the discipline.

'Okay. I'm ready whenever you are.'

## Chapter Sixteen

'Have you got your car with you?' Whitney asked as they left the incident room and headed to the car park. She had a good feeling about this group. The more she thought about it, the more she realised it could definitely be their work.

'Yes. Why?'

'I thought it would be nice to drive in comfort for a change, if you don't mind taking it. It's about thirty minutes to this guy's workplace.'

Whitney was envious of George's top of the range Land Rover, which was in stark contrast to her old Ford Focus. It also amused her how much of a petrol-head George was. She'd never have guessed if she didn't know.

'Happy to take my car if you like. Let's stop for a pub lunch if we have time,' George suggested.

'We've all got to eat,' Whitney said.

They left the station and headed to the Land Rover. Whitney slid into the passenger seat, running her hands over the soft black leather seats. George expertly drove them to the Thorplands area, which meant driving through the centre of the city to the outskirts, and on to an industrial development which had been built about fifteen years ago.

Hamilton's was a huge operation and employed hundreds of people in the area. The locals weren't happy when the company first moved to the city and took the largest warehouse and office space on the Thorplands Industrial Estate. But they'd turned out to be a good employer and had become accepted. They parked in the large car park and walked into reception.

'We'd like to speak to Len White please. I'm DCI Walker, and this is Dr Cavendish,' Whitney said to the woman on the reception desk, flashing her warrant card.

'I'll see if he's available.'

They listened while she called him on the phone.

'He'll be with you shortly, if you'd like to take a seat,' she said, after ending the call.

They headed over to a waiting area, where there were a few easy chairs. Neither of them sat.

'The usual drill, I assume. You speak, and I listen,' George said.

'Like you need to ask.'

'I'm just checking. One day you might actually trust me enough to contribute.'

'It's not that I don't trust you. I prefer you to focus on what isn't said. It's what you're best at. It's a case of you sticking to your area of expertise and me sticking to mine. Okay?'

Had she said enough to pacify George? She hoped so. It wasn't as if she didn't mean it. She'd spoken the truth.

'How can I not agree, as you put it so eloquently?'

Their attention was diverted as a man in his early forties appeared. He was a few inches shorter than George, stocky with a round, shiny red face and cropped dark hair, dotted with grey flecks.

'I'm Len White,' he said.

'DCI Whitney Walker and Dr George Cavendish. We'd like to have a word with you.'

'What's this about?'

'Justice Hunters. Is there somewhere quiet we can talk?' Whitney said.

'My office.'

They followed him into a small room, which had his name and title, Warehouse Manager, on the door. The space was sparse and contained a cheap looking office desk, a four-drawer metal filing cabinet, and three chairs around a small coffee table. On the wall was a Chelsea Football Club calendar.

'We'd like you to tell us more about the group,' Whitney said once they were all seated.

'Why?' he asked.

'We're investigating the murder of a man who had been grooming young girls.' As they hadn't yet announced the second death to the media, she wasn't prepared to tell him, unless necessary.

'And you think we could have something to do with it?' He put his foot on the table and leaned on his knee, staring directly at Whitney.

'We're investigating all possibilities, including it being the work of a vigilante group.'

'My group doesn't murder people. Our aim is to find and expose these men. We've reported them to the police in the past, but they haven't bothered to investigate. So we use our own persuasive tactics instead.'

'The police can't always do anything, unless a crime's committed,' Whitney said.

'Or they don't have the resources or the inclination to,'

he said in a well-rehearsed patronising voice, ignoring what she'd said.

'This isn't the time for a discussion on police involvement. We'd like to know more about your group and what activities you're involved in,' she said.

He sighed, removed his leg from the table, and sat back in his chair. 'What do you want to know?'

'How many members do you have?' Whitney asked.

'There are twenty-five of us.'

'And how did you recruit them?'

'It depends. Sometimes they're people I've met when I've been out or through places I've worked. Other people join after being introduced by a member. We vet them first. We don't want any nutters in there.'

'Do they pay to belong?'

'Yes. Five pounds a meeting, and that covers the cost of drinks and nibbles.'

'How very sociable,' Whitney quipped, glancing at George and arching an eyebrow.

'We're a social group. Like any other.'

Yeah, right.

'I'd like a list of names of everyone in the group and their contact details,' Whitney said.

'Do I legally have to?' he asked.

'Legally no. But if you don't, we'd consider you to be obstructing a murder enquiry and take you to the station for questioning.'

He gave a sigh. 'Fine. I'll get it for you, but you're barking up the wrong tree. My people wouldn't murder anyone.'

'How often do you meet?' Whitney asked, ignoring his protests.

'Once a fortnight, in a pub near where I live. We hire a room they have at the back.'

'And what's on the agenda?'

'We discuss sexual predators online and how we're going to expose them. We also exchange any information we've received about offenders in the area. Whether anyone's heard of someone abusing children. Anything we discover, we talk about and decide what we're going to do.'

'And you don't think to involve the police with any of this?' Whitney asked.

'I'm sorry, DCI Walker, but as I've already said, going to the police doesn't work. Bringing groomers to justice is our aim. When I lived in London, I was a member of a group. We tried a number of times to get the police involved, and there was always a reason why they couldn't. In particular, they didn't have the resources to tail someone *just in case*. It seemed to me the only way of dealing with these people was to dish out the punishment ourselves, especially in respect of paedophiles who'd been released from prison and put into the community without any discussions whatsoever with the residents. Anyone like that should be kept separate from the rest of us. In fact, they should all be kept together in the same area. Away from parks. Away from children. Away from schools. They shouldn't be allowed anywhere near normal families.'

'Don't you think that's a bit unfair?' George asked. 'People can change. If they've done their time and undergone treatment, surely they should be allowed to live wherever they want.'

'I take it you don't have any children?' he asked.

'What's that got to do with it?'

'The fact you have to ask says it all,' he said, his voice flat.

'And when you say you dish out the punishment, what exactly does that entail?' Whitney asked.

'Nothing physical. We speak to them and make it clear they're not wanted around here.'

'And if they ignore you?'

'We make it our business to go where they are. We follow them, make sure they know we're there.'

'Intimidation, you mean,' she said, shaking her head.

'You call it intimidation. I call it protecting our community.'

'And was Russell Atkins on your radar at all?' she asked.

'No, he wasn't. The first I heard of him was when his death was on the news.'

'What were you doing on the evening of Thursday the tenth, between six and ten?' Whitney asked.

'I've already told you I don't know him.'

'We need to eliminate you from our enquiries. The date?'

'I had a day off work to take my wife to the hospital and look after the kids.'

'How long were you there?'

'She had a biopsy which took a couple of hours. Then we came home and I stayed with her, apart from when I went to meet the kids from school. She can vouch for me. We would have gone to bed around ten, which is our usual time.'

'We'll need to speak to other members of your group. When's the next meeting?' Whitney asked.

'Saturday at eight.'

She looked at George. 'Are you free?'

'I can be.'

'Right. We'll be there. What's the name of the pub?'

'The Red Lion. On the corner of Lincoln Street and Spencer Road. But I don't think that's a good idea.' A worried expression crossed his face.

'I think it's a perfect idea. And don't mention we're coming, or who we are when we arrive.'

'But—'

'But nothing. If I find out you've tipped them off, I'll haul you in for obstruction. I'd also like the list of group members please.'

'I don't have it here. I can give it to you on Saturday, if that's okay?'

'It will have to be. That's all for now.'

They all left his office, and he showed them out of the building.

'Do you approve?' George asked as they made their way across the car park and to her car.

'Of vigilante groups? No, of course not. But I understand why they do it. Was he telling us the truth about how they operate, do you think?'

'I didn't see anything in his manner to suggest he was lying. It doesn't eliminate the rest of the group, though.'

'Exactly. Well, we'll soon see. One thing's for sure. I've never spent a Saturday night with a group called Justice Hunters before. Who the fuck came up with that name?' she said.

'It sounds like something from a cowboy film,' George said.

'Although it could've been worse. They could've called themselves something like the *nonce nobblers*.'

# Chapter Seventeen

When George arrived at work on Thursday morning, she stopped at her pigeon hole to collect her post. She hadn't checked for a couple of days, as most of her correspondence came via email. There were only two envelopes in there, both coming through the internal mail, and she put them into her brief case.

When she got into her office, she hung her coat on the hook on the back of the door and sat at her desk. She opened the first letter, which was from the university grant application office, confirming receipt of an application she'd put into the European Research Fund. Why they couldn't send it electronically, she didn't know. She picked up the second envelope and opened it.

Dear Dr Cavendish,

Thank you for your interest in the position of Associate Professor in the Department of Forensic Psychology. Unfortunately, your application has been unsuccessful.

This is no reflection on your undoubted ability, however, there was a very strong field of applicants.

I hope you will continue with your good work in the department.

Yours sincerely,

Robin Delaney

Head of Department

What. The. Fuck.

She stared at the letter, reading the words over and over again. This was unbelievable on so many levels. First, she'd virtually been promised the job. Second, she was hearing the news via a letter. A damn letter. Wasn't she a valuable member of the department? Did that count for nothing? Shouldn't she have been given the courtesy of being told face-to-face before the letters were sent out?

She reached for a cigarette in her drawer, then changed her mind. She'd pay the head of department a visit, first. The man whose arse she'd covered so many times in the past, because of his ineptitude.

She grabbed her bag, stormed out of her office, and headed down the corridor until she reached Delaney's outer office, where his secretary, Sophie, sat.

'Is he in?' she barked.

'Yes, but…'

George didn't listen to the rest of what she was saying, as she'd already reached his door. She knocked twice and marched in without waiting for a response. She closed the door behind her.

'What's this?' she said, standing in front of his desk and holding out the letter. Her tone was icy cold.

'I hadn't realised you'd got it already. I was going to speak to you about it,' he said, avoiding eye contact.

She sat on one of the chairs facing his desk. 'I'm here now. Speak.'

'You know you're one of our most highly valued

members of staff. Your research is exemplary. Your courses are among the most popular in the department…'

'But,' she interrupted.

'I wasn't the only person on the Selection Panel. We also took into account feedback from the presentation and the familiarisation informal lunch, which you missed.'

George sucked in a breath. She wasn't going to lose it. It wouldn't achieve anything.

'I had an emergency and couldn't make the lunch. According to the selection criteria, it shouldn't have been considered. It wasn't as if I didn't already know everyone.'

'That's beside the point. You'd agreed to be part of the familiarisation and, as such, were expected to take part in all aspects of it.'

'So you're saying I didn't get the job because of missing the informal lunch. If that's the case, I'm taking it further.' She leaned forward in the chair and locked her eyes with his. He lasted about two seconds before looking away.

'It wasn't that. I didn't mean to mention it.' He was clearly flailing.

'Explain. Did I do badly in the presentation?'

'No. Your presentation was excellent. As I'd expected. You made some interesting observations regarding your work with the police.'

'Observations which I'm intending to follow up with a research study. I've already applied for funding. If it wasn't the presentation, it must have been the interview.'

'Not exactly.'

'What does that mean?'

'You answered the questions very well. But you did spend a lot of time on the work you've been doing with the police. Maybe you should've focussed a little more on the wider application of your discipline and the successes of your students on the programme in pursuit of their degrees.'

Now she was getting to the bottom of it. They didn't like her involvement with the police. Which was ridiculous.

'What you're saying is real world application of theory isn't considered to be important.'

'This is an academic university. Second only to Oxford and Cambridge. Practical applications, while viewed as important, are more the domain of the newer, less established institutions.'

She understood where he was coming from, even though she didn't agree. If working with the police was going to have a bearing on her research output, then she couldn't see what was wrong with stepping foot outside of the academic ivory tower in which they inhabited.

'I believe we can do both.'

'Yes, but the emphasis has to be on the academics.'

'So, to clarify, my performance in the interview was the reason I wasn't selected for the position,' she said.

'It was everything combined. The presentation, the formal interview, and feedback from others.'

She noted he'd chosen not to mention again any part of the familiarisation.

Never in her career had she been unsuccessful in achieving her goals. This was something new, and she didn't like it.

'Are you saying my colleagues gave negative feedback, causing me to lose out on the position?'

Okay, she didn't mix much with others in the department, mainly because she was too busy. But also because she felt uncomfortable when with people, especially socially. She had an aversion to small talk.

'Not negative in so many words. Their main area of

concern is you're not as committed as you used to be. Your attention is more focussed on working with the police.'

'Is that what you think, too?' she challenged.

He shifted awkwardly in his seat.

'Well, it doesn't help your case by keeping to yourself all the time and not being a contributing member of staff.'

'I object to your comment. I contribute very much. I'm head of the departmental research committee. I regularly have my research findings published in the local and national press. My students perform very well. But because I don't hang out in the staff room gossiping, I don't count as a contributing member of staff? Frankly, you have your priorities all wrong.'

'I'm sorry you feel that way. If it's any consolation, I wanted you to be offered the position. But I was outvoted.'

'Who did get the position?' she asked, not sure if she cared.

'Greg Barnes.'

'The Scottish guy?'

'Yes.'

She shook her head. This wasn't happening. She'd worked so hard for this promotion, and some jumped up nobody from Scotland, who she hadn't even heard of, secured the post. She'd had it with him; she was getting out of there.

'Thank you for your time,' she said as she stood.

'Don't do anything stupid,' Robin said.

Stupid? What did he mean? Was he expecting her to attempt suicide or something? She'd never entertain anything like that. Her best friend in school died, and George found the body. She remembered it as if it was yesterday. No. Suicide would never be on her agenda. Ever. Nothing was worth that much.

'What do you mean?' she asked, wondering if she'd made an unwarranted leap by thinking he meant suicide.

'Don't hand in your resignation. We need you here. There will be other Associate Professorships available in the future.'

She found that hard to believe. Someone had to die, or leave, for it to happen, and the APs they had at the moment were way too settled to consider moving.

'When I make my decision, you'll be the first to know.' She marched out of the door without a backwards glance.

Wait until next time he needed his arse covered. Because she wouldn't be the one to do it. He could stand or fall by himself.

## Chapter Eighteen

'Detective Superintendent Jamieson is looking for you,' Ellie said as Whitney bumped into her in the corridor on her way to the incident room.

Damn. That was all she needed. His interference.

'Okay, thanks. I'll go see him now.'

She hurried to his office, and when she arrived, he was, as usual, on the phone. His door was ajar, and she knocked gently. He beckoned for her to come in, and she sat down opposite him. She glanced around his office, which was neat and tidy. The wall was adorned with certificates of his achievement. None of which were from the police. Although she tried to forget about his background, every time she was in this room it came rushing back to her.

It would be fine if he never interfered with investigations and got on with all the paper pushing which was the prerogative of his job, but there were times when he did get involved, and that was when she wanted to shove his precious Oxford University degree certificate up his arse.

He finished his call and looked at her. 'Where are we with the murder cases?'

'We know both men have been using SnapMate to attract young girls. So far, we've spoken to two of the girls Russell Atkins had been grooming but can't track the third. They both have alibis, as do their parents. We're in the process of trying to find a girl Keane had been grooming and looking to see if there's any overlap with Atkins.'

'Do you have any leads regarding the murderer?'

'They sent a letter to the local radio station detailing why murders were being carried out. For the moment, they've agreed not to broadcast it. I suspect there'll be more bodies if we don't catch the offender soon.'

'That's all we need. Another serial killer in Lenchester. What happened to the lovely city where people enjoyed a peaceful existence?'

'All cities have their problems. There's no such thing as the perfect place to live,' she said.

'What has the pathologist come up with?'

'Dr Dexter confirmed the murders were carried out by the same person. Our second victim also had his genitals removed, cooked, and fed to him. We're not sure, but we believe the murderer could be a woman.'

Whitney smiled to herself as the colour drained from his face. She enjoyed letting him see the other side of policing, the not so glamorous side, which was very different from attending functions wearing a shiny uniform.

'Well, make sure you—'

He was interrupted by Whitney's phone ringing. She pulled it out of her pocket and glanced at the screen. It was her mum.

'Sorry, sir. I need to take this. It might be an emergency.' She stood up and walked out of his office, standing beside the open door. 'Hello, Mum.'

'Hello, Whitney. How are you?' her mum said.

'I'm fine. You've phoned me at work. Is there a problem?'

'A lady from social services is here, and she wants me to let her do some cleaning.'

'Let me speak to her.'

'Hello,' a voice said.

'This is Whitney Walker.'

'Your mother's social worker asked me to call round and do some cleaning.'

'Why didn't Jean tell us in advance?' Whitney asked.

'I believe she told your mum when she was last here. It's not a regular visit. I've come in to help tidy things up a bit.'

'Okay, thank you. Put my mother back on.'

'Hello, Whitney.'

'It's fine, Mum. Jean arranged it. She thought you'd like some help, as you're finding it hard to clean everything. Don't worry, it's all okay.'

'When are you coming to visit? We haven't seen you for ages. Rob wants to know, too.'

'Soon. I promise. At the moment it's very busy at work. You know how it is.'

'Okay, love. I'll let you go. Speak to you soon.'

Whitney ended the call and returned her phone to her pocket. What the hell was she going to do? It couldn't go on. She kept trying to put it to the back of her mind and not think about what the social worker had said, but she knew she couldn't put off the decision for much longer. It wasn't fair on Rob to let things continue. It wasn't fair on her mum, either. In fact, it wasn't fair on any of them.

'Have you finished?' she heard Jamieson calling.

'Yes, sir,' she said, walking back into his office.

'Having problems?' he asked as she sat down on the chair in front of him.

'Not really.'

'Is your mum ill?'

'She's got early onset dementia, although it seems to be progressing quicker than we anticipated.'

Why the hell had she admitted that? It had nothing to do with him, and she didn't want his pity.

'I'm sorry to hear that, Walker. Are you the only person who can help, or do you have other members of the family?'

'It's all down to me, sir.'

He sat back in his chair and stretched out his arms over the back of his head.

'If you think it's going to be an issue, maybe you should consider stepping back from this investigation and letting someone else take over. Someone who can give it their full commitment.'

What the hell? He wanted to take her off the case? Every time something happened it was his first suggestion. His go-to response. She knew he didn't like her, but even so, it wasn't how he should operate. In his position, he should have his officers' backs. Not look to pull the rug out from under them whenever he could.

'It's perfectly fine. I can manage. I don't need anyone else taking over.'

'When we have a murder investigation, someone at your level has to commit twenty-four-seven. If you're having family issues, which I'm sorry for, I don't see how you can give the commitment required.'

'Have you had cause to question my commitment up to now?' She stared him in the eye.

He returned the stare for a few seconds. 'No,' he said.

'Exactly. This issue with my mother has been going on for some time. She hasn't suddenly developed dementia. We have a social worker who takes care of her, and occasionally I have to go and deal with something in work time. But as we work all hours God sends, I don't think it counts. Nobody in this job gets away without having their family life impinge on it. I'm no different. I don't need anyone standing in for me. Thank you for your consideration, but it's not necessary.'

Okay, they'd never got on, and he knew her feelings about the Fast Track scheme. But she got results, which is all he should go on. It was impossible to get on with everyone at work, and he should realise that. If she was a slack arse, it would be different, but she wasn't. She always worked harder than anyone else on her team. She didn't expect them to do anything she wouldn't.

'Well, if you think you can manage the investigation and your family issues, then we'll leave it for now. But if it comes down to you having to choose one over the other, then we'll need to reassess the situation.'

She could cheerfully slap the condescension off his face. Just let him dare try to remove her from the case, because if he did, he'd regret it.

'Sir.'

'What are your plans now regarding the murders?'

'We need to give another press conference to announce the second victim and give a few more details. In particular, we need to mention SnapMate, the teen friendship app. What we won't yet mention is the exact nature of the mutilation and the feeding of the parts.'

'I'll arrange the conference to take place first thing tomorrow morning. We'll do it together.'

'Yes. And we won't mention the letter to the radio station, either,' she said.

'Agreed.'

'Hopefully, after the press conference, someone will come forward with information, and we'll have further leads to go on. At the moment, all we have is the Snap-Mate app, the grooming, and traces of good-quality carpet on the bodies.'

'And you think this might be the work of a woman? Is she going to have the strength to lift a body wrapped in carpet?' Jamieson asked.

'The carpet could've been in the boot of a car. Some women are strong enough to lift bodies. Or it could have been the work of more than one person. We're following all avenues. We've interviewed the leader of a local vigilante group, and Dr Cavendish and I are attending the next meeting.'

'Let's make sure we catch the person, or persons, before they do this again. Not that I expect the public to be too sympathetic. Once they know these men have been grooming young girls, they might believe taking them off the streets is a good thing.'

'Yes, sir. I'm well aware of that. But we still have to mention it in the press conference, if only to highlight the dangers of using these apps. They're like paedophile paradise. I don't know if you've ever looked at one, but there seems to be no real security. These kids put up all sorts of personal details about themselves.'

'It's worrying. Unfortunately, with the Internet, these sites proliferate. Are there any similar murders outside of Lenchester?' Jamieson asked.

'Not identical. It does seem the perpetrator is targeting men in Lenchester. It's what the letter implied, too. There's obviously something about the city which is important. Maybe the murderer lives locally. Or something happened to them here.'

'Okay. You get back to the investigation. And remember what I said regarding someone else taking over if you need to concentrate on family issues.'

'It's all absolutely fine, thank you, sir. I'll see you for the press conference tomorrow morning.'

She left his office and headed back towards the incident room. What was it about the man that he wound her up so much? She longed for the days when Don Mason was her superior officer, but he'd retired years ago. He knew how to treat people and understood about family life. As long as you gave one hundred per cent to the job, when issues cropped up he was fine with you dealing with them.

It wasn't as if Jamieson didn't allow his family life to intrude. She'd been in his office many times before when he'd been taking social calls. Why he had it in for her, she didn't know. Actually, she did. It was because she wouldn't kowtow to him and all his *I went to Oxford University* crap.

Because she didn't care. What concerned her was how he did his job as a police officer, and as far as she was concerned, he didn't do it very well. Maybe the top brass were impressed with his metrics and the bullshit coming out of his mouth, but when it came to the real stuff, like supporting his officers and being able to discuss things, he was sadly lacking.

She knew she wouldn't be able to relax after the confrontation with Jamieson, so she pulled her phone out of her pocket and called George. 'Do you fancy going out for a drink tonight? We can discuss the case,' Whitney asked after she answered.

'Has something else turned up?'

'No. I wanted to go over everything.'

'Okay. I could come out if you want me to,' George said.

Whitney sensed the hesitation in her voice.

'Don't worry if you can't make it,' she said, giving her a way out.

'It's fine. What time?'

'I'll pick you up at seven.'

'Won't you be staying late working on the case?'

'I've been here since six this morning and deserve a break. If anything crops up in the meantime, I'll let you know.'

'I'll see you later, then.'

## Chapter Nineteen

George stared at the second hand on her kitchen clock. Why on earth had she agreed to go out for a drink with Whitney this evening? She was going to be the worst company ever. She'd rather sit at home on her own and wallow in self-pity. Not that she usually engaged in it, but after the way she'd been treated by the university, she deserved it.

She was tempted to take the matter further but knew better than to make a decision without being calm and in control. She was only thirty-four, so becoming an associate professor was a long shot, but she'd proved herself. She'd raised the department's profile to a high level, both inside and outside the university.

Her colleagues had always known she'd been working with the police, and now they were saying she was devoting too much time to them, to the detriment of her work. It was the biggest load of crap she'd heard, and she was really pissed off about it.

It was already six-thirty, and too late to cancel Whitney. Plus, it wasn't her fault, and if she needed help on the case, then George would oblige. In the meantime, she'd have a cigarette in the back garden. She pulled one out from the pack in her bag and was about to go out into the garden when there was a knock at the door. Damn, Whitney was early. She put the cigarette back and went to answer.

Whitney stared at her. Her usual upbeat demeanour was gone, and her mouth was downturned and her eyes glassy.

'What's wrong?'

'How do you know something's wrong?' Whitney frowned.

'It's written all over your face.'

'I've got trouble at home, and Jamieson's breathing down my neck, as well. To be honest, I was going to cancel drinks this evening. I'm not going to be good company.'

'Same here,' George said.

Whitney gave a hollow laugh. 'Look at the two of us.'

'Let's not go out tonight,' George suggested. 'I've got a bottle of wine in the fridge. We can have some crisps and dip and then talk.'

Had she suggested that? Since when did she ask anyone in for a drink and a chat? Never. Because she never knew what to talk about. In the past, the thought of making the offer wouldn't have entered her head.

'Good idea. Although I can't drink too much, as I'm driving.'

'If the worst comes to worst, you can always stay here. I've got a spare room,' George offered, again wondering if some alien had taken over her head space, because she'd never offered anyone to stay the night.

Whitney followed her into the kitchen. George opened the fridge and pulled out a bottle of her favourite New Zealand Sauvignon Blanc. She opened it, filled the glasses, and handed one to Whitney, who was sitting at the table. They clinked their glasses and both took a sip.

'So, who's going first?' Whitney asked.

'You can,' George said, not knowing whether she was ready to offload just yet.

'Where to begin,' Whitney said as she sighed. 'You know I told you about my mum and her strange behaviour?'

'Yes.'

'She's got a lot worse in these past few months. It's early onset dementia.'

'I'm so sorry,' she said.

Unfortunately, it was what she'd thought it might be when Whitney had told her about her mum's erratic behaviour. She hadn't wanted to say anything because these things sometimes took a long time to take hold. It seemed this wasn't the case for Whitney's mum.

'We have a social worker. She's very nice and thinks it's time Mum went into a home so she can be looked after properly.'

'It's often for the best in these cases,' George said.

'Yes, if it was only Mum. But what about my brother, Rob? What's going to happen to him?'

Whitney had mentioned her brother in the past, and she knew he'd suffered from brain damage after being attacked when he was younger. She didn't know how independent he was.

'I take it he can't look after himself?' George asked.

'No, he's not capable. Only the other week, the social worker called in just in time to prevent a fire occurring, as he was doing some cooking and a tea towel was resting on the hob. He hadn't noticed, and Mum was in another room.'

'Has the social worker suggested anywhere for him to go?'

'She said there are some nice places where he can live semi-independently, and there's always a carer on hand. She wants me to go and have a look, but I can't face it.'

Whitney rested her head in her hands and groaned.

'I know this can't be easy for you, but you have to think about what's best for Rob, long term.'

'Yes, but I don't want him to be locked up.'

'You don't know what it's like until you check. You're assuming it's going to be bad. Visit first, before you make a decision, and if you think it's suitable, take Rob and see what he thinks.'

'You're right. It could work out very well. But I feel guilty for not being able to do more for them. I can't afford to give up my job to look after the pair of them. We need my money. I'm still supporting Tiffany while she's at university. Even though she gets a student loan, it doesn't cover everything. I have to work. Not to mention how much it would hurt to leave. My job is my life.'

'You mustn't feel guilty. Your mum would hate the thought of you giving up everything you fought so hard for. You love your job. You're brilliant at it. I can't see you doing anything else.'

'But how am I supposed to juggle what's going on at home with trying to do my job? While I was with Jamieson earlier, Mum phoned. It gave him the opportunity to pass comment about me having to be available twenty-four-seven. He even offered to find someone to take over. We both know it wasn't out of the goodness of his heart.'

'I thought after the last case he was leaving you alone. Especially as we solved such high-profile murders and made him look so good,' George said.

'The trouble with solving any case is, once it's over, it's

forgotten. It's always the current one which counts. The one you stand or fall on. Well, that's Jamieson's view. He wants to keep his profile at a very high level all the time. One bad result and it could come crashing down.'

'I think it's ridiculous. He should value what you do for the force.'

Whitney's eyes brimmed with tears. 'Thanks. You're a good friend. You always manage to cut through all my emotional crap and see everything for what it is, in a logical way. I've said it before and I'll say it again. I wish I could be more like you; then I would be able to make decisions without feeling like the whole world is tumbling down on top of me.'

'I'm not so sure,' George said. 'I try to keep calm, but I think I did a *Whitney* on my head of department today.'

'Why? What did you do?' Whitney asked.

George picked up a glass and took a healthy swig of wine, enjoying the warmth of the liquid as it slid down her throat.

'I heard today I didn't get the job.'

'What?' Whitney exclaimed.

'It went to someone else. Someone with no substantial track record of research in the field. Furthermore, my head of department didn't even have the decency to tell me face-to-face. I learned of the decision from a letter. Can you believe it? A letter. He could have told me himself, before I actually received it. It would have been the fair thing to do, considering my standing in the department.'

'I can't believe it. I thought you were a dead cert for the job. You thought so, too.'

'It's taught me one thing. Don't count your chickens because they can run out on you. Stupid analogy, but you know what I mean.'

'Did he give you any feedback as to why you didn't get it?'

Should she tell her? Knowing Whitney, she'd take responsibility for everything because she'd got George involved in the investigations. But it wasn't Whitney's fault. The fault was her own.

'Yes.'

'What did he say?'

'I don't want you to take this personally,' she said.

'What do you mean?'

'Basically, feedback from the interview, the presentation, and the lunch, which I missed, was I'm focusing too much on working with the police and not enough on my work at the university.'

Whitney's jaw dropped, and she instantly regretted telling her.

'Hell, George. I'm so sorry. This is all down to me. I was the one who called you when we found the body.'

'Don't say any more, because it's not you. I made the decision to help, and I don't regret it one bit. What I do regret is assuming because I'm so high profile in the department I'd get the job. I won't make that mistake again.'

'You're not planning on leaving, are you?' Whitney asked.

'No, I love my job. I love researching, and I love working with students. But I also love working with you, because it's the practical application of everything I've been studying over the last few years. I'm going to reassess my priorities and goals. If I don't become a professor, then so be it.'

'You're being very calm about this,' Whitney said. 'By now I'd have been throwing things at the wall and anyone who stood still long enough.'

'I don't feel calm inside,' George admitted.

'You're certainly not showing it.'

'Because if I do, the university has won. The same for you and Jamieson.' She thumped the table. 'We can't sit here feeling sorry for ourselves. We've had our five minutes of moaning.'

'Agreed,' Whitney said. 'The only thing I can think of is we have to throw ourselves into this investigation and solve the case. Then we can prove to all those arseholes, well, to your head of department and Jamieson, they've messed with the wrong people.'

'Good idea,' George said, though she wasn't quite sure how solving the case was going to make any difference to people in her department, other than proving what they thought about her divided loyalties was correct. But she didn't care. She wanted to carry on working with Whitney.

'Okay, let's have a toast,' Whitney said.

George picked up the bottle and refilled their glasses. She suspected she might have an overnight guest.

'Here's to solving the case and proving our superiors are a couple of wankers who don't deserve us,' Whitney said, clinking her glass against George's.

'To our wanker bosses,' George agreed, laughing.

## Chapter Twenty

Whitney followed Jamieson into the press conference. Her head was thumping, and she wished she hadn't drunk as much wine as she had the previous evening. Then again, it was good to spend time with George. They'd got through two bottles, and with only crisps and dip to soak it up, the pair of them were pretty legless by the time they'd gone to bed.

She glanced around the conference room. As usual, it was full, with reporters in the seats and cameras at the back. Melissa, their PR officer, spoke first.

'Thank you for coming in. I'd like to hand over to Detective Superintendent Jamieson.'

'We're here to report there's been a second body found. Mr Kelvin Keane, from Lenchester. We believe the murder was committed by the same person who murdered Mr Russell Atkins. Both men were known to frequent the teen friendship site SnapMate.'

There were a few seconds of silence while Jamieson's words sunk in. Then the place erupted, and so many questions were shouted out, it was impossible to discern any of the words spoken.

Melissa leaned to the side and pulled the mic in front of her.

'One question at a time. Eric?' She nodded at one of the reporters in the front row.

'Are you saying both men were looking for teen girls to *befriend*?' Eric asked.

Jamieson slid the mic so it was in front of Whitney. She glanced at him. What was it with the guy that anything contentious he passed on to her? She ignored the thought at the back of her mind that it made sense for him to do so, seeing as she was the one who knew the case best.

'That is what we believe,' she said.

'Were they approaching underage girls?' Eric continued.

'Yes,' she confirmed.

'Paedophiles. Grooming young girls?' another reporter called out.

She ignored the comment, as she didn't want to be drawn too far down what was clearly an obvious track.

'Where was the body found?' a woman towards the back asked.

'Near the disused railway station in Cross Street,' she said.

'And had the body being mutilated in the same way as the first?' another reporter asked.

'I'm not able to discuss any details relating to the victim's body. But we would ask members of the public to come forward if they have any information.'

'Do you expect people to help catch someone who has murdered two paedophiles?' the same reporter asked.

A question Whitney had been asking herself.

'Irrespective of what these men have allegedly been doing, we still need to solve their murders.'

'Do you believe this to be the work of a vigilante group?' another voice called out.

'We're not ruling out anything at this stage. We will keep you informed of any progress, where we can.'

Melissa brought the press conference to a close, and Whitney and Jamieson left together.

'Where are we on the vigilante group angle? Have you looked into it?' Jamison asked.

'As I said yesterday, we've interviewed the leader of a local group, and I'm attending their meeting on Saturday with Dr Cavendish. We're covering all bases, sir.'

Was he trying to catch her out? Did he think she'd been lying to him?

How dare he question her ability? She'd show him.

## Chapter Twenty-One

George pulled on her jeans and T-shirt and stared at herself in the mirror. What did one wear for a vigilante group meeting? Who would be there? What were their backgrounds? What would be the proportion of men to women? She expected there to be more men, but maybe she was being stereotypical. When it came to aggressive behaviour, men outnumbered women. But, on the other hand, women were often fiercely protective of their families. So, it could be a mixture of both.

She'd been researching different vigilante groups around the country. Some were more political than others. Some focussed on online grooming and some on outing paedophiles in the community. She understood why people would want to take the law into their own hands, especially if they'd been subjected to abuse themselves. But where would it end?

A knock at the door interrupted her thoughts, and she grabbed her bag and ran down the stairs. She picked up her coat, which was on the end of the wooden bannister, and answered the door.

'Ready?' Whitney asked as she stood there under an umbrella. 'It's just started spitting.'

'Yes.' George pulled the door shut and ducked under Whitney's umbrella. 'Are you sure you don't want to go in my car?'

'I don't think your posh car will fit in as well as mine in the area. We don't want to stand out,' Whitney said.

'Good point.'

The journey took twenty-five minutes, by which time the rain had virtually stopped. They parked on the road and walked into the pub. A typical street-corner local which was already heaving, with groups of people standing around the bar and seated at the oblong tables filling the bar area. A pool table stood in the far corner and a dart board in the corner opposite. They navigated the crowds to get to the bar.

'We're here for the Justice Hunters meeting. Where's the room?' Whitney asked.

The man behind the bar looked them both up and down. 'I haven't seen you here before,' he said.

'This is our first visit. Len White invited us. The room?'

'Next to the ladies' toilet, over there.' He pointed to the left of the bar. 'Do you want a drink to take in with you?'

'I thought drinks were provided,' Whitney said.

'Beer, wine, and soft drinks. No spirits,' he said.

'We'll be fine then,' Whitney said.

They walked into the room and sat at the back. Behind them was a table with food and drinks. Already, most of the seats were taken. The chairs were in rows facing a table at the front, where Len White was sitting with a woman beside him. She was young, looked only in her twenties, had shoulder-length blonde hair and was wearing a leather jacket.

Scanning the rest of the room, George noticed there

was a mix of people. Their ages ranged from twenties right through to a couple who looked like they were well into their sixties, maybe early seventies. Towards the front, George caught sight of someone she knew from the university. Dave Milton, a lecturer in the criminology department. They were both on the resources committee. He'd been at her presentation. Should she go over and find out whether he was one of those who'd put the boot in?

'Is everything okay?' She started as Whitney elbowed her in the ribs.

'What? Yes. I've seen someone I know.'

'Here? Where?' Whitney frowned.

'Front row, at the end on the right. The guy with dark curly hair.'

'How do you know him?'

'He's a lecturer in the criminology department. Dave Milton.'

'I see him. Don't you like him?'

'What makes you say that?'

'Something to do with the evil eye you're giving him.'

'He was at my presentation. Probably one of those who fed back about my lack of focus.'

'You don't know for certain,' Whitney said, resting her hand on George's arm.

'I suppose not. I got the impression everyone had given detailed feedback, but maybe I'd misunderstood. For all I know, Dave didn't say anything at all.'

'What's more interesting is why he's here,' Whitney said.

'Agreed. Is he a vigilante? Or perhaps he's researching into them. If so, is it covert? He won't be happy to see us, either way, in case we give him away.'

'Has he seen you yet?'

'I don't think so. I'll speak to him after the meeting. It

might give us something more to investigate, especially if he can give us the run down on some of the members.'

'Welcome, everyone,' the girl at the front said. 'I see some new faces. It's good to have you here. After the meeting, when we mingle over drinks, please introduce yourself to everyone.'

George breathed a sigh of relief. For a moment she'd thought they were going to have to stand and say who they were. Which wouldn't have gone down well. At least now they could speak to people individually afterwards.

Len White stood. 'We've arranged training for anyone interested in acting as a decoy online to trap any predators. If you want more information, see me at the end of the meeting.'

For the next hour, they listened to various people outlining what they'd been doing in respect of outing any suspected child sex offenders. Everyone cheered when it was announced one offender, who'd recently been released into the community, had been hounded out of his house and had left the area.

Were they enjoying what they were doing? It seemed for some, children's interests weren't their top priority. And what about the mental health of the people in this group? Did some of them have problems?

'Thank fuck it's over,' Whitney whispered in George's ear. 'I'll be doing background checks on many of these.'

'Come on, let's *mingle*,' George said as she got up from her chair. 'Shall we split up?'

'Good idea. Why don't you speak to the guy you know, and I'll chat with some of the others?'

George walked over to where Dave was standing on his own in the corner, holding a glass of fruit juice. 'Hello, Dave.' She looked down at the short guy, who was wearing jeans and a Nirvana T-shirt.

Colour drained from his face. 'Dr Cavendish. What are you doing here?' He glanced anxiously from side to side.

'I was about to ask you the same thing,' she said, arching an eyebrow.

'I've been attending the meetings for a few months,' he muttered.

'Who recruited you?'

'The woman talking to Len, the leader. Nikki Bosworth. She introduced me.'

George looked over to Len, who was talking to the blonde woman who'd spoken earlier. 'How do you know her?'

'She's one of my mature students. She told me about the group and invited me to attend.'

'Is this for research purposes?'

'Yes, but no one knows, apart from Nikki.'

'She's happy for you to research this group, of which she's a part, and not tell them?' She shook her head.

'It's a joint venture. She's doing a Masters on vigilante groups and their positive uses in society. We'll do a combined paper on it once she's completed.'

'Does anyone else in the group know?' Had he considered the ethical implications?

'Not at the moment. She's going to tell them before it gets published.'

'And what if they refuse to give consent?'

'We won't be able to publish. But it shouldn't be an issue, as none of them will be named.'

'Glad to hear it. The university has ethical guidelines for a reason.'

She sounded preachy, but she had strong feelings about ethics in research and had seen in the past how some of her colleagues tried to flout them if it suited their purpose.

'What are you doing here?' he asked.

'I'm with the police, and we're here to talk to the members.'

'Of course you are.'

'Meaning?'

'At your presentation you talked about working with the police on their cases. Why else would you be here? You're hardly the type to join a group like this. It had to be the reason,' he said.

'Did you hear I didn't get the job?' she asked, conscious of the fact she was steering away from her true purpose.

'I heard a rumour,' he said.

'It seems a lot of people at the university weren't happy with me working alongside the police, and they let their feelings be known. Were you one of them?' she asked.

He averted his gaze and shuffled from foot to foot. 'Not exactly.'

'What does that mean? Did you, or did you not, question my commitment to the university?'

'No, I didn't. But I might have mentioned something to the person I was sitting next to at your presentation. I said you must have spent a great deal of time with the police, considering how involved you were in the capture of the campus killers.'

'And the fact it was being used for my research didn't come into it, I suppose?'

'It was a passing comment. I didn't realise it would be interpreted that way and go against you. I'm sorry. If it's any consolation, I thought you should have had the job.'

She let out a long sigh. Going over what happened wasn't going to change anything. She needed to compartmentalise it.

'Me too. But there's no point dwelling on it now.'

'Agreed. What do you want to know about this group?'

'We're investigating the murders of two men known to

groom young girls for sex. From what you've observed so far, is there anyone we should be paying particular attention to? Anyone you feel might go a step too far?'

'There are some who are quite open about their criminal records. One has been imprisoned for assault. Some of them, I believe, may have mental health issues. I'm not pointing the finger at anyone, but, as I'm sure you're aware, many people who join groups like this do so because of something in their past.'

'Who's the person with the criminal record?' she asked.

'Jimmy O'Brien. He's standing by the table with a sausage roll in one hand and a drink in the other. He's wearing jeans and a checked shirt.'

George looked over at the guy Dave mentioned. 'Is there anything else about the group you think we should know?'

'Most of them are coming from the place where they want to prevent children from being pursued. But some of them are in it because they enjoy the hunt. They thrive on confrontation, and bringing down these people is a legitimate way for them use their pent-up aggression.'

'I assume you're using the term *legitimate* loosely,' George said. 'Is this the only group you're studying?'

'Yes, because it's the only one I've been able to get into. There have been some research papers written on other groups. I think they're all fairly similar in their makeup. Some of them go further than others.'

'In what way?' she asked.

'Some are happy to name and shame, whereas others will take it further and then it becomes aggressive. Particularly setting up stings where they trick men who've been grooming girls. The groomer believes he's meeting a young girl, but he isn't. The group turns out in force and confronts the man, sometimes physically and always with cameras. They'll either put it up on social media or pass their information on to police. Sometimes both.'

'Thanks. That's useful to know. I'm going to have a chat with DCI Walker. Let me know if you think of anything else which might assist us.'

She made her way to where Whitney was standing, talking with one of the female members, a woman in her early sixties with short grey hair and dressed conservatively.

'They get what they have coming to them,' she was saying to Whitney.

'And you don't feel taking matters into your own hands can make things worse?' Whitney asked.

'How can it? If these people didn't commit such horrendous acts, we wouldn't have to go after them.'

'You could leave it to the police,' Whitney suggested.

'What are the police going to do, that we can't do a lot better? And quicker. Look around you. All these people are committed to bringing down sexual predators. Do you think the police have the time? Of course they don't. They're far too busy. They should be thanking us for easing their workload.'

Clearly Whitney hadn't told the woman who she was. Probably a good thing, or she wouldn't have got so much information.

'It's been good talking to you—' Whitney paused.

'Vera,' she said.

'I'm Whitney.'

'Will we see you at our next meeting?' Vera asked.

'I'm not sure. I'll try to make it.'

Whitney turned to face George. 'Shall we get something to eat?'

'Okay,' George said, assuming she was joking, as there was nothing on the table that remotely interested her.

Sausage rolls and sandwiches with curled up ends, which had clearly been made hours ago, were not her food of choice.

They headed towards the table and stood to one side where no one could hear them.

'Did you learn anything?' Whitney asked, her voice so quiet George could hardly make out the words.

'Dave Milton is doing some undercover research. He's here at the invitation of Nikki Bosworth, the blonde girl who spoke at the beginning. She's also doing research, for her Masters degree. As far as I'm aware, no one else knows about their projects.'

'Undercover, like us. I didn't tell anyone we're the police, as I thought we might get better answers if we're just chatting.'

'Makes sense. And did you get anything?'

'They're not backwards in coming forwards. They're more than happy to explain what they do. What they get up to stinks, especially the way they flush out these people online,' Whitney said.

'They would say the ends justifies the means.'

'I get that. If anything had happened to Tiffany, I'd have broken every law on the planet to seek revenge.'

'I don't think you would. You'd have placed your faith in the justice system,' George responded.

'Once I'd found him then, yes, I would have handed him over to the police. If he got away with it, then all bets would be off.'

'We're talking hypothetically here, because Tiffany's fine. So, let's not go down that road,' George said.

'You're right. One thing's for sure, someone within the agencies involved with sexual offenders' release is sharing this information. They seem very well informed.'

'It doesn't surprise me. These are emotive issues. Do you want us to mingle again?'

'I think we've done as much as we can tonight. Let's grab a drink somewhere away from here. Len White handed me the list of members earlier. In the morning I'll get the team to run background checks on all of them and decide who we need to bring in for questioning.'

## Chapter Twenty-Two

'Morning, team,' Whitney said as she walked into the incident room. 'Last night, George and I went to the Justice Hunters meeting. It was extremely informative, and I have a list of all the members for you to run background checks on. I already know at least one of them has a criminal record, so Frank, if you can focus on him, Mr Jimmy O'Brien, and Ellie, Doug, and Sue, I want you to share the rest.' She handed Doug the list.

'Yes, guv,' they all responded.

'Matt, I want you to come with me. We're going to pay another visit to Len White. I want more in-depth information on how they go about their work. Actually, no. Scrap that. We'll interview him here, and George can observe. Contact him to let him know you'll be picking him up. Ellie has his number.'

'On it,' Matt said.

The incident room door opened, and George came in holding a large white box.

'Doughnuts all round.' She placed it on the table, and everyone made a beeline for them.

Whitney thought back to when she first met George. She'd have no more brought in a box of doughnuts than fly to the moon. She was single-mindedly focussed on the task at hand. She only ever talked about work and didn't discuss anything else. Whitney liked this change in her. It didn't detract from how smart she was. She was the cleverest person Whitney had ever met.

'Now you'll be everybody's best friend.' Whitney took a bite of the jam doughnut in her hand and licked off the sugar from around her mouth.

'I thought as it was Sunday, and you got everybody in to work, it would be a nice treat. What are the plans for today?'

'We're going to get Len White in, and you can observe the interview. I want more information on Justice Hunters. Now we've been to a meeting, we understand the group more. I'm still of the opinion one of them could be the perpetrator. What do you think?' she asked the doctor.

'Difficult to say, but getting to know the group and the way it operates is certainly going to help us get into the mind of the person, or persons, carrying out the murders. The murderer definitely has the vigilante mentality, as illustrated by the letter sent to the radio station.'

'Exactly. And as we believe there could be more than one perp, let's see what White has to say. We know he's got an alibi for the first date, but it doesn't mean he wasn't involved in the setup,' she said.

'Are you going to tell him about the letter?' George asked.

'Do you think I should?'

'Yes. I can interpret his reaction and see whether he's really shocked or pretending. If you allow him to read it, I'll get a much better idea.'

'Will do. Even if he had no part in the murders, by

seeing the letter he might be able to direct us to who he thinks could be responsible.'

'What time is he coming in?' George asked.

'Matt's going to pick him up, so hopefully soon.' She walked to where Matt was standing. 'Have you spoken to Len White yet?'

'I got his voicemail. I'm about to try again.'

Whitney listened as this time Matt got through. Sounded like White was giving him some grief. Matt diffused the situation and agreed to pick him up in fifteen minutes. He was a good cop. He'd always been conscientious, and more and more he was able to think for himself. She'd have no hesitation in recommending him for DI once he'd done his exams. Although every time she'd broached the subject, he brushed it off. Perhaps George could shed some light on his reticence.

Matt ended the call, grabbed his jacket, and left the incident room, as she wandered over to Frank's desk.

'Any joy?' she asked.

'Jimmy O'Brien is thirty-five and has a rap sheet as long as your arm, starting from when he was a juvenile. Initially stealing from shops, then he progressed to burglary and later assault. He's been out of prison for the last twelve months after serving three years of a five-year term for grievous bodily harm. He attacked a man in his fifties who cut him up in his car at a junction. He followed the man, and when he got out of his car, O'Brien beat him senseless.'

'Charming. What about jobs? Where has he worked?' Whitney asked.

'This is where it gets interesting. He worked as a butcher's assistant in his late teens.'

'Interesting, indeed. He knows how to use a knife.' At last they were getting somewhere. 'Continue checking and then help the others looking into the rest of the group.'

She went back to the board. George was staring intently at it.

'Jimmy O'Brien looks promising. We'll speak to him after we've interviewed Len White. Remind me what your lecturer friend said about him?' she asked.

'Mainly, he's quite open about his criminal record and appears proud of it. Are you sending someone to bring O'Brien in for questioning?' George asked.

'No. I'll go around to his house after the interview with White. You can come, too.'

Whitney wrote *Justice Hunters* up on the board and underneath put the names Len White and Jimmy O'Brien. At least she now had something to report to Jamieson. She'd speak to him tomorrow when he came into work.

'Guv?' She looked up as Doug came over to them. 'Did you check this list of club members?'

'No.'

'Beryl Murphy's a member. Kelvin's mother.'

Crap. She could kick herself for not checking last night. 'Stepmother,' she corrected.

'What do you want to do?'

'Phone her and arrange to pick her up this afternoon. Tell her we have a few more questions about Kelvin.'

She wrote *Beryl Murphy* on the board and turned to George. 'Do you think she could do it? I know she's not his actual mother. But even so.'

'Parents have murdered their children in the past.'

'Murder, yes. But to feed him his mutilated body parts. That's beyond my comprehension.'

'You met her, I didn't. What do you think?'

'Her husband, Keane's father, is dead. When he was alive, he had a thing for young girls. There's a pattern.'

'Certainly a reason for her to join Justice Hunters. How did she take the news about Keane?'

'She acted like she didn't care. I couldn't tell whether she knew what he was up to or not. We'll know more after we question her later. In the meantime, we have Len coming in. He'll be able to tell us more about the woman.'

Within forty-five minutes, Matt had returned, having collected Len White and deposited him in one of the interview rooms.

Whitney wore an earpiece, and George stood by the two-way mirror to get a good view of what was going on.

'Thank you for coming in, Len,' Whitney said as she walked into the room with Matt following. They sat opposite him.

'I didn't have much choice,' the vigilante said. 'I thought I told you everything you needed to know when we spoke last week.'

'I'm going to record the interview. It's easier than writing everything down. Is that okay with you?'

'Do what you want,' White said, his arms folded tightly across his chest.

'You need to soften him up a bit,' George said in Whitney's ear. 'Or he'll dig his heels in, and you won't get anything out of him.'

'We appreciate you coming in to help us. We have some questions for you, following the meeting, and after doing background checks on some of the members.'

'Okay.' He unfolded his arms and sat back in the chair.

'What do you know about Jimmy O'Brien?' Whitney asked.

'I take it you're picking on him because of his criminal record,' White said, shaking his head. 'Just because he's been in prison, doesn't mean he'll go off on his own to murder men who groom children. There's an art to finding these men. We have techniques.'

'Perhaps you could enlighten us more on these *techniques*,' Whitney said.

'There's the hint of a smug expression on his face,' George said. 'He likes you coming to him for information. It's making him feel important. Keep going.'

'We entice men to take the bait and start to groom who they believe are teen girls.'

'This is very helpful. Can you give me an example of the words your people use when they're trying to trap a paedophile?' Whitney asked.

'We get our people to ask naïve questions. That always seems to get the nonce going. We also get our decoy to state their fake age within the first two or three messages. Which is usually either thirteen or fourteen. They tell him they're having problems at home or school and have no one to confide in. All these things are designed to draw out these monsters.'

'This is entrapment,' Whitney said.

'Call it what you like. If we can stop even one of them from grooming a young girl for sex, in my book, it's all that matters.' He leaned forward and locked eyes with her.

'Does that mean you condone murder?' Whitney asked.

'That's not what I said.'

'Look, Len. We have two dead bodies on our hands, and we're expecting more. We know the murderer is someone with vigilante beliefs.'

'How do you know?' White frowned.

Whitney pulled out a copy of the letter from the folder in front of her and slid it over for him to read.

His brow lifted. 'This doesn't sound like any of our members,' he said.

'He's surprised by the letter but is also uncertain. The expression on his face and the hesitation in his voice, when he denied it being one of his members, makes me think, in reality, he doesn't know,' George said.

'How can you be so sure?' Whitney asked.

'Because I'd have heard if any of my members were planning to go on a murdering rampage like this.'

'What about Jimmy O'Brien? Is he capable of this behaviour?'

'He would be capable of the murder, but this letter wasn't written by him. He can hardly write his name.'

'Do you think he could be working with another member of your group?'

'Keep going,' George said. 'He's getting very uncomfortable. We might get something good.'

'It's possible. That's all I can say. But I still can't see Jimmy being the murderer. I mean, mutilating a body. It doesn't seem like him.'

'You'd be surprised what people do in a fit of passion. The removal of genitals included,' Whitney said.

'You're getting into his head,' George said.

'Bloody hell,' Len exclaimed. 'Talk about the punishment fitting the crime.'

'It's not public knowledge. And we want it to stay that way.'

'People have a right to know.'

'They will find out when we're ready to tell them. Getting back to Jimmy, who does he hang out with most in the group?' Whitney asked.

'No one in particular. He mixes with everyone. I sometimes have a drink with him in the pub, as he doesn't live too far away.'

'What about women in the group? Is he particularly friendly with any of them?' Whitney continued.

'He sits next to Vera at most meetings. I don't know if they see each other outside of the group.'

'What can you tell me about Vera?'

'Vera's been with us since we started. She's sixty-odd and used to work at Hamilton's as a project manager but had to take early retirement because of ill-health. She has bad asthma. I don't know much about her personal life, other than she has a daughter who she doesn't see much. There's some history there, but I don't know what it is.'

'How did you introduce her to Justice Hunters?' Whitney asked.

'We were outside having a smoke break, and we got talking. I told her about the group, and she asked to join.'

'Smoking? I thought she had asthma.'

'She did, and smoking made it worse. It probably contributed to her having to retire early.'

'We'll look into her,' she said.

'I can't see how she'd be able to do it. She walks with a stick and can hardly breathe. I'm fairly sure the only time she goes out is when she comes to one of our meetings.'

'What about Beryl Murphy?'

'Why do you want to know about her?' He frowned.

'Is she a proactive member?' she asked, ignoring his question.

'Not really. She attends meetings. Keeps herself to herself, most of the time.'

'Who introduced her to the group?'

'I don't remember. She's been coming for about a year. Why?'

'She's the second victim's stepmother.'

'You're kidding?' His eyes widened.

'He's definitely surprised,' George said.

'No. Not kidding. You were told in confidence, and I don't want to find out you've blabbed it to anyone.'

'Okay.'

'I think that's everything for now,' Whitney said. 'If you think of anything which might help the investigation, contact us immediately. Remember, don't discuss the mutilation or the contents of the letter with anyone. You were shown it in confidence.'

'I won't.'

'DS Price will take you out.'

After White and Matt had left the room, Whitney went to see George.

'What do you think?' she asked.

'He was telling the truth. The revelation about Beryl Murphy was a surprise. He had suspicions about Jimmy O'Brien, though, despite what he said. We definitely need to interview him as soon as possible.'

'It's where we're heading next.'

## Chapter Twenty-Three

They went back to the incident room, got Jimmy O'Brien's address, and then left the station. He lived in a rough part of the city, in a block of flats well known to the police, as they were forever being called there to deal with fights, domestics, and gang trouble. Whitney parked her car in one of the free spaces outside the block. Hers was the newest one there, and that was saying something.

Walking into the building, they were immediately assaulted by the disgusting smell of stale urine. There was litter strewn across the concrete floor.

'What the fuck?' Whitney said as she narrowly missed treading in some dog shit.

'Don't they have cleaners?' George asked, pulling a face and skirting around a pile of old food wrappers.

'Yeah, every day someone comes around with a duster and polish.' Whitney rolled her eyes. 'But they obviously missed a bit.'

'So, no then?'

'You've never been in a place like this before, I take it.'

'No.'

'Welcome to the seedier side of the city. The common areas might get a wash down every few weeks, if they're lucky.'

'What floor's he on?' George asked.

'Right at the top. Fifteen.'

'I hope the lift's working.'

'There's one way to find out.'

They walked past the open staircase of the old 1960s building until they came to the lift. Whitney pressed the button and grimaced as her finger stuck to it. The metal door opened, and they stepped in.

'Thank goodness. I didn't fancy walking. I'm not that fit,' George said.

'Me neither.'

The lift groaned as it came to a halt on their floor. They walked along the open walkway until they arrived outside Jimmy O'Brien's flat. Whitney knocked on the door and waited a minute before knocking again, only louder. A woman from the next door flat opened her door and poked her head out.

'If you're looking for Jimmy, you'll need to make more noise. He didn't get in until late last night and was pissed out of his skull.' She closed the door behind her without waiting for an answer.

Whitney banged again, so hard the glass in the window frames shook. After a while they could hear someone walking towards them. The door opened and Jimmy O'Brien stood there wearing only a pair of blue and red striped boxers, the elastic around the top frayed. His hair stuck out in all directions. He'd clearly just woken up.

She held out her warrant card. 'DCI Whitney Walker and Dr George Cavendish. We'd like to speak to you.'

'What's this about?' he growled.

'We'd rather speak inside,' she said.

He shrugged and held open the door for them to walk in. The whole flat smelt stale. He showed them into the lounge and drew the curtains.

'Would you mind opening a window as well?' George asked.

He turned to face her. 'You'll be asking me to dust and hoover the place next.'

'Just the window will be fine.'

'It must have been quite a night, if you've only just got up.' Whitney shifted the pile of magazines on the couch to one side and sat down with George next to her. O'Brien was on an easy chair opposite. He pulled on a dark green T-shirt which had been resting on the arm.

'Certainly was. Can I get you both a coffee?'

'No thanks. I've recently had one.' As much as she was desperate for a caffeine fix, looking at the state of the place she didn't want to risk it.

'Okay. What do you want?'

'We'd like to ask you about your role in Justice Hunters,' Whitney said.

He smacked his forehead with his hand. 'That's where I recognise you from. You were at the meeting last night.'

'Yes, we were. We're investigating two recent murders which I'm sure you've heard about in the media. The victims were grooming young girls.'

'And you think a Justice Hunter member is responsible?'

'We're investigating all avenues and it's one of them. What do you think about these murders?' she asked, knowing it was a strange question to start with, but she wanted to see where it led them.

'They got what they had coming to them. Anyone who thinks it's okay to groom young girls for sex doesn't deserve to live on this planet.' O'Brien wagged his finger in their direction.

'Do you know anything about these murders?' she asked.

'Only what I've heard on the radio and seen on the telly.'

'I understand you've got quite a string of convictions against you,' she said.

'So what? It doesn't mean I'm going to go out and murder two perverts. Why do cops always think anyone with a record is guilty of other crimes?' He glared at her.

'You're part of a vigilante group whose sole purpose is to expose and eradicate paedophiles and sexual grooming. You have a record for violent behaviour. Of course we're going to talk to you.'

'Justice Hunters doesn't break the law,' he snapped.

'Debatable. Many vigilante groups are very close to being illegal in their activities,' she said.

'I didn't murder anyone, whatever you think.'

She glanced at George, who was staring at O'Brien intently. Had he given anything away?

'We'd like to know where you were between the hours of six and ten on the evening of Thursday the tenth, and between ten at night Monday the fourteenth and two in the morning, Tuesday the fifteenth.'

He was silent for a while. 'On the first date I was at work, doing the night shift.'

'Where do you work?' Whitney took out her notebook and pen from her pocket and began writing.

'In a warehouse on Thorplands. Hamilton's,' he said.

'Where Len White works. Did he get you the job?'

'No. The Job Centre did.'

'How long have you been working there?'

'I'm casual. Just go in when they need me. What's it got

to do with anything?' He reached over and pulled out a cigarette from the pack on the table. 'Want one?' he asked, looking at Whitney and George in turn as he lit up. They both shook their heads.

'Will Hamilton's be able to provide you with an alibi?' she asked.

'Yes.' He blew smoke in her direction, and she made sure not to act like it bothered her. He was doing it for effect. She knew that.

'What about the second date?' she asked.

'I wasn't working then. Maybe I was at the pub? I don't remember,' he said, shrugging.

'Until two in the morning?'

'I know the landlord.'

'Which pub?' she pushed.

'Look. I don't know if I was there on the night you said. I'm just saying I could've been. I don't remember. Okay?' His fist was clenched by his side.

Whitney instinctively moved her hand so her Taser was in easy reach.

'You were a butcher's assistant when you were younger,' she said.

'Years ago. Why?' He frowned.

'You're familiar with cutting flesh and using knives?'

'Oh, I get it. The bodies were chopped, so you think it's me because I know how to use a knife. Well, I've got news for you, lady. Hundreds and thousands of people can use a knife. It's not hard.'

'True, but not all of them are ex-cons who've been convicted for violent crimes and are also part of a paedophile hunting group. So you can see why we're interested in you.'

Whitney leaned forward in her seat, resting her arms

on her knees. She fixed him with a stare, and he shifted agitatedly.

'Well, I didn't do it.' His voice rose. 'Even if I don't have an alibi for the second murder, I do for the first, so that should count me out.'

Whitney exchanged a glance with George. The interview was pointless until they had some concrete evidence. They should probably leave before he got himself so riled he'd do something they'd all regret.

She stood, and George followed.

'I'd like the name of your supervisor at Hamilton's so I can check with them. I understand you're very friendly with Vera Smith?'

'I wouldn't say *very* friendly. Why?'

'Do you see each other away from the group?' she asked.

'We have met up sometimes.'

'What for?'

'When we've been trying to nab men online, she's helped. She's much better on computers than me. She understands them. I don't use them much.'

'So you leave the technical stuff to Vera, and once you've arranged to meet these men, to expose them, you get involved. With the physical threats?'

'Has anyone complained about me? We speak to these men when we meet them, that's all. We put the meeting up on social media, which is what Vera does. She's not the only person in the group who can do it, but I like working with her.'

'A funny combination,' Whitney said.

'Because she's clever and I'm thick. Is that what you mean?'

'I didn't say that. If you can let me have those details, we'll be going.'

'I can't remember his name. I've got it written down in the kitchen.'

He got up and left the room.

'There's got to be more to it than he's letting on,' Whitney said.

'Agreed,' George said.

He came back in and handed Whitney a piece of paper with the name of his supervisor and a phone number.

'Before we go, do you ever work with Beryl Murphy?'

'Who?'

'She's a member of the group. Has been for about a year.'

'I don't know her.' He shook his head.

'Tall. Walks with a stoop. In her sixties. Does that jog your memory?'

'Oh, yes. Now I remember. Miserable cow. When she does come to meetings, she doesn't speak to anyone. She sits at the back on her own. She's never worked on anything with me. I don't know about the others.'

Whitney stood. 'Thanks for your assistance. We'll be in touch if we need to speak further.'

They left the flat, and she breathed in some refreshing clean air. How the hell anyone could live like that, beat her. She should be used it by now, seeing as she'd been in enough shit-hole places in her time as a police officer, but for some reason it affected her today. It was probably the sleaziness of O'Brien she didn't like.

'What's your verdict?' she asked George.

'I agree there's no way he could have written a letter to the radio station. He certainly doesn't have the verbal skills or the vocabulary. When you asked him about Vera, his whole demeanour changed. Did you notice the way he crossed his arms? It's an indicator he's protecting a secret. Subconsciously, his arms were acting as a barrier.'

'They could be working together. She'd be able to write the letter.'

'It definitely needs further examination,' George said.

'We'll interview her and check her background. I'll phone the office now and get her details. We'll go straight there.'

'What about Beryl Murphy? Isn't she coming in?'

'Crap. I forgot.' She checked her watch. 'We should still have time. She'll have to wait if we're running late.'

## Chapter Twenty-Four

Whitney pulled out her phone and keyed in the shortcut to the incident room.

'Lenchester police, DS Price speaking.'

'Matt, it's me. Put me onto Ellie, please.'

'Hello, guv,' Ellie said.

'What have you found out about Vera Smith?'

There was a few seconds of silence, other than the click of computer keys. 'No record. She worked for Hamilton's for many years and had to leave for health reasons. She's on the sickness benefit, as she's not eligible yet for her state pension.'

'Family?'

'Husband died several years ago. One daughter, but I don't know where she lives.'

'Give me her address. We're going to pay her a visit.'

'One Rushton Crescent.'

'Thanks. We'll see you later.' She ended the call and popped her phone back in her pocket. 'Right, we're off to Rushton Crescent. A much nicer area.'

They drove across the city to the Warkworth Estate.

Vera's house was a traditional 1930s pebble-dashed semi-detached. It had a big bay window with smaller stained-glass windows above it. The front garden was grassed and in dire need of mowing. They parked in front of the free-standing garage and headed up a concrete path lined on both sides with small stones. There was a brass knocker on the dark red painted door. Whitney knocked twice, and within a few seconds they could hear someone shuffling towards them.

The door opened. 'I was expecting you.'

Whitney held out her warrant card. 'DCI Walker and Dr Cavendish. I take it you're Vera Smith, and Jimmy's been in touch.'

'He phoned to tell me you'd been to visit, and he thought you'd be coming to see me.'

'He wasn't wrong. May we come in?' Whitney asked.

Vera held open the door and they walked in. The house smelt fresh and clean, a stark contrast to Jimmy's. It made a friendship between the two seem even more bizarre.

'Come through to the kitchen, I've just boiled the kettle. Would you like a cup of tea or coffee?'

'Coffee would be great, thanks. Milk, no sugar,' Whitney said, grateful to finally have one.

'Same for me,' George said.

They followed her to the kitchen. She used a multi-coloured stick and walked slowly, each step seeming an effort. Her breathing was laboured. They sat down at the kitchen table while the older woman made the coffee.

'You have quite a way to go for the Justice Hunters' meetings,' Whitney observed.

'It's the only club of its kind in the area, so I have no choice. Plus, I know Len, and I wouldn't want to go anywhere without knowing anyone. Especially not a club like that.'

'What do you mean?' Whitney asked.

'Most of us in the group joined with the best of intentions. But you can't be sure of everyone.'

'What about Jimmy?'

'Jimmy's had a tough life. He didn't have it good when he was a child, and he ended up in trouble. He's paid the price. Now he wants to give something back.'

She passed them both a coffee, and Whitney wrapped her hands around the mug and inhaled the intoxicating fumes. 'And you don't believe by being aggressive and threatening these people he's doing more of the same, only in the so-called legal way?' Whitney asked.

'DCI Walker, and by the way that was very sneaky of you coming to our meeting and not saying who you were.' She arched an eyebrow.

'I told you my real name. I was off duty and wanted to come and see what it was all about. Len knew who I was. I didn't deceive anyone,' Whitney responded.

'That's your view. Anyway, as far as Jimmy's concerned, things happened to him as a youngster, which is why he's so committed to our cause. It's nothing to do with his criminal record. I'd be no good confronting the men we expose, so we use Jimmy, who's good at it.' Vera's voice was matter-of-fact.

'How far would you go when dealing with men who groom young girls? What do you think about the fact two were murdered?' Whitney asked.

'I could say they got what they deserved. But I don't believe in taking another person's life. There are other, more effective, ways of dealing with them. They should be imprisoned and exposed on social media. The public should know who they are. That's far worse, in many respects, because they have to live their lives and continually pay the price for their perversions, with everybody knowing about it. So, in answer to your question, I'd rather they weren't murdered. As for them being mutilated, that's a different matter and is something I could live with.'

Whitney finished her coffee and placed her mug on the table. 'What do you know about Beryl Murphy?'

'I've spoken to her a few times. She's not an active member of the group. Why?'

'We're looking into all members of the group. Thank you for your help. Before we go, please can you let me know where you were on Thursday the tenth between six and ten in the evening, and also Monday the fifteenth from ten in the evening until two in the morning. So we can eliminate you from our enquiries.'

'Both days I was at home and recovering from my shifts at the local Oxfam shop. I was tired and in bed by nine.'

'How do you manage with your asthma and walking disability?' Whitney asked.

'I don't do any sorting or pricing. I sit behind the counter and take the money. I'm not so decrepit I can't do that. If I'm having a bad day, I phone and don't go in. It's not like at work, when I could be letting everyone down because projects needed to stick to a strict deadline. This gets me out of the house and stops me from feeling like an old has-been.'

'We'll be off now. If you think of anything to help our investigation, here's my card.' She handed it to Vera.

They headed back to the car. Once inside, she turned to George.

'So?'

'I believe she was telling the truth. Nothing she said made me think otherwise.'

'I'm thinking about putting a tail on Jimmy O'Brien to

see what he gets up to. We also need to check his alibi. He still could be the murderer with someone's help, even if it's not Vera. Let's see what our interview with Beryl Murphy uncovers, and I'll decide.'

After grabbing some lunch from the café around the corner from the station, they went back to Whitney's office. Beryl Murphy had only just been brought in, which gave them time to wolf down their sandwiches.

'Ready?' Whitney asked as she wiped the crumbs from her mouth with a paper napkin.

'Yes. Do you want me in with you or looking on?' George picked up her bottle of water and tipped it into her mouth.

'Come in with me. Matt's tied up.'

Whitney picked up the investigation folder from her desk, and they went downstairs to the interview room where Doug had left the woman.

'Hello, Beryl. Thanks for coming in,' she said as they entered. She placed the file in front of her. The only thing in there were photos of the victims, but she always took in a file when interviewing. It showed she meant business. At least, that's how she saw it. She hadn't asked George for her opinion.

'I didn't have a choice.' The woman was dressed a lot smarter than when they'd last seen her, in a pink blouse buttoned up to the top and a grey cardigan. A gold cross hung around her neck.

'We have a few more questions to ask you,' Whitney said.

'When can I have Kelvin's body? I want to arrange the funeral.'

'The coroner's office will let you know; it's not in my jurisdiction. We'd like to ask you about Justice Hunters.'

'Why?' The woman's lips pressed together.

'Our investigation has led us to the group. We discovered you're a member. Would you like to tell us more about it?'

Beryl shifted in her seat and kept her gaze averted from Whitney's. 'There's nothing to tell. I joined last year after reading an article about them. I wish they'd been around when my husband was doing his thing. I'd have set them onto him.'

George and Whitney exchanged a glance.

'What about Kelvin?' she asked. 'Did you tell them about him?'

'No. I didn't know what he was up to.'

'If it's true, why didn't you seem surprised when I told you? You must have had your suspicions,' she pushed.

'He spent a lot of time on his phone and on his computer. But I don't know how to work them, so I couldn't check what he was doing. Okay, yes. It did cross my mind he might be like his father, but until I knew for sure, I kept it from the group. It turned out I was right. It doesn't matter now. Someone beat me to it.' She took hold of the cross around her neck and twisted it in her fingers.

'You approve of what happened to him?'

'He was murdered and mutilated. That's all I know.'

Whitney pulled out a photo of Kelvin and slid it across the table. 'This is what was done to him.'

The woman glanced at the photograph and she paled. 'God help him,' she muttered.

'The other victim, Russell Atkins, was mutilated in the same way.'

'Do you know the other victim?' George asked.

'Um… um…'

'It's a simple question,' Whitney said. 'Do you know him?'

'Yes.'

Whitney's heart pumped in her chest. They had a connection between the two victims. But was it enough? Forensics hadn't come up with anything they could use. Certainly the carpet in the woman's house wasn't good quality, like Claire had found in the fibres.

'In what capacity?'

'I used to clean at the Atkins' house.'

'Maidenwell is miles away from where you live. Why didn't they employ someone more local?'

'It's half an hour on the bus. There's a shortage of cleaners out there. All the posh people want someone in to clean for them.'

'How long were you there for?'

'Six months, five years ago.'

'Why did you leave?'

The woman bit down on her bottom lip. 'They let me go. Accused me of stealing.'

'And did you?' Whitney locked eyes with her, and she visibly squirmed. 'The gold carriage clock?'

'Yes,' the woman said as she lowered her eyes.

'We're not interested in whether you stole it. I want to know about you and Russell Atkins. When was the last time you saw him?'

'Not since they sacked me.'

Whitney drew in a breath. There wasn't a lot more they could do. They needed to investigate the woman further.

'We may wish to speak to you again, so don't leave the area. For now, we have no further questions. I'll call DC Baines and ask him to take you back home.'

Whitney and George left the interview room.

'How did you know to ask about Atkins?' she said to George once they were in the corridor.

'Gut instinct,' George said, shaking her head. 'Yes, I

know that's your territory, but I had this feeling and was correct.'

'But does it mean she murdered the two of them? Or is it a coincidence?'

'That's what we need to investigate. Have you decided whether you're going to put a tail on O'Brien?' George asked.

'We'll check his alibi first.'

She didn't trust O'Brien as far as she could throw him. If he was their killer she'd nail him for it.

## Chapter Twenty-Five

*The next one's lined up, and everything's coming along nicely. It's so easy. All I had to do was log into SnapMate and create a fake profile. No one bothers to check. It's ridiculous. But good for me.*

*I found a list of dos and don'ts online, to make sure my intended target won't guess he's being set up. To protect my identity, I go through a special network which keeps everything I do private by creating a multi-layered encryption. No one will find me. It never ceases to amaze me; there's nothing that can't be done on the Internet these days.*

*This latest pervert has already started asking questions with sexual undertones. I act innocent and naïve, pretending I don't understand.*

*But I do.*

*He's going to suffer. Big time.*

*I told him I was only thirteen, and he responded by saying what a perfect age it was. That I should be treated like a flower in bud. And he wanted to be the one to help this flower bloom.*

*He'll get more than a blooming flower from me, the sick, perverted bastard.*

*I didn't respond. Just told him how easy he was to talk to, and how I wished I had someone like him in my life because everything was so hard at the moment. I told him school sucks, my best friend has fallen out with me, and my parents treat me like a child instead of an adult.*

*He swallowed the whole lot. The stupid prick.*

*Even though he hinted, I didn't send him photos of me naked. I sent one of a young, fully-clothed teenage girl.*

*He sent a photo of himself and told me it was him when he was younger and then admitted to being in his late teens. Of course I know that's not the truth, as I know what he really looks like. He told me his real name, and I googled him. What an idiot. I found out for sure he's a disgusting pervert. He's at least thirty-five.*

*When he asked to meet, I said I couldn't get out in the evenings. He suggested I skip school. After pretending to deliberate for a while, I said yes but would have to meet somewhere close to school.*

*Of course he agreed, and we arranged to meet in a quiet spot I know very well.*

*And that's as far as I am with this arsehole.*

*Knife sharpened, sedative ready for the syringe, and I have everything ready to carry out the deed.*

*I'll arrive half an hour before him so I can set up and make sure he doesn't get away. I hope he enjoys his breakfast because it's the last meal he's going to have.*

*Apart from the special dinner I'm going to prepare for him.*

*He certainly won't be enjoying that.*

*But I'll enjoy watching. I'll also enjoy the look on his face when I take out my knife and he realises exactly what's going to happen. He won't be able to scream because his mouth will be taped up. He won't be able to do anything while he's being subjected to everything he deserves.*

*I really should take photos to show my other victims so they know what's going to happen to them. But where's the fun? It's better to let them think I'm just a silly woman who's eventually going to let them go.*

*But we all know how wrong they are.*

# Chapter Twenty-Six

George sat at the table in the university café, her hands wrapped around a steaming mug of hot chocolate. It wasn't what she usually drank, but she fancied something sweet and warm. The case was a puzzle. It seemed most likely they'd find the murderer in a vigilante group. Then again, this was at odds with what Vera said about it being far better to leave the men suffering the consequences of their actions, rather than being dead. In which case, who wrote the note to the radio station? It certainly wasn't Jimmy, so either he was working with someone else or he wasn't involved.

In the mix was Beryl Murphy. But was she too obvious, because of the connection between her and the Atkins'? Would she have been capable of writing the note? The language was very feminine. The person who wrote it was articulate, intelligent, and well read. They were fully aware of the political implications of what they were doing and what was happening in the country. Was that Beryl Murphy? On the face of it, no. But they needed to know more about her.

As to the nature of the deaths, you couldn't get more personal than mutilating the genital area. The fact the murderer suffocated the victims, pointed to the death itself not being as important as what happened beforehand. The murderer got off on the mutilation, so the victims could no longer groom young girls. Grooming was key. And if they didn't solve it, there would be more bodies. The letter told them there were more to come.

'George.' She glanced up at the sound of her name and smiled as she saw Tiffany standing beside her, holding a can of drink.

'Are you on your own?' she asked.

'I'm meant to be meeting some friends, but they haven't arrived yet.'

'Join me.' George gestured to the empty seat opposite her at the table.

Tiffany placed her drink on the table and pulled out the chair. George noticed how relaxed she seemed, unlike the previous times they'd spoken when she was permanently agitated.

'Are you working with Mum on the two murders?'

'Yes. Just mulling over the evidence we have. Which isn't much. Not that I'm allowed to talk about it. How are you doing? You seem a little better. Are you?'

'It's helped seeing the counsellor you suggested. We've gone from weekly to fortnightly. She's really happy with my progress.'

'Excellent. What about the nightmares?'

'I haven't had one for a while.' She smiled, and it lit up her whole face. She'd inherited Whitney's striking good looks, with curly dark hair and arresting chocolate brown eyes.

Without thinking, George reached over and covered Tiffany's hand with hers. 'I'm proud of you.'

Tiffany blushed. 'Thanks, George. I couldn't have done it without you and Mum.'

'We did it together,' she said.

There was an easy silence for a few moments.

'Do you have a minute?' George turned to see Yvonne, a professor in her department, holding a mug in one hand and a plate with a Danish pastry in the other.

She looked back at Tiffany.

'I'll leave you to it,' the young woman said. 'My friends are over there now.' She pointed in the direction of a group of students sitting at one of the large circular tables.

'If you're sure?'

'Of course.' She picked up her can, smiled, and left.

'Is it important?' George asked Yvonne.

'I wanted to know how you're holding up,' her colleague replied.

'What do you mean?'

'After the interview, and with Greg Barnes getting the position. It can't have been easy, especially as we all thought you were a dead cert.'

'Put it this way, I've felt better. But there's not a lot I can do about it.'

'Have you spoken to Robin and asked him why?'

'You mean you haven't heard?' George said, her body tense. 'Because you must be the only one.'

'No one said anything to me. I'm sure I would've heard if it was common knowledge.'

'The university isn't happy with the amount of time I'm working with police. Not only the "university",' she said, making quote marks with her fingers. 'It seems my colleagues aren't happy about it either. At least that's what I've been led to believe. Feedback from all sides was I lack focus. Me, lack focus? Have you ever heard such crap? When I look at the amount of time many of our colleagues spend in the staffroom ducking out of work when they can, I want to scream. But I'm the one without focus.' Her fists were tightly balled.

'It's ridiculous. I think part of it stems from jealousy.'

'Why would anyone be jealous of me?' George frowned.

'Try because you're so successful at what you do. You don't need the validation of other people. You don't take part in petty office politics, and I guess some of our narrow-minded colleagues thought they'd take the opportunity to stick the boot in.'

'Well, they've succeeded. I hope they feel good about it.'

'So, now what? Are you thinking of leaving?' Yvonne asked.

'Where would I go? I'm settled here. I have my house and a job I enjoy. And I'm putting all the theory into practice working with Whitney.'

'That's another thing they're jealous of, because you're getting involved in something exciting, whereas they're stuck here in their own little cocoons.'

George laughed. Yvonne was right. Even if she wasn't going to be associate professor, she had so much more going on. Not to mention the plaudits when she produced her research paper on working with the police and the murderous twins.

'I should listen to you more. I'm going to get on with my work as normal and keep my connections with Whitney.'

'Are you working with her at the moment?' Yvonne asked.

'Yes, the two murders where the men were mutilated. It's not an easy case.'

'I'm not surprised. I guess the public aren't keen to get

involved. They were paedophiles. Why would anyone want to help?'

'The trouble is, we can't let people get away with murder because we don't like their victims. It's important justice is brought against sexual offenders, but it doesn't mean allowing them to be murdered.'

'You're right, of course. Did you actually see the bodies?'

'I did, and it was not a pleasant sight. Pretty gruesome really.'

George's phone rang and she glanced at the screen. Whitney. 'I'm going to have to get this.'

'Hello.'

'Where are you?' Whitney asked.

'At work. Where do you think?'

'We've got another body. How soon can you get here?'

Crap. An additional body meant more evidence for the profile, but she wished another person hadn't lost his life. She glanced at her watch. She had a class in thirty minutes. It was only for an hour and then she'd be free.

'A couple of hours. Are you at the scene?'

'Yes, I'm here with Claire. It's the same MO. Why don't you meet me at the morgue, and we'll go over everything with Claire? In the meantime, I'll get back to station. I need to sort out putting a tail on O'Brien. Turns out his alibi isn't watertight. According to the chap he worked for, he was there at the start of the shift but then disappeared, which is why he hasn't been employed since.'

'Are you going to bring him in?'

'Not yet. We don't have any evidence linking him to it.'

'What about Vera?'

'Her alibis checked out, and from her interview I'm not convinced she's involved, but nothing's certain and she remains on our radar. And then, of course, there's Beryl

Murphy.' Whitney sighed. 'Lots of possibilities but nothing concrete.'

'We'll work it out together. I'll see you later.'

George finished the call and placed her phone back on the table. She glanced up at Yvonne.

'No wonder you continue working with the police. It's so exciting. When you were talking, your whole demeanour changed. You love being part of it, don't you?'

'This is only our second case together, but it makes such a change from being stuck in academia.'

'Have you thought about going into private practice and working full-time with them?'

'It's crossed my mind, but I love my research, my students, and the lecturing. I could do without the petty politics surrounding the place, but, that aside, I want to stay. It's perfect as it is. One foot in each camp.'

After articulating it to Yvonne, George realised she didn't want the associate professorship. If she'd been given the position, it would have severely impacted on her work with Whitney and the police. She would've been given more responsibility at the university and been a lot more involved with the higher echelons. Losing out was for the best. Her pride had been dented, but she could live with it.

'I, for one, am glad you're staying. You're the sanest person I know around here. If you left, I'd miss not having your take on things. The way you don't allow emotions to cloud your judgement.'

George smiled to herself. At one time she'd prided herself on her ability to detach from her emotions. Now, after working with Whitney, she wasn't so sure she wanted to be like that all the time.

She picked up her mug of chocolate and finished it.

'I'd better go and get ready for my next class,' she said.

Two hours later, George was in her car driving to the morgue. After pulling into the hospital car park and parking around the back, she walked into the building and down the corridor. Pushing open the door, she heard voices coming from Claire's office area.

'You can't blame yourself,' Claire said.

'Well, I do. She desperately wanted the job. But instead of supporting her, I constantly contacted her, assuming she'd drop everything and be at my beck and call,' Whitney said.

'Has she blamed you?'

'Of course not. You know what George's like. So typically stiff upper lip English with that posh upbringing of hers. She takes it on the chin. But whatever she says, we all know it was down to me.'

George couldn't allow this conversation to continue, so she walked into the office. 'Have you finished discussing me?'

'What are you doing here? I wasn't expecting you for another twenty minutes.' Whitney's face was flushed. Guilt?

'I managed to get away sooner than I thought. Anyway, back to your conversation. I don't appreciate being discussed. What happens at work is my business. No one is to blame except me, and that's that. Do you understand?'

Whitney and Claire exchanged glances. 'Yes, boss,' Whitney said, saluting.

Claire laughed, and after a few moments Whitney joined in, closely followed by George.

Perhaps Whitney had a point about her typical Englishness. But she couldn't help her background.

'Have you seen the body yet?' she asked her, changing the subject.

'No, I was waiting for you. Can we have a look now, Claire?'

'Good idea, and then I can get back on with my work. I've wasted far too much time acting as an agony aunt and not enough time doing my job.'

They followed her to the stainless-steel tables and the body of their latest victim.

'Have you identified him?' she asked.

'Yes. He was wearing one of those medical ID bracelets because he's diabetic, and the killer left it on his wrist. His name is Tony Adams. The team are getting more information for me,' Whitney said.

Whitney's phone pinged, indicating a text had arrived. She pulled it out of her pocket and glanced at the screen.

'It's from Ellie. Tony Adams, aged thirty-five. Lives at 20 Ascot Grove with his wife, Dawn, and family. He's an insurance broker. We'll go there next. Sorry, Claire. Carry on.'

Claire pulled down the arm of the overhead light, illuminating where she'd cut open the body and sewn it back up.

'The penis and testicles have been removed, only this time the work is a little neater. Possibly because the murderer has become more confident in what they're doing. The body was naked, as before, apart from the bracelet and his socks. There are ligature marks around his wrists and ankles from being tied up, again with cable ties. I looked at the stomach contents, and he was fed his genitals. There was a tiny hole in his leg from where he was injected. I've sent his blood to toxicology for testing, to confirm it was a sedative. Time of death, between eight p.m. and midnight on Tuesday.'

'Any trace evidence?' Whitney asked.

'There was semen under his fingernails, possibly from masturbation and not washing his hands after. There are also carpet fibres on the back of his head. I'm going to check whether they're from the same carpet as the previous two victims.'

'Do we know yet where the carpet comes from?' George asked.

'Not yet. I've got someone working on it. Interestingly, mixed in with the carpet fibre I found bits of straw. They weren't present in the other two victims, though I'm going to go back and have another check to make sure nothing was missed.'

'So the body could have been laid on top of some carpet which was lying on straw?' Whitney asked.

'That's a likely scenario.'

'Could the murders have taken place in a barn?' George suggested. 'The soil under the first victim's fingernails could have come from a farm area.'

'Again, it's possible,' Claire said.

'Well, at least we're getting somewhere. Next step is to find out more about Tony Adams and whether he had a predilection for young girls. We'll leave you to it, Claire. Once you have the tox results and have written your report, please let me know,' Whitney said.

'Don't I always?' Claire rolled her eyes towards the ceiling before turning her back on them.

George and Whitney left the morgue and made their way down the corridor to the double doors leading outside.

'What you heard before,' Whitney started.

'Forget about it. It doesn't matter. And for the record, it really isn't your fault. Funnily enough, earlier I had an epiphany about the whole thing.'

'A what?' Whitney exclaimed.

'An epiphany. It means…'

'I know what it means, it's just I don't know anyone who'd use it in everyday conversation. Anyway, tell me about this *epiphany*.'

'I don't want to be a professor. I'm happy being senior lecturer.'

'What the hell made you think that? I thought your academic career was what you valued most.'

'It was. Until I started working with you. I've realised the academic world is only half-fulfilling. The other half lies in the application of my discipline. Working in the real world and seeing how theory can actually help.' She gave an embarrassed laugh. 'I probably sound pompous, but it's how I feel. Staying as a senior lecturer means I can have the best of both worlds. So in actual fact, my backstabbing, two-faced colleagues—'

'Whoa… too much emotional stuff, if you don't mind,' Whitney interrupted.

'By going behind my back, they did me a huge favour. I certainly don't blame you one iota for what happened.' She paused for a moment. 'Actually, I do, because if we hadn't met, and I hadn't started working with you, we wouldn't be together discussing the case.'

Whitney shook her head. 'This is getting way too deep.'

'Don't you like deep?' she teased.

'Not at the moment. Right now, we need to see Tony Adams' family and break the news to them. Not something I'm looking forward to.'

# Chapter Twenty-Seven

Whitney parked outside the home belonging to Tony and Dawn Adams. It was a modern semi-detached house in one of Lenchester's newest developments. All the houses looked identical, like small boxes, but they were very popular, especially with first-time buyers. The road was adjacent to a small park area, which had swings and other play equipment for young children. She grimaced. If he was a paedophile, it would've been the perfect location for him, especially if he liked young children as well as teenaged girls.

'Ready?'

'Yes,' George said, picking up her bag, which she'd placed next to her feet, and opening the car door.

As with most new houses in the development, there was only a couple of yards between the pavement and the newly painted, white front door. Whitney knocked and waited. A woman in her early thirties answered; two children who looked around three or four followed close behind.

'Dawn Adams?' Whitney said.

'Yes,' she said.

'I'm DCI Whitney Walker and this is Dr George Cavendish. We're with Lenchester CID. Please may we come in?' She showed her warrant card.

'What's it about?'

'We'd rather speak to you inside.'

She opened the door wider and stepped aside, allowing them to enter. 'What is it?' she repeated, panic etched across her face. 'Has something happened to Tony?'

'Is there somewhere we can sit down to talk without the children?' Whitney said. She hated this part of her job so much. There was no way to make it any easier. Dawn Adams already knew there was something wrong.

'Wait here and I'll put the TV on for them.'

They stood in silence until she returned, and then followed her into the kitchen. Whitney waited until they were all seated at the table.

'I'm sorry to inform you, we have found the body of a man we believe to be your husband. We've preliminarily identified him from the medical ID bracelet he was wearing.'

Dawn stared at them as though she hadn't quite understood what she'd been told.

'Are you sure it's him?' she said. 'He went away to a conference two days ago. I'm expecting him home tonight. It could be someone else.'

'Do you have a recent photo of him?' Whitney asked gently.

'Over there on the fridge.'

Whitey stared at the photos. They were an attractive, happy family at an amusement park. The type you'd see on washing powder commercials. Except beneath the façade was something dark and despicable. 'I'm sorry, Dawn, but our victim is your husband. There's no mistake, but we will need you to make a formal identification.'

Dawn leaned on the table and let out a low moan. 'No. No. He can't be dead. He can't. What am I going to tell the children?'

'Is there someone we can call for you?' she asked.

'My mum lives in the next street.'

'What's her name and number? I'll phone and ask her to come around,' George said.

Dawn gave her the details, her voice mechanical, and George left the room and went into the hall.

'Don't say anything to the children just yet. Wait until your mum arrives. Hopefully, Dr Cavendish will manage to get in touch with her and she'll be here soon.'

'What happened to him?' Dawn choked back a sob.

'We're treating his death as suspicious. His body was found in a woodland on the edge of the city.'

'I don't understand. He was in Leeds; how can he have been here in Lenchester?'

'When did you last speak to Tony?'

'Yesterday morning when he left. He said it would be too difficult to speak while he was away because they had no free time. He was due home this evening. He…' Tears dropped from her eyes and rolled down her cheeks.

George walked into the room and stood beside Dawn. 'I've spoken to your mum and she's going to be here in five minutes.'

They remained silent while the distraught woman cried, until she finally pulled herself together and sat upright in the chair.

'How was he murdered?' Dawn asked.

'We won't know for certain until we've heard back from the pathologist,' Whitney said.

This part of her job sucked. The woman was entitled to know what had happened to her husband. Whether she could cope with it was a different matter. Her life was never going to be the same again once it was in the public domain.

'Does this have anything to do with those other two men?' she asked, looking at Whitney and then George.

'There are some similarities, and it's an area we will be investigating,' Whitney conceded.

'It said on the TV the other men's tackle had been removed, and they were both grooming young girls online. Tony would never do anything like that.'

'Like I said, there are some similarities between the cases, but I don't want to go into detail until we have all the facts. Are you up to us asking you some questions about Tony?' Whitney asked gently.

'Yes, I think so,' Dawn said.

'You mentioned he went to a conference in Leeds. Do you have any details about it?'

'No, I don't. You'll have to ask his work, Pyke Insurance Brokers.'

Whitney knew of the firm; they were the largest in the area. She'd been to school with Arthur Pyke's daughter.

'How did he get to the conference?'

'He drove. Have you found his car?' Dawn asked.

'Not yet. But we're looking for it. Does he have a laptop or a computer he uses at home?'

'He has a laptop which he takes with him wherever he goes.'

'Do you have a family computer?'

'No. I have my tablet and the children have their own.'

Children so young with a tablet? Crazy. They'd be having their own mobile phones next.

'Had Tony been acting suspiciously? Did he go off on

his own for periods of time?' She hated broaching the subject, but it had to be done.

'This house isn't large enough to disappear in, especially when you have two small children. The only time he's alone is if I take them out somewhere or if we go to my mum's. This has to be a case of mistaken identity. There's no way he'd ever go after young girls. He wouldn't. I know him. We've been together since we were in our early twenties. He couldn't possibly do anything like that. I...' Her voice cracked and a low groan spilled from her mouth.

There was a knock on the front door. 'I'll go,' George said.

After a few minutes, during which time she could hear muffled voices, George came back in. 'This is Mrs Watson, Dawn's mum,' she said to Whitney.

The woman rushed to her daughter's side and pulled her close. Dawn broke down sobbing again.

'I think she's had enough,' Mrs Watson said.

'I understand,' Whitney said. 'We'll come back another time. We do need a formal identification of Tony, sometime today or tomorrow.'

'I'll bring her down,' Mrs Watson said.

Whitney pulled a card from her pocket and gave it to her. 'You can reach me on this number. I'm very sorry for your loss, Dawn.'

They left the house and were about to get into the car when Whitney's phone pinged. She looked at the text. 'They've found his car in Wessex Street. SOCO is already there. Let's take a look, to see if there's anything which might be of use. I also need them to go to the Adams' house, but it will have to wait for now.'

They drove to Wessex Street and headed towards the cordon which had been placed around the car.

'A BMW. He must have been doing well,' she muttered to herself.

'Good afternoon,' one of the forensics team said as they approached.

'Jenny. Colin. How are you both doing?' Whitney said.

'Could be better,' Colin said.

'But could be worse,' Jenny kidded.

Whitney pulled on some disposable gloves and opened the passenger door, noting the laptop on the front seat and the phone connected to a mount on the dashboard. 'Have you finished with these?' she asked Jenny, who was busy snapping with her camera.

'Yes.'

'Great. Put them in a bag for me and I'll take them back to the station.'

Jenny picked up the laptop and phone and dropped them into separate bags. 'Here you are,' she said, handing the bags to Whitney.

'Thanks. We'll leave you to it.'

She was anxious to get back and have the phone analysed.

As soon as they arrived at the station, Whitney made a beeline for Ellie's desk. 'Here's the victim's phone. Go through it and see what you can find. Send his laptop to Mac's boys.'

'Okay, guv. I've got a message for you from Detective Superintendent Jamieson. He wants to see you in his office as soon as you return,' Ellie said.

Whitney rolled her eyes. That was all she needed. She supposed she'd better get it over with. 'Okay. I'm on my way. I want a background check on Adams. Someone needs to interview his family, friends, and colleagues. CCTV close to the site of the body also needs examining. Ask Matt to distribute the work.'

Jamieson's door was shut, so she knocked and waited. After there was no reply, she knocked again and pressed on the handle to open the door. He was sitting behind his desk with his chair turned, so all she could see was his back.

'Sir? You wanted to see me?'

He took a few seconds before swivelling around to face her.

'Walker, come in,' he said.

Red circles lined his eyes. Had he been crying?

'Is everything okay?'

His eyes glazed over, and he was silent for a few seconds. 'Yes, I'm fine. It's just … Just … it's something personal. Nothing you can help with.'

'You wanted to see me?' she repeated.

'Yes, I want to know about the case now we have a third victim. We'll need to do another press conference.'

'It's the same MO as the previous murders. We're waiting on final details from Dr Dexter. We've found the victim's car and belongings. CCTV is being looked at and we'll be speaking to those people who were close to him. We've interviewed members of a local vigilante group, and I have one of its members being tailed. We suspect it could be a man and a woman working together, and we're putting together a profile.'

'Can you handle the press conference on your own?'

She stared at him. Something serious must be wrong if he wanted to keep out of the limelight. But she wasn't the person to ask about it.

'Of course, sir. I'll liaise with Melissa in PR and arrange a time.'

'Tell me something. You're a single parent. How do you cope?'

So that was it. He was getting a divorce.

'It wasn't easy, but I had help from my folks and we managed. We had to. Why do you ask?' she said before having time to stop herself. Did she really want to go down this road?

'My wife has left us. Me and the kids.'

'Sorry to hear that, sir. How old are your children?'

'Fourteen and fifteen. Both girls.'

Whitney winced. Two teenage girls to look after. She wouldn't wish it on anyone.

'It takes some adjusting, but I'm sure it will be fine.' She hoped she was convincing. Because if he treated his kids in the same pompous way he treated the people he worked with, she imagined there would be fireworks.

'She's moved in with the father of one of my daughter's friends. Broken two marriages. Two families. How could she?'

Whitney moved uncomfortably in her seat. This was the first time he'd talked about anything really personal, and she wasn't sure how to deal with it. Especially as tomorrow he'd undoubtedly be back to his usual officious self. Did she make George feel this way when she was blurting things out?

'I'm not sure. It's hard to know what to do in these situations. Maybe you should take some time off work,' she suggested.

'I think I might. I'll leave you to get on with the investigation. It goes without saying you keep our conversation to yourself.'

'Of course, sir. I won't mention it to anyone.'

'Good. You can go now. The next time I see you, we'd better be further along in the investigation. We have a serial killer on our hands, and people will be demanding answers.'

She'd known he'd be back to his old self soon, but this must be a record.

'Yes, sir. I'm onto it.'

# Chapter Twenty-Eight

Whitney headed back into the incident room, still contemplating the weirdness of her boss spilling his problems.

'Is everything okay?' George asked.

'Why?' She frowned.

'The look on your face.'

'It's Jamieson. He's got a few personal issues, and for some strange reason he decided to confide in me. I'm trying to fathom why.'

'Easy. He wanted someone he could trust,' George said, shrugging like it was no big deal.

'Me? The thorn in his side. The person who won't put up with his ridiculous idiosyncrasies.'

'Yes, exactly. He knows you'll tell it as you see it. Maybe it's what he needed,' George said.

'Maybe,' she said, not totally convinced.

She picked up a pen. On the map, she marked where Tony Adams's body had been found, and also where they'd located his car. She had more important things to worry about than Jamieson.

'Okay, the body was found about a mile from his car,

and when we look at where the other two bodies were located, they're all within a three-mile radius of each other. What does it tell us?' she asked George.

'It confirms the murderer is a local or has an extensive knowledge of the area. They know the places to leave the bodies where they'll be found fairly quickly, but not where they'd be caught depositing them. As for the car, if Tony Adams had arranged to meet the killer, thinking he was meeting a teen girl, we need to look at areas close by. Potential meeting places. We should also ask ourselves how the murderer accosted and sedated him without anyone seeing.'

'That's what bothers me. How would the offender move a sedated body?' Whitney said.

'Injected sedatives can start working within a few minutes. While the victims were half sedated, the murderer might have managed to move them,' George suggested.

'Alternatively, what if Adams didn't want a scene, so he agreed to get in the car to talk? Assuming he knew how vigilante groups operate once they'd found a paedophile, he'd want to persuade them not to expose him by filming him for social media. He also wouldn't want them to inform the police. And if our murderer is a woman, he wouldn't have felt so threatened. Once she'd got him in the car, it would be easy for her to stick a needle in him.'

George was silent for a moment. 'It seems a more likely scenario,' she agreed.

'Guv,' Ellie said, coming up to them. 'I've gone through the phone contacts and got into his texts. He had a meeting arranged with someone called Vi at three o'clock on Sussex Street, by the telephone box.'

'Around the corner from Wessex Street, where he parked his car.' Whitney pointed at the street on the map.

'Does it say where exactly they were going to go? A café maybe?' she asked Ellie.

'No. Vi suggested the meeting place and said they could go somewhere to talk but didn't say where. I know the street, and there aren't any cafés close by. It's secluded and backs onto Springford Park. There are no houses on the Sussex Street side, as it leads into an industrial estate.'

'An ideal place to lure someone. What else did they say about the meeting?'

'Nothing, apart from how much he was looking forward to seeing her and how lovely she looked in her photo.' Ellie grimaced.

'Is her photo on his phone?' George asked.

'Yes. Nothing intimate, just a picture of a young girl with long blonde hair, who looks about thirteen or fourteen,' Ellie said.

'Was Vi's photo on either of the other two victims' phones, by any chance?'

'No. I checked both of them. There's no crossover.'

'Damn. That would've made things too easy,' George said.

'Back to Tony Adams. Is there anything else from the texts?' Whitney asked, sensing they were beginning to put the pieces together.

'He'd been messaging with Vi every day for several weeks,' Ellie said. 'More so during the week, rather than weekends.'

'That makes sense. If he was with his family, he wouldn't be able to text so freely,' George said.

'What were their conversations about?' Whitney asked.

'She told him all the problems she had at home. How her parents were treating her like a child and she was fed up of them not letting her grow up. He told her he wouldn't be like that. He could tell how mature she was for her age, and he wished he could do something to help her.' Ellie grimaced again. 'The sick pervert. It makes my skin crawl.'

'Mine, too. But we have to put our feelings to one side and concentrate on catching the murderer.' She sympathised with the young officer. When Whitney had been her age, she'd have felt the exact same way. But they couldn't cherry-pick which laws to uphold.

'Who actually suggested the meeting?' George asked.

'She did.'

'Interesting,' George said, nodding. 'It would have confirmed to him he'd done a good job.'

'Wouldn't he suspect anything was wrong?' Whitney said.

'Why? He thought he was talking to a young girl. Remember, people believe what they want to believe. The thought he was being duped probably didn't even enter his head. He's a respectable man with a good job and young family. He was no doubt convinced he was invincible. Ellie, how long has he been a member of the site, and what other girls has he been talking to?' George asked.

'I got into his account directly from his phone. According to his status, he's been a member for twelve months. I'll look back into all of his chats and see what I can find,' Ellie said.

'Good. I want details of anyone he's met up with,' Whitney said.

'Yes, guv.'

'Were you able to track down Bea, the girl who Keane had arranged to meet?'

'No. I asked Mac to take a look, and I'm still waiting to hear back.'

'Okay, carry on checking out Tony Adams' past messages and look at the conversations Keane had with

Bea so we can compare them with conversations Atkins had. See if we can pull anything together which might help.'

'Can Ellie manage all that?' George asked.

'Of course she can. She's the best researcher this force has ever had.' Whitney smiled at the blushing young officer.

'It won't take me long to extract the information you need,' Ellie said. 'What would you like first?'

'It doesn't matter,' Whitney said as she went over to the board and wrote the name Vi under Tony Adams' name.

Her phone rang.

'Walker.'

'It's Frank. O'Brien's sitting in Diablos café in Wood Street with a young girl and an older woman.'

'How long's he been there?' she asked.

'We tailed him here from his house. He went in about twenty minutes ago, the woman arrived five minutes later, and the girl has just joined them. They're sitting by the window, and I can see them from where we're parked on the other side of the road.'

'Describe the older woman.'

'Short grey hair, in her early sixties, small.'

'Sounds like Vera Smith. Keep an eye on them. We'll be there shortly. If they leave, tail the girl so we can find out who she is.'

'Okay, guv.'

She ended the call and turned to George.

'Jimmy O'Brien and Vera are meeting with a young girl in a local café. Let's go and see what they're up to.'

The café was situated next to the bus station, and she parked in a side street out of sight. They walked around the corner, keeping on the side of the café. She spotted Frank in his black Vauxhall Astra but didn't go over in case they were seen by Jimmy and he attempted to scarper.

'What's the plan?' George asked. 'Do you want them back at the station?'

'We'll go into the café and sit with them. I think we'll get more from them if we keep it low key. We'll pretend to be surprised to see them in there.'

George pushed open the door and they headed inside. Whitney glanced to the right and saw the three of them engrossed in conversation. Vera was sitting on one bench next to the young girl, who was next to the window, and Jimmy sat opposite.

She turned and made her way towards them, with George following.

'Jimmy. Vera,' she said as she approached.

The shocked expressions on their faces were almost comical. They couldn't have looked guiltier if they'd tried.

'DCI Walker,' Vera said. 'What brings you here?'

'I could ask you the same thing.'

'We…we…' Vera glanced furtively at the young girl beside her.

'Vigilante work?' Whitney suggested. 'I'm sure you won't mind if we join you.' She slid in next to Jimmy, and George sat next to Vera.

'Would it matter if we did?' Jimmy growled.

'We can always do this at the station.'

'Do what? We're not doing anything.' Jimmy's body stiffened. 'We're out having a coffee. Is it about the murders? Because, if so, I've already given you my alibis. So stop hounding me just because I've got a record.'

'Jimmy, calm down.' Vera leaned over and rested her hand over his clenched fist. 'What do you want to know, Chief Inspector?'

Whitney glanced at the young girl next to Vera, who'd

kept her head lowered and had avoided looking in her direction.

'Perhaps you could introduce me to your friend.' She nodded at the girl.

'This is Polly; she's my goddaughter. Polly, say hello to the Chief Inspector and Dr Cavendish.'

The girl glanced up. 'Hello,' she muttered.

'How old are you, Polly?' George asked.

'Sixteen.'

That surprised Whitney. She'd have put money on her only being thirteen or fourteen.

'Do you often hang out with Vera and Jimmy?' George asked.

The girl flushed a deep shade of red. 'No.'

'So why today? Are you doing some vigilante work for them?' Whitney said.

Polly turned her head and stared out of the window.

'We're not doing anything illegal,' Vera said.

'Then enlighten me; what are you doing? Actually, let me guess. You're using Polly as a decoy.'

'We haven't got anything planned. We're talking to her about it, to see if she'd be interested in helping us,' Vera said.

'And are you, Polly?' she asked.

She shrugged. 'I don't know,' she muttered.

Whitney let out an exasperated sigh. No good could come from getting youngsters involved in this sort of work.

'Jimmy. Vera. What were you doing Tuesday just gone, between eight and midnight?'

'I was at home alone, watching telly until nine, and then I went to bed,' Vera said.

'Jimmy?' she asked after a few seconds, as he clearly wasn't going to answer.

'At the pub,' he grunted.

'Can anyone vouch for you?' she asked.

He leaned back in his seat and folded his arms tightly across his chest. 'Ask Len. We went out for a drink together,' he finally said.

'To discuss Justice Hunters work?' She tried to make eye contact, but he stared straight ahead.

'Maybe.'

'Which pub?'

'The Red Lion.'

'What time did you leave?'

'I don't remember. I had a skinful. It was late.'

'How did you get home?'

'Taxi.'

'Do you have the name of the taxi firm?'

He turned his head and glared at her, his eyes bulging. 'No, I fucking don't. Go to the pub and ask them, and stop trying to trip me up. I didn't kill anyone. Leave me alone and start looking for the real culprit.'

Whitney stared right back into his eyes. She'd faced off against much worse than him. His size and aggression didn't intimidate her. 'That's exactly what we're doing. And by the way, your alibi for the first murder didn't check out. According to your supervisor at Hamilton's, you left early.'

'Well, I was there for some of the time,' Jimmy said, his tone not so aggressive now.

'Where did you go after you left Hamilton's?' she asked.

'Home. And before you ask, no one can back up my story.'

'Why didn't you tell us the truth before?'

'Why do you think?' Jimmy retorted.

'Has there been another murder?' Vera asked, interrupting.

'Yes, there has,' she said.

'Good,' Jimmy snapped. 'We don't want filth like that on our streets.'

Whitney caught George's eye. It was time to leave. They were getting nowhere fast. Jimmy would continually proclaim his innocence, and at the moment, they had nothing to tie him to the crimes.

# Chapter Twenty-Nine

On the way back to the car, after meeting with Jimmy, Vera and Polly, Whitney's phone rang. It was Becky from Radio Lenchester. Crap. She probably wanted permission to use the letter. But she couldn't. Not yet.

'Hello.'

'I've got another one,' the head of news said, dispensing with any formalities.

'A letter?'

'Yes. It arrived in the post today. I've only just got to my desk, so I'm not sure what time it arrived.'

'Have you opened it?'

'No, because I recognised the way my name and address were typed and thought it was from the murderer. Plus, I don't get many personal letters, as everything comes via email. Do you want me to open it?' Becky asked.

'No. Don't do anything. I'm coming over. I should be there within twenty minutes.'

'Okay. I'll see you then.'

George frowned. 'What's that about?' she asked as Whitney ended the call.

'Becky from the radio station. There's another letter from the murderer. She didn't open it because she recognised the typing on the envelope.'

'Do you want me to come with?' George asked.

'No, it's fine. I'll go on my own. I'll drop you back at the station.'

'Okay. Let me know if you need me. If not, I'll pop in tomorrow morning. Now the students are on Easter break, it's easier to come and go as I please.'

'I'll text and let you know one way or the other.'

'How's it going at work, now?' Whitney asked once they were in the car and driving towards the station.

'Fine. I'm keeping my head down, so you don't have to keep asking me all the time. Nothing's going to change, and when the new associate professor arrives, I'll treat him exactly the same way as I treat everybody else.'

'In other words, you won't be speaking much to him.' Whitney grinned.

George scowled in her direction, and then the muscles around her face relaxed. 'You're so funny,' she said, rolling her eyes towards the sky.

When they got to the police station, George got out and Whitney carried on to meet with Becky. There was a small car park at the back of the radio station, and she managed to find a space. She walked in the front door and up to reception.

'DCI Walker to see Becky Ellis.'

She waited while the receptionist called, and after a few minutes Becky came downstairs to greet her.

'You got here quickly,' Becky said.

'I had the siren on.'

They hurried up the stairs into the sales area and through to the newsroom where there were five people sitting at desks working. Becky led Whitney into her office, closing the door behind them.

'I need permission to release the first letter soon. I can't hang onto it for much longer. Management will go ballistic if they find out.'

'Let's have a look at this latest one and we'll discuss it,' Whitney said as she looked at the type written envelope sitting face up on the desk.

Becky pointed to it. 'Look at the way this person has put my name. Ms R Ellis c/o Lenchester Radio Station, and the address. It's so formal and very different from the way most people send a letter.'

'You're right.' She'd discuss with George what the formality meant.

After pulling on some gloves, she picked up the enve-lope from the desk and turned it over in her hands, looking to see if there was anything suspicious about it. It was the same as the last one. An innocuous white envelope.

She slid her finger under the seal and opened it as care-fully as she could. The sheet of white A4 paper had been neatly folded.

*Dear Rebecca Ellis,*

*I am writing to you again because you seem to have disregarded my first letter. This was either because you didn't receive it, or you chose to ignore it.*

*If it is the latter, you obviously have no sense of what's important in life and you don't deem my mission newsworthy. If that is the case, shame on you. You don't deserve to be in the position you are. It is important for people to know the ineptness of our legal system and our police force, for allowing men like Russell Atkins, Kelvin Keane, and Tony Adams to go free. Yes, I'm telling you the name of my latest conquest, so you know for sure I'm the one who is ridding the world of these monsters. Action is eloquence.*

*I have attached a copy of my original letter and expect to hear an item on the radio outlining exactly what I've done and why I did it. I will give you until the end of the week. If nothing is aired, I will go to one of the newspapers, and you will have lost your scoop, as they say in the media world.*

'A third victim?' Becky asked. She'd been reading over Whitney's shoulder.

'Yes, we're announcing it later.'

'What now?'

'Leave it with me while I discuss with my Super how much we can let you release as a news item.'

'At the moment, you're in control because I've agreed not to say anything, but the papers won't be so accommodating. If they get hold of it, you won't have any choice in the matter. The news will be spread across the pages. What I'd like to do is to read out both letters on air or release extracts from them,' Becky said.

'That's why I'm going to talk to Detective Superintendent Jamieson,' Whitney said. 'As soon as I know anything, I'll be in touch. I appreciate you not opening it before I arrived.'

Whitney folded the letter and envelope into separate evidence bags.

'Have you got time to look at one of the studios this time?' Becky asked.

She didn't want to appear too keen, like a radio station groupie. Or "anorak" as they were known in radio land, according to Becky.

'Yes, I think so. Who's on at the moment?' She actually knew Steve Evans was presenting. He was one of her favourites. She always listened when she was in the car.

'It's the afternoon show with Steve. I'm sure he won't mind us going in to have a chat.'

She followed Becky downstairs to reception and through the back to where the studios were. They stopped outside a door which had the *on air* light illuminated.

Through the glass, Steve was talking into the microphone.

'We'll wait until he's finished and has put on the next track,' Becky said. 'It shouldn't be too long.'

'Sure.'

Her phone rang and she it pulled from her pocket.

'Sorry, I've got to get this,' she said as she checked the screen and saw it was work.

She walked away and answered the call.

'Walker,' she said.

'Hello, guv,' Matt said. 'We need you back here, PDQ. Amy Bond called in, without her mother. She wants to talk to you about Russell Atkins.'

## Chapter Thirty

Whitney rushed into the station, stopping at the incident room to collect Matt so they could speak to Amy Bond together. What did she want to tell her? Would it help progress the case? This could be the break they were looking for.

'Is Amy on her own?' she asked Matt, finding him sitting at his desk.

'She's with a friend. I've put them in interview room one and said you'd be with them as soon as you returned.'

'Did she elaborate at all?'

'No. She was very cloak and dagger. All I could get out of her was she had something to tell you, and she wouldn't speak to anyone else.'

'Shouldn't they be in school?'

'School broke up at the end of last week for Easter,' he said.

Of course. She should've known. Tiffany was off uni at the moment and working most days at the garden centre close to where they lived. Even straight after the kidnapping, her daughter had kept on with the job. Whitney had been glad because it gave her some normality during such a harrowing time.

'Okay. Let's see what she's got. George believed she wasn't telling us everything in her previous interview, but we didn't push it because we didn't want to cause difficulties with her mother.'

When they entered the interview room, Amy was sitting next to her friend, chatting. They both looked older than their fourteen years, as they were wearing make-up and trendy clothes. When Amy noticed her, she blushed.

'Hello, Amy. I understand you want to talk to me,' Whitney said. 'You already know DS Price. He's going to sit in with us. And you are?' She looked directly at Amy's friend.

'I'm Sasha Newman.'

'It's good of you to be so supportive. Amy, would you like to talk to us alone, or would you prefer if Sasha stayed?'

'Sasha knows everything, so if it's okay, I'd like her to stay,' Amy said.

'Of course. Legally we can't interview you without an adult present, but if you're only here to give us some information, that's different.'

'I want to tell you about Billy, who you said was Russell Atkins, but I don't want anyone to know, especially not my parents.'

'I can't promise anything. It really depends on what you tell me. I know it's hard, but this is a criminal investigation, and we have to catch the murderer. If you tell us anything helpful, we'll be extremely grateful. But there's a chance your information might not stay within these walls. Do you understand?'

Amy nodded.

'I'd like to record our conversation, if that's okay with you?'

'Do you have to?' Panic shrouded the young girl's face.

'Not if you'd rather I didn't. I'll take notes.' Whitney didn't want to push it, so she opened her notebook and took a pen from her bag. 'What do you want to talk about?' she asked gently.

'You asked if I'd ever met him before, and I said no. Because Mum was there. It wasn't the truth. I did arrange to meet, thinking it was Billy, but he turned out to be an older man. We met in the park. I was sitting on a bench, and he came to sit next to me. He started talking, and I said I was waiting to meet someone. He told me it was him. I got up to leave, but he grabbed hold of my arm and made me sit back down. He…' Her voice cracked, and tears filled her eyes.

Whitney passed her a tissue from the box on the table. 'Take it steady. I know this is hard, but you're doing the right thing by telling me.'

Amy wiped her eyes and sniffed. 'After he made me sit down, he started being nice and talking about how well we got on. He said we were friends. He had hold of my hand so I couldn't get away. I didn't know what to do. I couldn't get to my phone, as it was in my bag. So I pretended to play along and talked to him, hoping he'd let go of me and I could run.' She started to cry again.

'Would you like a glass of water?' Whitney asked.

Amy nodded.

'Matt, could you get some water?'

They sat in silence when he left the room, while Amy drew in some breaths to gather herself. 'Before I could make my getaway, he reminded me of some photos he had. For a laugh, we'd exchanged naked photos of ourselves.' Her voice faded.

'They weren't among the photos you sent to me,' Whitney said.

'I deleted them.'

Matt came back into the room with two glasses of water, which he put down in front of the girls. Amy took a sip.

'After he reminded you about the photos, what did he say?' Whitney asked, sensing it was about to get even more painful for the young girl.

'He told me again how much he liked me and didn't want me to leave. He said he'd booked a special room for us to have lunch in private. I told him I had to go home, but he laughed and told me not to be stupid, because he knew I'd arranged to be out for the day so I could meet him. It was during the last half-term in February. He said if I didn't go with him he'd make sure photos of me were put everywhere on the Internet, and he'd send them to my parents and all my friends.'

If Russell Atkins wasn't already dead, Whitney could've murdered him herself. No one with even a shred of decency would do something like that. She tensed in antici-pation of what was coming next.

'You're doing really well, Amy.'

'He took me to a small hotel, where he'd rented a room. He ordered room service and we had lunch. All the time, he was saying how much he liked me and how this was going to be such an enjoyable time. I knew what he wanted, and I couldn't get out of it. Even when he went to the bathroom and I thought about running away, I remem-bered the photos. I couldn't do that to my family. Or myself.' She went silent, and her eyes glazed over as she stared into space.

'Did he force you to have sex with him?' Whitney asked.

Amy nodded and leaned forward on the table, burying her head in her arms. Sasha put her arms around Amy's shoulders. She looked at Whitney over the top of Amy, shaking her head. She was a good friend.

'Amy, you've been really brave telling us what happened, and I'm sure we're going to be able to keep this between us. We have a specialist team here who can help you with what's happened. Would you like me to make an appointment for you? It's all strictly confidential.'

Amy glanced at her friend, who nodded. 'Yes, please.'

'I'll do it now.' She picked up her phone from the table and went out of the room. She keyed in the number.

'Maureen Ash speaking.'

'It's DCI Walker here. I'd like to make an appointment for an Amy Bond to speak to you. She was subject to a sexual assault some months ago, and I've suggested she meet with you. Can you see her now?'

'Yes. I'm free at the moment.'

'I'll bring her up. She's with her friend.'

Whitney ended the call and went back into the interview room.

'Maureen Ash is available. I'll take you up there in a moment.'

'Okay.'

'If you want to speak to me again, here's my card. You can phone any time, day or night, if you want someone to talk to.'

Amy gave Whitney a watery smile. 'Thank you. It was horrible reliving it, but you have to know the truth so you can see what a monster he was. I'm glad he's dead. And I don't care if you never catch the person who did it.'

'I understand how you feel, but it's my job to find and

punish criminals. We can't leave it for people to take the law into their own hands.' Her words sounded trite, especially considering what Amy had gone through. 'Would you like me to arrange for someone to take you both home after you've spoken to Maureen?'

'No, thanks. We're going for coffee. I'm not expected back until after five.'

Whitney took them to Maureen's office. Her body tensed as she watched the young girl go in. Would she ever trust anyone again? If she was Amy's mum, she'd want to know what had happened, but only Amy could tell her.

Whitney returned to her desk. Something had to be done. This killer wasn't going to rest at three victims. She pulled out her phone and keyed in George's number.

'Hello, Whitney.'

'I've just talked to Amy Bond. She came in to see me. You were right about her lying. That lowlife arsewipe Atkins raped her, threatening to reveal the naked photos she'd sent him.'

George was quiet for a moment. 'The bastard. I'm not surprised. What about the letter?'

'Definitely from the murderer and, again, very articulate and political. I'll show you when you come in. Right now, I've got a plan which I think is the only way we can catch our killer. We're going to run our own sting. We already know quite a bit about the murderer, and we've seen the messages they've sent. It will work. Come in tomorrow morning and we'll set it up. Because if we don't, we know there's going to be another murder.'

'Good idea. I'll be with you at eight, if that's not too early?' George said.

'Eight's fine. We need time to get it all sorted. I'll see you in the morning.'

She ended the call and went to Jamieson's office, as she

needed him to sign off on the idea. She knocked on the door and waited for him to call her in.

'Yes, Walker?' he asked.

'I'd like permission for us to run a sting on the Snap-Mate site. We need to catch the murderer, and this seems the best solution.'

'Do you have any leads at all?'

'The murderer sent another letter to the radio station. At the moment they've agreed not to release either of them, but I don't know how long I can hold them off.'

'Maybe they should release them. It might help us. Someone from the public could come forward with evidence.'

'It could also incite further crimes against paedophiles. The way the letters are worded, I don't want to risk it.'

'Okay, your call.'

Whitney's eyes widened. He never ceased to surprise her.

'Thank you, sir. Now about this sting. We'd like to put the wheels in motion tomorrow. It involves creating a fake profile on the site and pretending to be an eighteen-year-old boy.'

'Who are you going to use?'

'Dr Cavendish. With her knowledge of the criminal mind, she'll know what language is needed to carry out the sting.'

'Wouldn't a male officer be better?'

'I don't believe so.'

'Do we have any other expertise on the force we can leverage?'

'Not at such short notice, but I know of someone we could ask to assist us.'

'Okay. You get on with it, and leave the paperwork to me.'

'Yes, sir.'

She left his office and hurried back to hers. She was going to visit the homes the social worker had suggested for Rob and her mum, shortly. But before that, she had a call to make, and she suspected this person would be very surprised to hear from her.

# Chapter Thirty-One

'Listen up, everyone,' Whitney said once they'd arrived in the office the next morning. 'I have a plan to catch the murderer. We're going to operate our own sting. We'll set up a profile on SnapMate as an eighteen-year-old boy. But we want the murderer to think he's an older man posing as a young boy. The offender will be acting like a thirteen or fourteen-year-old girl.'

'It seems complicated. How are you going to do it?' Frank asked.

'George is going to be our decoy. Okay?' Whitney asked, looking directly at her.

Whitney hadn't mentioned her role when they'd talked last night. If she'd known in advance, she would've done more research into the specific language used by teenagers when they were online, especially the language boys used. She would've also liked to study the things the victims said in the chats, to see if she could pinpoint any errors which led the murderer to realise they were really older men. But she still had time. Although, if they wanted to be caught, she needed to make some mistakes. Not so many as it became obvious, though.

'No problem. Do we need permission to do this?' she asked.

'Spoken like a true copper,' Whitney quipped. 'I've already been to see Jamieson and heard first thing this morning he's had it approved by the powers that be. So, it's good to go. I've also arranged for someone to come in to give us some advice.'

George stiffened. Why ask her to participate in the sting because of her expertise and then get someone else in to help? Was it another psychologist? That would be an insult.

The phone on Whitney's desk rang, and she answered it.

'Walker.' She paused for a moment. 'Ask someone to bring her up.' She ended the call. 'And it looks like she's here already.'

A couple of minutes later, in walked Vera Smith.

George hadn't seen that coming.

'Hello, Vera,' Whitney said. 'It's good of you to come in.'

'What's it about?' Vera asked as she headed over to where Whitney and George were standing.

'We're planning a sting to trap the murderer and would like your help in setting it up.'

'Why would I want to do that? We've now got three monsters off the street. If we stop this person, others are left to carry on grooming and abusing young girls.'

'You've changed your tune,' Whitney said. 'When we last spoke, you said you'd rather they weren't dead, but punished. You know we can't let this carry on. We want to rid the online sites of paedophiles, the same as you do. But we can't allow vigilantes to do it on our behalf. Especially when *doing it* consists of murder. It's very different from threats, or exposing them on social media, or handing them over to the police. We can't allow these murders to continue.'

'You're right. And I stand by what I'd originally said. It's not in our interest for them to die,' Vera replied, nodding.

'Thank you. What we need from you is an idea of how we should be behaving, as you've extensive experience on these sites.'

'We have people posing as young girls attracting these older men. What you're asking is the other way round. It's not something we've actually done in the past, obviously.'

'Perhaps you can give us an indication of the protocols to follow when on this sort of site.'

'One thing to consider is some of the men who are attracting young girls to groom often have very low key conversations on the actual site. They may comment on a girl's posts, but there's rarely anything suggestive or personal. If you look at someone's profile, and the messages being left or the conversations, you wouldn't be able to ascertain who was the groomer. They cleverly persuade the girl to take their conversations off site.'

'And how do they do that?' Whitney asked.

'They send the girl a private message and ask if they could talk away from the site. They would use any app where they can be private. They wouldn't use video, obviously, because they want the girl to believe they're a teenager.'

'Okay, we can do that once we've identified who the murderer is.'

'And how are you going to do that?' Vera asked.

'That's where you can help us further. We want to

appear like a groomer and need to know how the 'young girl' will act towards us,' Whitney said.

'There are two ways we work. Either we pursue them, or we encourage them to pursue us. When we operate stings, we get our people to use specific phrases and to act in defined ways to draw the predators in.'

'Can you tell us what they are?' Whitney asked.

'It's important for the girl to appear childlike and innocent. They will state their age early on to make sure the man's aware they are underage. We get them to ask leading questions to incite a sexual response, even though they act as if they don't know what they've said. Once we get to this stage, it's usually done privately off the main page. But it doesn't always happen. Some groomers will be more open online. Usually the less experienced ones.'

'So the girls act differently depending on the type of predator,' George said.

'Yes. It's difficult to be precise because every sting is different. Every groomer is different. They don't all act in the same way. They have their own idiosyncrasies. Some keep everything totally private and off-line. Others will be openly flirty, for everyone to see. The main thing is, you have to be prepared to go with the flow and see where it takes you. Sorry, that's all I can give you.'

Vera's one-eighty was interesting. She'd suddenly become very helpful. Was it because of her preference for the men not to be killed and instead made to suffer throughout their lives? Or was there another reason?

'Actually, you've helped a lot,' George said. 'It means we're less likely to expose ourselves because there's no set pattern we have to adhere to.'

'Good point. I have an appointment in forty minutes. Is there anything else you need from me?' Vera asked, looking back at Whitney.

'No. We appreciate you coming in to help. Frank will show you out.'

Vera picked up her bag and was escorted out of the incident room.

'Ellie, I want you to set George up with a profile on SnapMate.'

Whitney and George followed Ellie to her desk and stood behind while she logged onto the site.

'What do you want call yourself?' Ellie asked.

'Shall I go by George?' she asked Whitney.

'That would work. At least you won't slip up when signing your name or something,' Whitney said.

'Do I need a surname?'

'Most people put an initial or numbers. They don't usually give their full name. Some of them have little sayings,' Ellie said.

'Just call me GeorgeW, then,' she said.

'As in George W Bush?' Whitney said, laughing.

'Not at all. I was using your last name initial, as we don't want it to mean something. If someone sees GeorgeC, and it turns out to be a person we'd already interviewed, they might twig.'

'Good idea. GeorgeW it is.'

'I've got a better idea. What about george1207,' George said.

'Let me guess, your birthday is the twelfth of July,' Whitney said. 'That's original.'

'Now you know, I'll be expecting a gift.'

'Except that makes you more traceable. It's 101 of what not to do,' Ellie said.

'I'm feeling old. Why don't we know this?' Whitney said.

'You think of a name, Ellie,' George suggested, as she was out of ideas.

'How about livetoplayfootball?'

'Seriously?' She'd never have come up with that name in a thousand years.

'Yes. It's a typical user name.'

George was only in her thirties, yet all this was passing her by. She felt like an alien in her own world.

'What else do you need to know?' Whitney asked.

'Where George lives and the area she wants to meet people.'

'Put I'm from Lenchester and would like to meet girls within a ten-mile radius, or however you'd word it.'

'I'll put Lenchester and surrounding areas. Now we need your interests.'

'Football, obviously. Music, seeing live bands. What else does an eighteen-year-old boy do?'

'Gaming,' Ellie said.

'Shall we say I'm at college or in the sixth form at school?' George asked.

'Either would do,' Ellie said.

'Put school, then.'

'You can add more about yourself and the person you want to meet.'

'Say I'd like to meet a fun-loving girl who also likes intimate conversation,' George said.

'It sounds too adult,' Ellie said.

'Isn't that the aim, in a roundabout way? We want to give ourselves away a little,' she said.

'But not too much. Remember, men who groom young girls have researched into it and know how to act,' Whitney said.

'What do you suggest, Ellie?' George asked.

'Let's say you want to hang out online with a girl, to be friends,' the young officer said.

'Yes, much better. What else do we need?' Whitney asked.

'A photo of a young man around eighteen. Do you have one?' Ellie asked.

George thought for a moment. The only photo she had was of her brother when he was eighteen, and that was years ago.

'Not a recent one. Does that matter? Will people be able to tell?'

'It depends on the clothes he's wearing. Actually, we can use a stock photo,' Ellie said.

'Good idea, because even if the murderer recognises it as a stock photo, it will mean she'll know she's onto a predator,' Whitney said.

'Let's find someone.' Ellie opened up another window on her computer and called up a website full of images. 'What about him?' she said after a few seconds of scanning.

George and Whitney leaned in to look at the photo of a good-looking young boy with blond hair curled slightly around his ears. He had a cheeky smile and dimples.

'He looks perfect,' George said.

'Agreed,' Whitney said.

'I'll buy the image through my account,' Ellie said.

'How come you have an account for these photos?' Whitney asked.

'I do websites for people in my spare time,' Ellie admitted, biting down on her bottom lip. 'But please don't say anything, I'm not sure if my contract allows me to do it.'

'Your secret's safe with us,' Whitney reassured her.

Ellie uploaded a photo and made a few adjustments to the profile. 'Okay, that's it. You're officially loaded.'

'Now what?' George had absolutely no idea about these sites. She'd never been on one or ever been tempted.

'We can add more things to your profile, if you think it will help. A list of likes and dislikes, and answer some of the questions suggested,' Ellie said.

'Does everyone do that?' she asked.

'No. Some people just put their name, photo, and a few details.'

'That will be best for now,' Whitney said. 'We can always answer some of the questionnaires down the track, if we find no one's biting.'

'We have to wait for your account to be approved. They'll email the new address we've set up for you, and then we'll confirm it. Once that happens, you're free to interact on the site. Oh wait, here's the confirmation email,' Ellie said. 'I'll confirm and send it back now.'

'Do I need access to the email?' George asked.

'Yes, to log into the site. Any private messages will be sent directly to your profile. You can carry on conversations, as they're recorded. We might need them as evidence,' Ellie said.

George marvelled at how proficient Ellie was. Whitney was always praising her, but it was good to actually see her in action.

'Let's hope we don't have to wait too long for a bite.'

## Chapter Thirty-Two

'While we're waiting for something to happen online, let me show you a copy of the latest letter sent to the radio station,' Whitney said to George.

Following Whitney into her office, she saw the letter on the desk. She picked it up and examined it.

'Hmmm. She's not happy about being ignored. And once again we have the Shakespearean quote.'

'What quote?' Whitney grabbed the letter from her and stared at it. She was quiet for a moment while she read the letter. 'Is it "action is eloquence"?'

'That's the one.'

'I suppose you're going to tell me which play it came from as well, aren't you?'

'Not if you're going to poke fun at me.'

'Come off it. You know you want to tell me.'

'Okay, it's from *Coriolanus* and spoken by Volumnia.' George couldn't help flashing a smug smile in Whitney's direction.

'I've never even heard of the play before.'

'It's one of his tragedies. The other being *Anthony and Cleopatra*. I…' She paused.

'What?'

'I've had a thought. Let's go back to the incident room.'

She half-walked, half-ran into the room, with Whitney following close behind. Stopping at the board, she stared at it intently.

'Are you going to let me in on this thought of yours?' Whitney said.

'The connection between them all. It's Shakespeare.'

'Explain.'

'Well, we already have the two Shakespeare references in the letters, *King Lear* and *Coriolanus*. And look at the names of the girls who arranged to meet our victims: Cleo, Bea, and Vi.'

'Cleo, short for Cleopatra. That's one. But Bea and Vi?' Whitney asked.

'Beatrice from Much Ado About Nothing.'

'Vi is short for Violet.'

'No. It's Viola from *Twelfth Night*.'

'Bloody hell. Our murderer uses fake names from Shakespeare's plays, which means we're looking for a Shakespeare buff who wants to rid the world of predators. More to the point, it makes it much easier for us to identify the girls who start chatting with you. We've just got to look for someone with a name that fits.'

'Not just any Shakespearean name. All three women used so far are strong and fearless. It's got to be the name of one of his powerful female characters.' She nodded her head, pleased to have made such an important connection. 'It's our final confirmation the murderer is a woman.'

'But we still don't know if she acts alone or has an accomplice. Strength is required to move the bodies.'

'True. But not impossible for a woman to do. And once we apprehend her, if there's an accomplice, they'll be somewhere close, so we should be able to find them, too.'

'Working out this connection is going to make our sting much easier to complete,' Whitney said.

'Agreed. We should go online to see if we've had any response to my profile.'

They headed over to Ellie's desk. 'Anything?' Whitney asked.

'Not yet. It's the school holidays. Most girls will still be in bed this early in the morning.'

'But we're not after a teen girl,' George reminded her.

'If our murderer is pretending to be a teen girl, he or she will adopt the habits of one. It means getting up late when it's not a school day. Not being able to speak during lesson time when she's at school. Not being around in the evening during dinner time. All these things have to be taken into consideration,' Ellie said.

'It all makes sense. Now we're in, can we look through the profiles of girls from around the area? We might be able to identify the murderer ourselves and then approach her,' George said.

'Yes, we can do that,' Ellie said.

'Why don't I sit next to you and go through them myself while you're getting on with your other work. Can you log me in from this computer?' George pulled out the chair in front of the desk and slid the keyboard over to Ellie, who logged her in and opened the site.

'I'll help,' Whitney said, sitting to the left of George.

They scrolled through the site, viewing the different profiles. George couldn't believe the number of teens who actually joined. She was clearly way behind everything. She'd always believed meeting people online wasn't popu-lar, but she'd been proved wrong. It seemed an accepted way to meet people. Would she try it herself? She doubted it.

'So, we're looking for a name we can link to Shakespeare?' Whitney said.

'It's certainly a start. There are lots of different names we could look at. Take this entry.' George moved the mouse so the arrow highlighted someone called Rose. 'This could be a link to Rosalind from *As You Like It*. Let's look into her profile.' She clicked on the name and picture of a girl who looked around sixteen or seventeen. 'I don't think this is her; she looks too old.'

'Often the younger ones make themselves up to look older,' Whitney said.

'True, although if she's our murderer, she'll want to come across as sweet and innocent. Let's look at her details. She lives near Rugby, which is in our catchment area. She's about to take her GCSEs at school. Which would make her too old,' George said.

'Where are the profiles of Cleo, Vi, and Bea?' Whitney asked.

'They don't seem to be here,' George said.

'They've been taken down,' Ellie said.

'If they're no longer showing, I'm assuming there will still be records of them on the site database?' Whitney said to Ellie.

'I would've thought so. The company hasn't been very helpful up to now. But it could be they're not able to assist. Even with the private texts and emails, our IT guys weren't able to track any of these girls. The murderer is smart and has been using a special network to block us finding out where she is. I'll ask Mac to contact them again, to see if they'll give us anything.'

'It's worth a try. Right, we've established it's not Rose, so there's no point in us approaching her.'

'There's a Hermione from Lenchester,' George said. 'The name could reflect Hermia from *A Midsummer Night's Dream*. Looking at her profile, she seems the right age. The photo is of a cute younger girl. Shall I reach out to her?'

'Yes,' Whitney said.

'What shall I say?' George asked.

'Just say hi and ask what she's doing,' Ellie suggested. 'But you might not get a response straightaway.' She leaned in towards George. 'Actually, it's showing she's online at the moment, so you could be in luck.'

George made contact and waited, but there was no response. They continued looking through other profiles.

'There's a Dee. She could be Desdemona from *Othello*.' Whitney grinned at George.

'I thought you didn't know any Shakespeare.'

'I don't, apart from *Othello*, because we had to study it for our English literature GCSE. But I surprised you, didn't I?'

'You did. Dee looks young and lives locally, so I'll make contact. She's online at the moment,' George said, now knowing what to look for. She said hello, and again they waited.

There was a ping, showing Hermione had replied. George opened it and all it said was NM. HBY.

'What the hell is NM?' she asked.

'It means *not much*,' Ellie said. 'You asked *what you been doing?* Now you need to answer because she asked you back. HBY means *how about you?*'

'Okay, I'll put *hanging out with my friends*, if that's okay?'

'No. It's too early in the day. Try SSDD,' Ellie said.

'Meaning?'

'Same stuff, different day.'

'I'll never get the hang of this,' George said.

'I've an idea. Hang on a minute.' Ellie went into

Google and, after searching, printed off a sheet of paper which she handed to George. 'Here you are. A list of 100 acronyms teens use when texting or online.'

George scanned the list. 'Seriously, they say IWSN as in *I want sex now*? And NIFOC is *nude in front of computer*?'

'Show me.' Whitney grabbed the list from her. 'Bloody hell. I'm glad Tiffany is past this stage. I couldn't have coped.'

'At least now I can be more convincing when I converse,' George said.

She continued engaging in an inane conversation with Hermione regarding her friends, family, and pets. They got quite a discussion going. George told her she was seventeen and doing A-levels. She also found out Hermione was fourteen.

She then got a reply from Dee, and they had a chat. Dee was fifteen and lived in Lenchester. There was nothing flirtatious about the chat.

'I don't know whether either of these are the murderer,' George said.

'Give it time. You have to build up to it by getting to know them. The more time you spend chatting with these girls, the more they'll learn to trust you and start to confide more personal stuff. Then you'll be able to tell if they're the person we're looking for.'

Once again, George was impressed by Ellie. She had good insight.

'Agreed, except the longer it takes, the more likely it is we'll have another victim. There has to be a way to speed up the process.'

The message board pinged.

'Look. This is someone new. They're reaching out to me, and not vice versa.' She opened up the message. 'It's from someone called Juleslovesyou. Interesting.'

'From *Romeo and Juliet*. She's not a strong female character. She's a fourteen-year-old girl who thinks she's in love,' Whitney said.

'Actually, she's thirteen and is one of Shakespeare's strongest heroines. She refused to marry the Count of Paris, despite her father trying every conceivable way to make her. She dug her heels in and wouldn't be swayed. She was brave and showed enormous determination and courage.'

'I stand corrected. What does she say?' Whitney said.

'She's asked me what I'm doing.'

'You stay and chat, I've got to head out. The social worker is meeting me and Tiffany at Mum's house in an hour, and I want to get there first to explain to her and Rob what's going to happen.'

George reached over and placed her hand on Whitney's arm. 'You're making the right decision. Especially now you've seen the places you want them to move into. It's difficult now, but it's for the best in the long run.'

'I know.' Tears filled her eyes and she brushed them away. 'Ignore me. I'll be fine once everything's sorted. Wish me luck.' She gave George a wave before leaving the incident room.

George stared at her retreating back. Their friendship had grown into something special. No way when they'd first met would Whitney have allowed herself to cry in front of her. It took some serious trust. Would she ever cry in front of the officer? One day, maybe.

## Chapter Thirty-Three

Whitney picked up Tiffany so they could go together to see her mum and Rob. This was a family discussion, and she wanted her daughter to be a part of it.

'Are you sure about this?' Tiffany asked.

'I'm not sure about anything. All I know is we can't let Granny and Uncle Rob live on their own any longer. It's too dangerous. I couldn't live with myself if something happened which could've been prevented if they hadn't been alone.'

'What about if I move in with them?'

'That's a lovely thought, but totally impractical. You're out at uni during the day, have a part-time job, and a social life at night. Not to mention how cramped it would be. Have you seen the size of the third bedroom? It used to be mine, and I had a lot less stuff than you. There wouldn't be room for all your clothes, let alone your computer and textbooks.'

'I suppose you're right, but it doesn't seem fair. Granny will hate having to move.'

'I can't bear to say this, but soon Granny won't know

where she is. It's Uncle Rob I'm more concerned about. What's he going to do if he's living in a place where he has no freedom?'

Whichever way she looked at it, no one was going to come out of this situation unscathed.

'But you said the place you went to look at was okay. Have you changed your mind?' The worried tone in Tiffany's voice jolted Whitney back to reality. The girl had been through enough. What she didn't need was for her mum to offload all her worries onto her.

'No, I haven't. It does seem suitable. I'm being silly.'

When she'd been to visit the home the social worker had recommended for Rob, she'd been pleasantly surprised. It was a detached house in a nice area of Lenchester, and there were six people living there, plus a full-time carer. They all had their own rooms, and there was a shared kitchen where they were allowed to make meals, under supervision. There was also a garden for them to sit in, and they were encouraged to grow their own vegetables and do some gardening. Not only did the full-time carer live-in, but during the day there were two others working, so there was always someone available to oversee what was going on. The residents were taken to any medical appointments, and to the local day centre where they could mix with other people.

They were lucky a space had become available, and Rob had been put to the top of the list because of the situation with her mum.

She'd also been to visit the home for her mum. It specialised in caring for people with Alzheimer's and dementia, and came highly recommended. Again, someone was looking over them, because there was a room available.

It was just hard to make the change. She was

dreading telling her mum and brother, because she knew they'd be scared until they were living in their new homes.

Tiffany rested her hand on Whitney's arm. 'Don't worry. It'll be fine, and we'll visit them regularly. Try not to feel guilty.'

Her daughter knew her so well.

'You're right, love. It's for the best. Right, we're almost here, so smiles on faces and let's look as if this is going to be an exciting transition for them.'

They got out of the car and walked up to the house. Whitney knocked and waited for her mum to answer.

'Whitney. Tiffany. How lovely to see you. An unexpected surprise,' her mum said.

'I told you we were coming round, Mum.'

They walked into the lounge. Across the room, Rob sat playing on his computer.

'Hello, Uncle Rob,' Tiffany said.

He glanced up from his game and gave them a beaming smile. Whitney's insides clenched. She hoped his happy disposition wouldn't disappear when she explained the changes about to happen.

'Mum, come and sit next to me,' Whitney said as she sat on the old sofa and patted the empty seat beside her.

Tiffany sat on the arm of Rob's chair, facing Whitney and her mum.

'Is there something you want to tell me?' her mum asked.

'Yes. Jean is going to be here soon, but I want to talk to you before she arrives.' She swallowed hard. 'I know things have been really difficult recently, and you're struggling to manage. So, I've found a lovely place for you to live, and also somewhere for Rob.'

'Will we be together?' her mum asked.

'It's not possible. But the places are close to each other, so you'll be able to visit. I'll make sure of it.'

Whitney glanced at Rob, who was still playing his game.

'Rob, did you hear what I said?' she asked.

'I'm not going anywhere,' he said, his eyes firmly fixed on the screen.

'You can't stay here on your own, and Mum has to live somewhere they can take care of her.'

He looked up and scowled in her direction. 'I told you. I'm not going anywhere.'

She drew in a calming breath. 'Why don't we visit the place I found before you decide. It's really lovely. You have your own room and even your own television.'

His face lit up. 'My own telly?'

He'd never been allowed a television in his room before because her mother felt he'd stay in there all of the time. Was it mean using it as a bargaining chip? Maybe, but she had to get him to come and see the place.

'Yes, and a garden where you can grow vegetables. You can plant seeds and watch them grow.'

When her dad was alive, they'd grown most of their vegetables, and Rob had really enjoyed helping him.

'I'll think about it,' he said.

'That's all I want you to do. When Jean arrives, we'll tell her we want to go for a visit, so you can see for yourself.'

'And I want to see, too,' her mum said.

It was ironic her mum seemed almost like her old self the day they were discussing moving her into a home. But Whitney knew this side of her wouldn't last, and she'd go back to being confused.

'First, we'll take a look at Rob's new place, and then go to yours, Mum. We'll go as a family. All four of us.'

'Who'd like a cup of tea and a biscuit?' Tiffany asked, jumping up. 'It'll be nice to have something before we go out.'

'Make mine a coffee please, love,' Whitney said.

'She's a good girl,' her mum said as Tiffany left the room.

'Well, you helped me raise her, so it's thanks to both of us.' Whitney took hold of her mum's hand and gave it a squeeze.

The doorbell rang, and she went to answer it. The social worker stood there, a worried expression on her face.

'When you called and left a message for me to come around, I thought there might be something wrong,' she said as she walked into the hall.

'Sorry, I didn't mean to alarm you. We've made a decision. I went to visit the places you recommended for Mum and Rob, and it's definitely the way to go. We're going to take a look together and wanted you to come with us. Do you have time?'

'The assessment I was meant to be doing today was cancelled, so yes, I do. I'll phone the office and let them know I won't be back for a couple of hours. How did they take it?'

'Mum was fine. She's been fairly lucid and understands it's for the best. Rob was unsure until I mentioned the TV he'd have in his room. That swayed it. I'm sure once he sees the place, he'll be happier.'

'It's a hard decision, but definitely for the best. I know you're feeling guilty about it, but you mustn't. Your mum's and Rob's needs have to come first.'

'I get it. The decision's the right one, and my guilt comes a long way behind. Come on. Let's round them up. You know how long it takes to get them ready for a trip out.'

## Chapter Thirty-Four

After spending the morning in the police incident room, George went back to the university to get some work done. There was a knock at her door, which was slightly ajar, and Robin Delaney poked his head around.

'Have you got a minute?' he asked.

'I'm rather busy.'

They hadn't spoken since she'd blasted him after finding out about the job, and she wasn't in the mood for a conversation now. She wanted to finish her work and go back online to see if there were any more messages for her. It wasn't that she wanted to jeopardise her "proper" job, because she realised her work with Whitney was going to be sporadic. But at the moment, her priority was helping solve the murders. She was up to date on her marking and lecture preparation, and the students wouldn't be around for several weeks.

'This won't take long.' He walked further into her office and sat on a chair opposite her.

'What do you want?' She gave her best intimidating stare, and he visibly squirmed in his seat.

'I know you're still upset about what happened, but I want to ask if you'd consider being a member of the university Research Ethics Committee.'

'Is this meant to be a "runners-up prize"?' She arched an eyebrow.

'Not at all. You head the department's research committee and have an excellent research record, so you're the natural choice of candidate.'

The natural choice to be on the Ethics Committee, but not to be associate professor. 'I'll think about it,' she said.

She wasn't going to let on she'd love to be part of the committee. Research ethics were extremely important to her and something she constantly drilled into her students.

'Let me know your decision by the end of the week. If you're not interested, I'll have to find someone else.'

'You could always offer it to our new associate professor, Greg Barnes. I'm sure he'd love the exposure so early in his career here.' She could've kicked herself. Sarcastic belligerence wasn't the sort of behaviour she usually indulged in.

'Not going to happen,' Robin said as he stood. 'I'll wait to hear from you.'

She stared at him as he left her office. So much for thinking she'd dealt with being passed over for the job. She pushed the thought to the back of her mind, as she had other things to focus on. Were there any more messages from Jules? Because her gut was telling her she could be the one.

Gut? Surely she wasn't channeling Whitney.

No. That wasn't going to happen.

She shook her head to get rid of any Whitney-inspired thoughts, because she really needed to finish her work. Then again, checking the site would only take a few minutes. She logged into the SnapMate app and put in her password. The message light was flashing. She had three messages. One from Vi and two from Jules. She read the one from Vi, which was about something funny her cat had done. Then she opened the first of the messages from Jules:

*I hate my life.*

Before answering, George read the second message:

*Sorry. You don't want to know my problems.*

Her body tensed. The second message didn't sound like a thirteen-year-old. But it was designed to elicit a response. Was she right about Jules being the one?

*I'm here if you want to talk. PM me.*

She was meant to be a guy of eighteen, so it seemed an appropriate reply. Jules was still online. All George had to do was wait for her to read the message.

After staring at the screen for a while, willing her to answer, she decided to go back to her uni work. But before she did, the message showed it had been read. Now she wanted a reply. She didn't have to wait for long. In less than a minute, one arrived in her private message box:

*I missed going to the dentist because I got home late. My mum went mad and grounded me. I said it wasn't my fault but she wouldn't listen. My cow of a best friend took my purse and I had no money to get the bus. I had to walk home and on the way I fell and ripped my new jeans.*

George didn't want to reply straightaway. She wanted to make sure what she said was enough to elicit more conversation and make her sound genuine. Except she needed to write it in such a way as to hint perhaps she wasn't who she said she was. It was a tricky path to follow. She eventually decided less was more.

*That sucks. Why did your mate do that?*

Was it enough? Would she respond?

*She's not my friend anymore. She turned everyone against me. She said I'm trying to take her boyfriend away from her. But I'm not. It's not my fault he keeps texting me.*

Should she say anything about these issues? She could ask for more details, but that seemed like a more girly thing to do. Boys didn't go in for all the gory details.

*How long have you been grounded for?*

That seemed a better way to go.

*I don't know. Why is everyone turning on me?*

Jules was trying to draw her in. She wanted George to believe her life was awful and hopeless, hoping to be seen as someone who could be groomed. Well, George was happy to oblige.

*I'm not.*

She debated whether to use an emoji but decided against it. Boys didn't use them like girls did. At least, that's what she thought. She'd have to check with Ellie.

*That's because you don't know me.*

And now the sob story. A perfect way to catch a predator. Leaving George able to make her move.

*I'd like to get to know you. You're so pretty and you have lovely eyes.*

Even though she was convinced Jules was an adult, it didn't stop her from feeling sick at how easy it was to lure a young girl.

*GTG Mum wants me.*

Jules signed off and George was left staring at the screen. Had she come on too strong, too soon? What if she didn't get a response? She hoped she hadn't jeopardised the operation. Whitney wouldn't be happy if she had.

She had a long night of worrying ahead of her.

# Chapter Thirty-Five

*The next sleazy predator is all lined up. It makes me sick when I think of how many there are in Lenchester alone. He thought he was being so clever acting like a teenage boy. But I can tell. It's the little things that give him away. Things he won't even realise.*

*Word choice.*

*Punctuation.*

*Adult perspective.*

*Just another pervert. But this pervert is going to pay the price.*

*I usually string it out for a while, because grooming typically can take several weeks, but this time I don't have that luxury. I've got a holiday booked and want to get this over with before I go. If I wait until after I come back, he might have moved on to someone else.*

*I can't let that happen.*

*It's a risk, but I can see from his profile he's only recently joined SnapMate. If he's new to this, it shouldn't raise any alarm bells. No one's life is going to be ruined again from livetoplayfootball because Juleslovesyou will make sure of it.*

*I still can't believe my letters to Radio Lenchester have been ignored. The only thing I can think of is the police interfered and refused for them to be made public. What sort of newsroom allows that to happen? The next letter I send, after I've disposed of liveto-playfootball, will be to the local paper. I'm sure they won't kowtow to police demands.*

*It was probably Walker thinking it was right to keep my letters secret. If she was any good at her job, there wouldn't be any predators in Lenchester. I doubt she'd even considered going after them.*

*That's why I'm here.*

*To deliver justice.*

*A special kind of justice.*

*Fatal justice.*

## Chapter Thirty-Six

Whitney walked into the incident room with a spring in her step. It had gone well with her mum and brother yesterday. Rob really liked the house, and the staff seemed lovely. He already had a friend there. A girl in her twenties who he recognised from the day centre he used to visit. Mum had cancelled him going, but as soon as he moved into the new place, he'd go back.

'Morning, everyone,' she called out. 'What have you got for me?'

'I've checked into George's account on SnapMate, and she's been engaging in conversation with one of the girls she was speaking to yesterday,' Ellie said.

'Do we have any idea yet whether one of them is our target?'

'George will know better. We'll ask when she gets here,' Ellie said.

The door opened, and they glanced up as George entered.

'Speak of the devil,' Whitney said.

'And good morning to you, too,' George said. 'Are you taking my name in vain?'

'Ellie was telling me you've been talking with one of the girls from yesterday.'

'Yes, I've been messaging Juleslovesyou. Have you seen the conversation?'

'Not yet. I've only just arrived, myself.'

'She could be the one, as she's already moved to being more personal, and we're speaking in the private message section. I'm hoping to continue the conversation today. We should arrange a meeting as soon as possible, in case she's chatting with others she plans to entrap.'

'Agreed. It's probably a little early, because if she's acting like a normal thirteen-year-old girl, there's no way she'll be up chatting at eight-thirty in the morning,' Whitney said.

'I'll keep an eye on the app and let you know as soon as she comes online,' Ellie said.

'Okay. George and I will take a look at Claire's report, which has come in.'

She went to her office with George following.

'You seem happy today,' George said.

'I took Mum and Rob to the homes I've found, and it went really well. Rob didn't want to go at first, but when he saw his bedroom and the rest of the house, he was convinced. Mum was a bit more reserved, but she seemed to like the place we've chosen.'

'When's the big moving day?' George asked.

'We're hoping to get it all sorted so they can move sometime next week. And then we've got to do something with the house.'

'Are you going to sell it?'

'Eventually. It needs a complete make-over so we can get as much money for it as possible. At the moment, it's a mess and needs cleaning and completely redecorating. I don't know when I'll have time. We've got the case to solve.'

'I'll help you when you're ready,' George offered.

'You can decorate and clean?' she arched an eyebrow.

'Of course I can. Is it so strange?'

'I wouldn't have thought you had time to do mundane tasks like that. I'd have bet you paid to someone to do it.'

'Well, you're wrong. I can strip wallpaper, wield a paintbrush, and make a basin sparkle. I also have green fingers. Unlike some people around here.'

'Ouch,' she said, laughing. 'I take it that's a swipe at my pathetic excuse of a garden.'

'Well, it certainly could do with some TLC.'

'As you're so keen to help with Mum's place, you can come around and do mine, too, if you like.'

She glanced at George. When they'd first met, there had been no banter. Their relationship had been awkward and professional. She knew George struggled in social situations, and it made her feel good the doctor was able to relax in her company. They made a good team.

'I'd love to. I'll do the garden, and you can cook us a meal. Oh no, I forgot you don't do cooking, either. I suppose that will be down to me, too.'

'I might not cook, but I can certainly shout us a take-away,' she responded.

'I'm glad everything's working out for you. It must be a huge weight off your mind. Let's have a look at this report from Claire,' George said, bringing the conversation around to work.

Whitney picked up the report, which she'd left on her desk. 'There's nothing different from what she's already told us. Apart from now the toxicology report's back and he'd been given a light sedative.'

'Is it the same sedative as the others?' George asked.

'I think so. Not strong enough to totally knock him out. Just enough to relax him and make him easy to deal with.' The phone on her desk rang and she picked it up. 'Walker.'

'Guv, it's Ellie. I wanted to let you know Jules is back online, if Dr Cavendish wants to come back.'

'We're on our way.' She put the phone back on the desk. 'Come on, Jules is active.'

They headed out of her office, towards the desk next to Ellie's.

'Are you going to speak first?' she asked.

'No. I'm going to wait to see if she sees me online and makes the first move.'

'You think it's best for her to take the lead?'

'On the one hand, if I'm acting like the predator, maybe I should be trying to lure her in as soon as possible. But on the other, we want to be sure she's the one. I think it will come through more if we let her lead us,' George said.

'That makes sense. The whole point is for her to be luring us to our demise.' There was a ping, and it showed a message had arrived for livetoplayfootball from Juleslovesyou.

'Well, it looks like she's made the first move anyway,' George said as she opened the message.

*Hiya WUU2?*

'What does that mean?' she asked.

'*What you up to*,' George said. 'I won't answer straight-away. I'll give it a few minutes. I've got to pretend I'm at home and in bed.'

'Look at you, down with the kids. How do you know this?' She grinned.

'I spent yesterday afternoon with Ellie, and she got me up to speed. Glad you're impressed.'

'You did a good job, Ellie,' Whitney said, nodding in her direction.

'Thanks, guv,' the young officer said.

After a few minutes, George decided to reply. 'I've got to make out we're kindred spirits. She's having problems with her parents, so I'll be having problems with mine.'

*NM apart from being ordered to clean my mum's car not happy about it HBY*

They didn't have to wait long for a response.

*I'm still grounded even though I told her it wasn't my fault. She never listens. She hates me and I hate her.*

'Right, let's take this steady and get her on side,' George said.

'Or get her to believe you think you're getting her on side,' she said as she shook her head. 'Talk about weaving a tangled web.'

'True. It's certainly complicated.'

*Sorry ur so upset wish I could help.*

'Is that what an eighteen-year-old boy would typically say?' she asked.

'Doubtful, but that's the point. If I'm pretending to be an eighteen-year-old boy and occasionally slip up, it confirms to Jules she's got the right person.'

'Got it,' she said.

*I wish we could meet up to talk*

'Bloody hell, that's quick,' George said.

'You must have been very convincing.'

'I don't know. It seems a bit soon to be suggesting a meet-up. From what I've seen, it doesn't usually happen this quickly.'

'Or maybe Jules isn't the one,' she said.

'Grooming typically can take weeks, but if she's convinced we're not who we say we are, then maybe she wants to trap us as soon as she can. Or she has another reason for moving this on quickly. Either way it doesn't matter. If we go to the meeting and see she's a young girl, we won't bother going up to her, so she'll think she's been stood up,' George said.

'Except our murderer could have a young girl working with her. The girl lures the man somewhere quiet, and the killer injects them and takes them away. If there's a young girl there, we'll stand her up and then tail her,' Whitney said.

'True. Anyway, it's worth following this through. I'll make the plans,' George said.

*Can you get away at all?*

The reply was almost instant.

*Not today. My mum goes to work tomorrow so I can sneak out of the house without her knowing.*

'Don't suggest anywhere too private and secluded because that might appear suspicious,' Whitney said.

*Okay. Let's meet in Orchid Café at Springfield Shopping Centre.*

They stared at the screen, waiting for a response.

*No. I want to go somewhere quiet where we can get to know each other.*

George arched an eyebrow. 'This has to be our murderer. There's a sexual undertone, and all I've suggested is for us to talk.'

'Yes.' Whitney punched the air.

*Where?*

*Abingdon Park near the lake on the far side by the trees.*

The park was vast, and where the girl had suggested wasn't a place young people usually went. They tended to congregate by the fountain.

'That would work,' Whitney said.

*Okay what time?*

*11?*

*Cool. See you then. GTG.*

George signed off. 'We've done it.'

'Right. I've got work to do making sure this happens,' Whitney said.

'I've got some jobs to do. When do you want me back?' George asked.

'After lunch.'

Whitney spent the next few hours dealing with the red tape involved in getting all the approval they needed. Jamieson gave clearance after risk assessments were made. She also made sure they had additional officers available for support.

Mid-afternoon, she went back into the incident room. George had also returned and was standing with Matt.

'Listen up, everyone. Stop what you're doing and make sure you can see the board.' She pinned up an aerial map of the Abingdon Park area.

'This is the meeting place,' she continued once everyone was settled. 'There are benches situated around the lake. Matt, you're going to be our decoy, and you're to sit on the bench closest to West Street. I want you wired.'

'Yes, guv,' the detective said.

'I want you to wait in a side street, out of sight, until fifteen minutes before the meeting time. Then walk over to the bench. Act furtive, then sit down. Listen to instructions from me, and report anything you notice.'

'And be prepared to get the needle, so wear thick trousers,' Frank said.

'Matt's fully aware of the possibility he might be injected with a sedative,' Whitney said. 'But before that happens, Matt, you have to get her to admit to what she's done, and what she intends to do. If we don't get this confession, she could walk. Our only evidence is carpet fibres and some straw. We need something concrete. Let's make sure no mistakes are made.'

'Understood, guv.'

'George and I will be stationed here, behind the trees.' She pointed to a clump of trees on the map. 'Doug and Sue, you sit on a bench on the opposite side of the lake, so you can keep an eye on everything. You can pretend to be a couple. We'll all have earpieces and will be able to hear what's going on.'

'What about me, guv?' Frank asked.

'I want you out of sight, here.' Whitney pointed to some bushes to the left of where Matt was going to sit. 'I'll have officers in cars placed at every road leading to the park. Does anyone have any questions?' Whitney asked.

'What if there are two of them?' Sue asked.

'There are five of us, plus Matt and the backup cars. We're also carrying Tasers. They won't get away. The meeting is set for eleven, so I want everyone there at nine-thirty. We want to make sure we're there before the murderer, who also might arrive early to check things out. Questions?' No one had any. 'Right. I'll see you all tomorrow. Let's nail this fucker.'

## Chapter Thirty-Seven

George glanced at her watch. It was fifteen minutes before the meeting, and Matt had already positioned himself on the bench.

'There's a teen girl walking around the lake.' Sue's voice came over the radio.

George grabbed Whitney's binoculars and held them up to her eyes, focusing on the area Sue and Doug were sitting. She spotted the young girl, wearing jeans and a hoodie. She looked around fifteen.

'A decoy?' she asked Whitney as she handed the binoculars back to her.

'Could be. Let's see what she does.'

The girl strolled casually around the lake. As she got within twenty yards of where Matt was, she stopped, stared in his direction, and pulled out her phone. She held the phone to her ear, all the time keeping her gaze on him.

'She could be calling the perp. Matt, go over and ask if she's Jules,' Whitney said.

He slowly rose from the bench and walked towards the girl.

'Hello,' he said once he was within a couple of feet.

The girl tensed and panic etched itself across her face. 'It's not her,' George said.

'Are you sure?' Whitney asked.

'Definitely. There was terror on her face when Matt approached. It wasn't put on. It was for real.'

'Matt, get back to the bench, pronto,' Whitney said.

'Sorry,' he muttered before turning back and walking towards the bench.

The young girl turned and ran off.

The radio crackled. 'A white Ford's turned slowly into West Street,' came the voice of one of the backup police officers over the radio.

'Thanks. Matt, be prepared,' Whitney said.

George kept her eyes focussed on the road and observed the car driving slowly past. She couldn't tell who was behind the wheel. The driver didn't stop.

'Is she sussing out the scene, do you think?' she asked Whitney.

'She could be.'

'She'll be back soon, then.'

'Did you get the registration number?' Whitney spoke into the radio.

'Yes, guv. We're running the plates now,' the officer said.

'Who was behind the wheel?' Whitney asked the officer.

'A woman on her own.'

While they waited, the car came back the other way and slowed down until it was level with the bench where Matt was now sitting. The driver pulled in and parked.

'It looks like this is it,' Whitney said to the rest of the team.

They waited for around five minutes before the car door opened and someone stepped out.

'What the fuck?' Whitney muttered.

George strained her eyes, cursing the fact her distance eyesight wasn't as good as it should be.

'What?' she asked.

'Can't you see who it is?' Whitney said.

'No. Tell me.'

'Diana Atkins!'

Bloody hell. Why hadn't she worked that out?

Mesmerised, they watched the woman stride over towards the bench. She was immaculately dressed in dark brown boots and a fawn, calf-length, double-breasted coat. A large tan-coloured handbag was hanging over her shoulder. When she reached Matt, she sat beside him, placing her bag on the bench to her left-hand side.

George and Whitney stood in silence, waiting for the conversation to commence.

'Hello,' Diana Atkins said as she smoothed out her coat beneath her.

'Hello,' Matt responded.

'Are you waiting for someone?' she asked, smiling at him.

'I am, yes.'

'Is it Jules?' she asked.

'Yes. How do you know?'

'It doesn't matter how I know. All that matters is she won't be coming,' she answered icily.

'Why not?' Matt asked, his voice remaining calm and in control.

'Because she doesn't exist, that's why.'

'Yes, she does. I've been speaking to her.'

'No. You've been speaking to me.'

'I don't understand,' Matt said.

George and Whitney exchanged a glance. He was good.

'You thought you could prey on a thirteen-year-old girl and abuse her. Well, you can forget it. It's not going to happen now, and it's not going to happen ever again.'

'What do you mean?'

'I make it my business to stop men like you.'

'You don't know anything about me.'

'I know plenty. You're all the same. Scum who don't deserve to walk this earth. This is it for you.'

'Really. And what can you do to me?' Matt taunted. 'You can't prove anything. I'll deny it if you go to the police.'

'I don't need to *prove anything*. The police won't be involved.'

'What then?'

Diana reached into the bag by her side and pulled out a small gun, which she lowered until it rested on the bench and was pointed at his leg.

'Gun,' Whitney whispered into the radio.

'This is what. If you move, I'll shoot,' Diana said.

'W-what do you want me to do?'

'Explain why you think it's okay to groom young girls for your perverted benefit. Make me understand.'

'Are you going to kill me?' Matt asked.

'I'm asking the questions, not you,' she said.

'Please answer me. Am I going to die?'

'Do you deserve to?' she responded.

George looked at Whitney. 'We can't let this carry on. Matt's life's in danger.'

'Okay, everyone, we're going in. Doug and Sue, get up slowly and act normal, as if you're going for a walk. Head towards the bench. Frank, come in from the other side, and we'll come around the back, disarm, and arrest her.'

George watched as Doug and Sue left the bench and ambled around the lake. She and Whitney went to the back of the trees and approached from behind. As they got closer, Whitney trod on a twig and it snapped. Diana's head flicked around, and she saw them.

Her eyes locked on Whitney. Furious.

Matt made a grab for her arm but not before she shot him in the leg. He let out an agonising shriek and fell to the ground.

George rushed over, pulling off her scarf, which she wrapped tightly around his leg, attempting to stem the flow of blood which was oozing down his trousers.

Whitney charged towards Atkins as she took off down the path. The woman ran headfirst into Doug and Sue, causing her to pause and attempt a detour. Before she had time to set off again, Whitney came up from behind, throwing herself forward and grabbing her around the legs, tackling her to the ground.

The gun was thrown from her hand, and Doug kicked it away.

Whitney stood and grabbed Atkins by the arm, hoisting her to her feet.

'Diana Atkins, I'm arresting you on suspicion of the murders of Russell Atkins, Kelvin Keane, and Tony Adams, and for the attempted murder of Detective Sergeant Price. You do not have to say anything, but it may harm your defence if you do not mention when questioned something which you later rely on in court. Anything you do say may be given in evidence. Do you understand?'

'I hope you can live with yourself. How many girls will have their lives ruined because you've stopped me?' the woman challenged.

'Take her away.' Whitney turned and headed back to George and Matt.

# Chapter Thirty-Eight

Whitney, George, and Doug walked down the corridor towards the interview room where Atkins was sitting with her solicitor. She preferred interviewing with Matt, but he was in hospital after the operation to remove the bullet from his leg.

She'd been in to visit him, and he was doing okay. Already talking about when he'd be back at work. But she'd make sure he didn't return until he was totally better. She'd be putting him forward for a commendation.

'Doug and I will interview. George, you can watch and listen from behind the two-way mirror.'

Whitney pushed open the door, and they walked in and sat down. She placed her folder on the table and prepared the recording equipment.

'Interview on March twenty-seventh. Those present: DCI Walker.' She nodded at Doug.

'DC Baines.'

'And please state your name,' she said to the prisoner.

'Diana Atkins.'

'And,' she said, nodding at the solicitor.

'Jeffrey Baker, solicitor for Diana Atkins.'

'Mrs Atkins, we'd like to talk to you about the murders of Russell Atkins, Kelvin Keane, and Tony Adams. Let's start with your husband. When did you first find out about his predilection for young girls?'

The solicitor leaned in towards her. 'You don't have to answer, Diana.'

'I want to answer. I want to tell them everything,' she said.

'I strongly recommend you don't. They can use it against you when we get to court,' he said.

'I want them to know my story, as I'm going to plead guilty. I'm glad they're dead and the world is rid of such monsters.'

The solicitor glanced at Whitney, frustration etched across his face.

'There will be a sentencing hearing. I advise against you going through with this,' he said.

'If she wants to speak, then let her,' Whitney said. 'You carry on, Diana, and tell us everything.'

The solicitor leaned back in his chair and shook his head. 'It's up to you,' he said, shrugging.

Diana sat upright and looked directly at Whitney. She could easily have been sitting in a Womens' Institute meeting rather than being charged with three atrocious murders.

'I discovered quite by accident Russell had joined SnapMate. We both had the same make and model of phone, and I accidentally picked up his. I keyed in my code to unlock it, and it turned out we were both using the same numbers. The year of his birth. I had no idea. Once I realised my mistake, I should have put the phone down, but you know what it's like. I started looking around and saw the app on there. I clicked on it, and that's when I realised what he was doing.'

'Why didn't you challenge him about it?' Whitney asked.

'I wanted to see how far he'd go. I monitored everything he did and, whenever I could, sneaked into his phone. For six months I did this, following him in person whenever possible. I saw his intentions towards these girls, so I decided to set him up.'

'With the intent to murder him?' Whitney asked.

'Yes. I had to put a stop to his behaviour. Even while he was trying to groom me, pretending to be a teen girl, he'd been doing the same to two other girls. I couldn't let it continue.'

'We are aware of these two girls and have spoken to them.'

'Do you know he blackmailed one of them into having sex with him? Luckily, I saved the other girl.'

Whitney didn't answer. She wanted to extract more information from Diana, without appearing to condone her actions.

'What happened when you met him?'

'He came to the place we'd agreed to meet and saw it was me. He tried to wriggle out of it and said he was doing it for a friend. I suggested we go somewhere to talk. When we were in the car, I injected him with a sedative and took him back home to the barn in one of the fields adjoining our house.'

'You mean the stable block?' Whitney asked.

'No, we have some fields adjoining our house and the barn is there.'

Whitney could've kicked herself. Why hadn't they searched there? They'd confined themselves to the house and immediate garden.

'Why did you decide to cut off his genitals and feed them to him?'

'After what he'd done, I wanted to take away his manhood. Making him eat it was to illustrate to him how depraved he was. Likewise, for the other men.'

'On all the bodies, you left on their socks. Why?'

'I hate feet and I didn't want to see them.'

Whitney sensed it was more than that.

'Why didn't you leave them fully clothed?' she asked.

'Because I wanted them to feel as vulnerable as they made those poor girls.'

'What made you decide to murder Kelvin Keane and Tony Adams? I understand Russell, because he was your husband, but why did you murder the others?'

'They deserved it. Every time they groomed and had sex with these young girls, they ruined their victims' lives forever. And I should know.'

'Did you experience something like that yourself?'

Diana's eyes glazed over, and she stared into space for a while. Eventually, she looked across at Whitney. 'Yes, I did.'

'Would you like to tell me about it?' Whitney asked.

Could there be extenuating circumstances? Something which would lessen her sentence when she got to court? Not that Whitney was advocating she got special treatment. That couldn't happen. The woman deserved to be punished for what she'd done, but if they understood the reasons behind it, the judge might err on the more lenient side, within the sentencing guidelines.

'My parents had lots of friends, and they'd see each other at dinner parties. I liked it when the dinner parties were at our house because of all the food, and sometimes I'd be allowed to stay up and talk to the guests. My favourite guest was Uncle Charles. He always paid me extra attention. We'd talk for ages. He seemed to understand me.' She paused, a pained expression on her face.

Whitney already knew what was coming. Uncle Charles.

'Carry on,' she coaxed.

'Their friends were at our house the day after my tenth birthday. It was late and I'd gone to bed. I was almost asleep when there was a knock at my door and it opened. I thought it would be one of my parents, but when I opened my eyes fully, I saw Uncle Charles standing there, looking down at me. He sat on the edge of my bed and rested his hand on the duvet. He pulled it back and looked at me in my PJs. He started stroking my body over my pyjamas and then eased his hand under the elastic of my bottoms. I told him to stop, but he kept on going, telling me I was enjoying it.'

Diana went silent. After a few seconds, Whitney spoke. 'What happened next?'

'He stopped and left my bedroom. On his way out, he told me what had happened was our little secret and if I told anyone he would pull the funding he'd promised my father for his business.'

Whitney swallowed hard. What a bastard. But it wasn't enough to turn her into a murderer. There had to be more.

'Did it happen again?'

Diana nodded. 'Every time he came around to the house, he'd somehow manage to appear in my bedroom. If I knew in advance he was coming, I'd try to arrange a sleepover at one of my friends' houses, but that didn't always work out.'

'Did he do more than touch you?' Whitney asked.

Diana nodded again and shuddered. 'He raped me. H-he made me do abhorrent things to him.' Tears formed in her eyes.

Whitney cringed. 'What things?'

'Suck his toes. The rancid smell of his feet still permeates my senses whenever I remember having to do it.' Disgust flickered in her eyes.

'Which is why you hate feet and left the socks on the victims,' Whitney said, now understanding.

'Yes.'

'How long did this go on for?' Whitney asked.

'Until I was thirteen and he had a stroke. It was just before I went away to boarding school.'

'Did you tell anyone about it?'

'You're the first person. I was so embarrassed and disgusted. But I couldn't let what I'd gone through happen to others. When I found out about Russell, I flipped.' She leaned forward and rested her head in her hands.

'Would you like a glass of water?' Whitney asked.

'Yes, please.'

'Doug will get you one. Interview suspended at fourteen hundred hours.'

Whitney left the interview room with Doug, who went in the direction of the water cooler, and she went in to see George.

'The poor woman,' she said, shaking her head.

'It explains a lot,' George said.

'But it doesn't excuse what she's done. She's still charged with three murders.'

'Her solicitor should get a psychiatric evaluation.'

'You think she could claim diminished responsibility?' Whitney asked, hoping it might be the answer.

'It would be up to the psychiatrist to decide. But I'm sure her history will have an impact on the sentence.'

'Good. I'm going to continue the interview and then have to see Jamieson. No need for you to stay if you want to get back to work.'

George glared at her. 'How many times do I have to tell you not to mention me going back to work?'

'I'm just saying, in case it's what you want to do. But as it's not, you can come with me to see Jamieson.'

## Chapter Thirty-Nine

Whitney knocked on the open door of Jamieson's office and walked in, followed by George.

'Sit down,' he said, beaming at them, in particular George.

Whitney tensed. What an arse. He was being extra nice because George was with her. Clearly he viewed George as academically superior and wanted to ingratiate himself. Or was she being super sensitive, for a change? She'd decide later.

'Thank you, sir,' she said.

'I want to congratulate you on a job well done. Now we've got the crazy lady off the street, everyone can sleep easier in their beds.'

An odd thing to say, considering Diana Atkins only targeted paedophiles.

'Well, I don't know about that, sir. She went after depraved men who groomed young girls on the Internet. I'd say she did us all a service.'

'We can't encourage vigilantism.'

'I'm not condoning it. Just saying we wouldn't have

these vigilantes if we were able to direct more resources to policing these Internet sites.'

'Agreed. But unfortunately, our resources are finite. Anyway, the case is now closed, but at least we have a budget for Dr Cavendish to continue working with us. Assuming you want to continue and it doesn't interfere too much with your work at the university,' he asked, smiling at George.

'I'll endeavour to fit it in,' George said.

Whitney smiled to herself at George's response.

'If that's all, we have a mountain of paperwork to tackle,' she said, anxious to get away.

'Yes, you can go,' he said.

They left his office and once they were far enough away so they couldn't be heard, Whitney came to a halt.

'What a sleaze. Did you notice how he was sucking up to you?' she asked, grimacing.

'Not really.' George shrugged.

'All smiles and being nice. It's because you're a doctor and hold higher academic qualifications than him. Does he know you went to Oxford, too?'

'If he does, it wasn't from me.'

'I bet he researched you online.'

'Does it matter?' George asked.

'I suppose not. But it does annoy me, the way he assumes he's better than me because of his fancy education.'

'But as we've already established, it doesn't make him a good police officer. You knock spots off him in that respect.'

'You're just saying that because I'm annoyed.'

'I'll be annoyed soon, too, if you don't stop being so silly.'

Whitney stared at George and started to laugh.

'Oh my God. Listen to us. We're like an old married couple.'

'What does that mean?'

'It means we've got to learn to put up with each other's quirks and ways of doing things. Then our relationship will be successful.'

'So, we're in it for the long haul, then?'

'You bet we are,' Whitney said.

**Book 3** - George and Whitney return in ***Death Track***, to face the notorious Carriage Killer. But how can they get into the mind of a killer who has already killed twelve times in two years without leaving a single clue behind.

Tap here to buy book 3 now.

GET ANOTHER BOOK FOR FREE!

To instantly receive the free novella, **The Night Shift**, featuring Whitney when she was a Detective Sergeant, ten years ago, sign up for Sally Rigby's free author newsletter at www.sallyrigby.com

## DEADLY GAMES - Cavendish & Walker Book 1

### A killer is playing cat and mouse....... and winning.

DCI Whitney Walker wants to save her career. Forensic psychologist, Dr Georgina Cavendish, wants to avenge the death of her student.

Sparks fly when real world policing meets academic theory, and it's not a pretty sight.

When two more bodies are discovered, Walker and Cavendish form an uneasy alliance. But are they in time to save the next victim?

*Deadly Games* is the first book in the Cavendish and Walker crime fiction series. If you like serial killer thrillers and psychological intrigue, then you'll love Sally Rigby's page-turning book.

Pick up *Deadly Games* today to read Cavendish & Walker's first case.

## DEATH TRACK - Cavendish & Walker Book 3

### Catch the train if you dare...

After a teenage boy is found dead on a Lenchester train, Detective Chief Inspector Whitney Walker believes they're being targeted by the notorious Carriage Killer, who chooses a local rail network, commits four murders, and moves on.

Against her wishes, Walker's boss brings in officers from another force to help the investigation and prevent more deaths, but she's forced to defend her team against this outside interference.

Forensic psychologist, Dr Georgina Cavendish, is by her side in an attempt to bring to an end this killing spree. But how can they get into the mind of a killer who has already killed twelve times in two years without leaving a single clue behind?

For fans of Rachel Abbott, L J Ross and Angela Marsons, *Death Track* is the third in the Cavendish & Walker series. A gripping serial killer thriller that will have you hooked.

## LETHAL SECRET - Cavendish & Walker Book 4

### Someone has a secret. A secret worth killing for....

When a series of suicides, linked to the Wellness Spirit Centre, turn out to be murder, it brings together DCI Whitney Walker and forensic psychologist Dr Georgina Cavendish for another investigation. But as they delve deeper, they come across a tangle of secrets and the very real risk that the killer will strike again.

As the clock ticks down, the only way forward is to infiltrate the centre. But the outcome is disastrous, in more ways than one.

For fans of Angela Marsons, Rachel Abbott and M A Comley, *Lethal Secret* is the fourth book in the Cavendish & Walker crime fiction series.

## LAST BREATH - Cavendish & Walker Book 5

**Has the Lenchester Strangler returned?**

When a murderer leaves a familiar pink scarf as his calling card, Detective Chief Inspector Whitney Walker is forced to dig into a cold case, not sure if she's looking for a killer or a copycat.

With a growing pile of bodies, and no clues, she turns to forensic psychologist, Dr Georgina Cavendish, despite their relationship being at an all-time low.

Can they overcome the bad blood between them to solve the unsolvable?

For fans of Rachel Abbott, Angela Marsons and M A Comley, *Last Breath* is the fifth book in the Cavendish & Walker crime fiction series.

**FINAL VERDICT - Cavendish & Walker Book 6**

**The judge has spoken……everyone must die.**

When a killer starts murdering lawyers in a prestigious law firm, and every lead takes them to a dead end, DCI Whitney Walker finds herself grappling for a motive.

What links these deaths, and why use a lethal injection?

Alongside forensic psychologist, Dr Georgina Cavendish, they close in on the killer, while all the time trying to not let their personal lives get in the way of the investigation.

For fans of Rachel Abbott, Mark Dawson and M A Comley, Final Verdict is the sixth in the Cavendish & Walker series. A fast paced murder mystery which will keep you guessing.

**RITUAL DEMISE - Cavendish & Walker Book 7**

**Someone is watching…. No one is safe**

The once tranquil woods in a picturesque part of Lenchester have become the bloody stage to a series of ritualistic murders. With no suspects, Detective Chief Inspector Whitney Walker is once again forced to call on the services of forensic psychologist Dr Georgina Cavendish.

But this murderer isn't like any they've faced before. The murders are highly elaborate, but different in their own way, and with the clock ticking, they need to get inside the killer's head before it's too late.

For fans of Angela Marsons, Rachel Abbott and L J Ross. Ritual Demise is the seventh book in the Cavendish & Walker crime fiction series.

## Acknowledgments

Fatal Justice was a challenging book to write, because of the subject matter, and I couldn't have done it without the help of many people.

First, I'd like to thank my partners-in-crime, Amanda Ashby and Christina Phillips, for always being there and helping me turn the seed of an idea into a complete novel. I'd be lost without you.

Thanks, to my editing team, Emma Mitchell and Amy Hart. Also, to Stuart Bache, thanks for another fabulous cover.

Last, but not least, thanks to my family Garry, Alicia and Marcus for your continued support.

## About the Author

Sally Rigby was born in Northampton, in the UK. She has always had the travel bug, and after living in both Manchester and London, eventually moved overseas. From 2001 she has lived with her family in New Zealand, which she considers to be the most beautiful place in the world. During this time she also lived for five years in Australia.

Sally has always loved crime fiction books, films and TV programmes, and has a particular fascination with the psychology of serial killers.

Sally loves to hear from her readers, so do feel free to get in touch via her website www.sallyrigby.com

Printed in Great Britain
by Amazon